A VAMPIRE GENEVIEVE NOVEL

GENEVIEVE UNDEAD

WARHAMMER™
HORROR

• THE VAMPIRE GENEVIEVE •
by Kim Newman

DRACHENFELS
GENEVIEVE UNDEAD
BEASTS IN VELVET (July 2019)
SILVER NAILS (July 2019)

THE WICKED AND THE DAMNED
A portmanteau novel by Josh Reynolds,
Phil Kelly and David Annandale

MALEDICTIONS
An anthology by various authors

PERDITION'S FLAME
An audio drama by Alec Worley

WARHAMMER™
HORROR

A VAMPIRE GENEVIEVE NOVEL

GENEVIEVE UNDEAD

KIM NEWMAN

WRITING AS JACK YEOVIL

WARHAMMER HORROR
A BLACK LIBRARY PUBLICATION IMPRINT

First published in 1993.
This edition published in Great Britain in 2019 by
Black Library,
Games Workshop Ltd.,
Willow Road,
Nottingham, NG7 2WS, UK.

10 9 8 7 6 5 4 3 2 1

Produced by Games Workshop in Nottingham.
Cover illustration by Toni Deu.

See Warhammer Horror on the internet at

blacklibrary.com

Find out more about Games Workshop
and the worlds of Warhammer at

games-workshop.com

Printed and bound by CPI Group (UK) Ltd, Croydon, CR0 4YY

WARHAMMER™
HORROR

A dark bell tolls in the abyss.

It echoes across cold and unforgiving worlds, mourning
the fate of humanity. Terror has been unleashed, and
every foul creature of the night haunts the shadows.
There is naught but evil here. Alien monstrosities drift
in tomblike vessels. Watching. Waiting. Ravenous.
Baleful magicks whisper in gloom-shrouded forests,
spectres scuttle across disquiet minds. From the depths
of the void to the blood-soaked earth, diabolic horrors
stalk the endless night to feast upon unworthy souls.

Abandon hope. Do not trust to faith. Sacrifices burn
on pyres of madness, rotting corpses stir in unquiet
graves. Daemonic abominations leer with rictus
grins and stare into the eyes of the accursed. And the
Ruinous Gods, with indifference, look on.

This is a time of reckoning, where every mortal soul
is at the mercy of the things that lurk in the dark.
This is the night eternal, the province of monsters
and daemons. This is Warhammer Horror. None shall
escape damnation.

And so, the bell tolls on.

INTRODUCTION

I've liked vampire stories ever since I saw Bela Lugosi as Dracula – on late night TV in 1970, when I was eleven. That viewing set me on a course for life.

In outlining *Drachenfels*, my first novel for Games Workshop, I realised I needed a heroine who didn't age in the decades between the prologue and the main story... After mulling it over, I realised that one solution was to make Genevieve a vampire. At that time, GW manuals had a page of stats and rules for the Undead, which wouldn't allow for what I had planned in the book. 'Couldn't she be an elf?' someone suggested at the meeting – a line that ended up in the novel – only for the then-supreme emperor Bryan Ansell to say they'd change the rules to let her exist. Bryan is not an uncontroversial figure in the history of the company and the franchise, but that decision turned out well.

Genevieve may be the first vampire in fiction to have been formed as a character (I knew who she'd be and what she needed to do) before it was settled that they'd be a vampire. Years later, the TV series *Being Human* was in development as a flat-share story about an agoraphobic, a rageaholic and a sex addict before they were turned into a ghost, a werewolf and a vampire. This is probably why she seemed fresh. I made her an eternal teen-ager – though in later incarnations she's put on a few apparent years – because there was still a sense that the GW books were aimed at a Young Adult readership. Oddly, she became the most grown-up character in either of her primary worlds.

She sat out *Beasts in Velvet*, the second Jack Yeovil novel, except for a cameo... Partly because the last line of *Drachenfels* seemed to end her story. But I did a prequel with her in the novella *Red Thirst* and that led to the three novellas which are collected here. *The Cold Stark House* and *Unicorn Ivory* were written for antholo-gies that didn't happen, so it seemed to make sense to write *Stage Blood* to make it into a self-contained trilogy. The other theme is homages to classic horror films, which is why the stories are steeped in gothic references and specifically rework ideas from *The Phan-tom of the Opera* (1926), *The Old Dark House* (1932) and *The Most Dangerous Game* (1932). Oh, and the twee side of fantasy is always caricatured by mention of unicorns – so I thought I'd write some-thing about dangerous, nasty, rhino-horned unicorns.

Genevieve became a signature character across my fictional multiverse. Reasoning that the Warhammer timeline is an alter-nate reality, I decided to incorporate her counterpart into the novel series I began with *Anno Dracula* (1992). Geneviève Dieu-donné of the *Anno Dracula* series differs from the Warhammer Genevieve Dieudonné by an extra accent – in 1989, typesetting from word processing files was in its infancy and accents were fiddly, so the Warhammer Genevieve lost one of hers – and a middle name, but they are cross-continual cousins.

I still like vampires a lot more than I like elves.

Kim Newman, 2018

'When he lost his love, his grief was gall,
In his heart he wanted to leave it all,
And lose his self in the forests tall,
But he answered instead his country's call...'

– Tom Blackburn and George Bruns,
'The Ballad of Davy Crockett'

Part One

Stage Blood

I

He had a name once, but hadn't heard it spoken in years. Sometimes, it was hard to remember what it had been. Even he thought of himself as the Trapdoor Daemon. When they dared speak of him, that was what the company of the Vargr Breughel called their ghost.

He had been haunting this building for years enough to know its secret by-ways. After springing the catch of the hidden trapdoor, he eased himself into Box Seven, first dangling by strong tentacles, then dropping the last inches to the familiar carpet. Tonight was the premiere of *The Strange History of Dr Zhiekhill and Mr Chaida*, originally by the Kislevite dramatist V.I. Tiodorov, now adapted by the Vargr Breughel's genius-in-residence, Detlef Sierck.

The Trapdoor Daemon knew Tiodorov's hoary melodrama from earlier translations, and wondered how Detlef would bring life back to it. He'd taken an interest in rehearsals, particularly in the progress of his protégée, Eva Savinien, but had deliberately refrained from seeing the piece all through until tonight. When the curtain came down on the fifth act, the ghost would decide whether to give the play his blessing or his curse.

He was recognized as the permanent and non-paying licensee of Box Seven, and he was invoked whenever a production went well or ill. The success of *A Farce of the Fog* was laid to his approval of the comedy, and the disastrous series of accidents that plagued the never-premiered revival of Manfred von Diehl's *Strange Flower* were also set at his door. Some had glimpsed him, and a good many more fancied they had. A theatre was not a proper theatre without a ghost. And there were always old stage-hands and character actors eager to pass on stories to frighten the little chorines and apprentices who passed through the Vargr Breughel Memorial Playhouse.

Even Detlef Sierck, actor-manager of the Vargr Breughel company, occasionally spoke with affection of him, and continued the custom of previous managements by having an offering placed in Box Seven on the first night of any production.

Actually, for the ghost things were much improved since Detlef took over the house. When the theatre had been the Beloved of Shallya and specialised in underpatronised but uplifting religious dramas, the offerings had been of incense and a live kid. Now, reflecting an earthier, more popular approach, the offering took the form of a large trencher of meats and vegetables prepared by the skilled company chef, with a couple of bottles of Bretonnian wine thrown in.

The Trapdoor Daemon wondered if Detlef instinctively understood his needs were far more those of a physical being than a disembodied spirit.

Eating was difficult without hands, but the years had forced him to become used to his ruff of muscular appendages, and he was able to work the morsels up from the trencher towards the sucking, beaked hole of his mouth with something approaching dexterity. He had uncorked the first bottle with a quick constriction, and took frequent swigs at a vintage that must have been laid down around the year of his birth. He brushed away that thought – his former life seemed less real now than the fictions which paraded before him every evening – and settled his bulk into the nest of broken chairs and cushions adapted to his shape, awaiting the curtain. He sensed the excitement of the first night crowd and, from the darkness of Box Seven, saw the glitter of jewels and silks down below. A Detlef Sierck premiere was an occasion in Altdorf for the court to come out and parade.

The Trapdoor Daemon understood the Emperor himself was not present – since his experience at the fortress of Drachenfels, Karl-Franz disliked the theatre in general and Detlef Sierck's theatre in particular – but that Prince Luitpold was occupying the Imperial box. Many of the finest and foremost of the Empire would be in the house, as intent on being seen as on seeing the play. The critics were in their corner, quills bristling and inkpots ready. Wealthy merchants packed the stalls, looking up at the assembled courtiers and aristocrats in the circle who, in their turn, looked to the Imperial connections in the private boxes.

A dignified explosion of clapping greeted the orchestra as Felix Hubermann, the conductor, led his musicians in the Imperial national anthem, 'Hail to the House of the Second Wilhelm.' The ghost resisted the impulse to flap his appendages together in a schlumphing approximation of applause. In the Imperial box, the future emperor appeared and graciously accepted the admiration of his future subjects. Prince Luitpold was a handsome boy on the point of becoming a handsome young man. His companion for the evening was handsome too, although the Trapdoor Daemon knew she was not young. Genevieve Dieudonné, dressed far more simply than the brocaded and lace-swathed Luitpold, appeared to be a girl of some sixteen summers, but it was well-known that Detlef Sierck's mistress was actually in her six hundred and sixty-eighth year.

A heroine of the Empire yet something of an embarrassment, she didn't look entirely comfortable in the Imperial presence, and tried to keep in the shadows while the prince waved to the crowd. Across the auditorium, the ghost caught the sharp glint of red in her eyes, and wondered if her nightsight could pierce the darkness that sweated like squid's ink from his pores. If the vampire girl saw him, she didn't betray anything. She was probably too nervous of her position to pay any attention to him. Heroine or not, a vampire's position in human society is precarious. Too many remembered the centuries Kislev suffered under Tsarina Kattarin.

Also in the Prince's party was Mornan Tybalt, grey-faced and self-made keeper of the Imperial counting house, and Graf Rudiger von Unheimlich, hard-hearted and forceful patron of the League of Karl-Franz, a to-the-death defender of aristocratic privilege. They were known to hate each other with a poisonous fervour, the upstart Tybalt having the temerity to believe that ability and intellect were more important qualifications for high office than breeding, lineage and a title, while the pure-blooded huntsman von Unheimlich maintained that all Tybalt's policies had brought to the Empire was riot and upheaval. The Trapdoor Daemon fancied that neither the Chancellor nor the Graf would have much attention for the play, each fuming at the imperially-ordained need not to attempt physical violence upon the other in the course of the evening.

The house settled, and the prince took his chair. It was time for the drama. The ghost adjusted his position, and fixed his attention on the opening curtains. Beyond the red velvet was darkness. Hubermann held a flute to his lips, and played a strange, high melody. Then the limelights flared, and the audience was transported to another century, another country.

The action of *Dr Zhiekhill and Mr Chaida* was set in pre-Kattarin Kislev, and concerned a humble cleric of Shallya who, under the influence of a magic potion, transforms into another person entirely, a prodigy of evil. In the first scene, Zhiekhill was debating good and evil with his philosopher brother, as the darkness gathered outside the temple, seeping in between the stately columns.

It was easy to see what attracted Detlef Sierck, as adaptor and actor, to the Tiodorov story. The dual role was a challenge beyond anything the performer had done before. And the subject was an obvious development of the macabre vein that had been creeping lately into the playwright's work. Even the comedy of *A Farce of the Fog* had found room for a throat-slitting imp and much talk of the hypocrisy of supposedly good men. Critics traced Detlef's dark obsessions back to the famously interrupted premiere of his work *Drachenfels*, during which the actor had faced and bested not a stage monster but the Great Enchanter himself, Constant Drachenfels. Detlef had tackled that experience face-on in *The Treachery of Oswald*, in which he had taken the role of the possessed Laszlo Lowenstein, and now he was returning to the hurt inside him, nagging again at the themes of duality, treachery and the existence of a monstrous world underneath the ordinary.

His brother gone, Zhiekhill was locked up in his chapel, fussing with the bubbling liquids that combined to make his potion. Detlef, intent on delaying the expected, was playing the scene with a comic touch, as if Zhiekhill weren't quite aware what he was doing. In his recent works, Detlef's view of evil was changing, as if he were coming to believe it was not an external thing, like Drachenfels usurping the body of Lowenstein, but a canker that came from within, like the treachery forming in the heart of Oswald, or the murderous, lecherous, spiteful Chaida straining to escape from the confines of the pious, devout, kindly Zhiekhill.

On the stage, the potion was ready. Detlef-as-Zhiekhill drained

it, and Hubermann's eerie tune began again as the influence of
the magic took hold. *Dr Zhiekhill and Mr Chaida* forced the Trapdoor Daemon to consider things he would rather forget. As Chaida
first appeared, with Detlef performing marvels of stage magic and
facial contortion to suggest the violent transformation, he remembered his own former shape, and the Tzeentch-born changes that
slowly overcame him. When, at the point Detlef-as-Chaida was
strangling Zhiekhill's brother, the monster was pulled back inside
the cleric and Zhiekhill, chastened and shaking, stood revealed
before the philosopher, the ghost was slapped by the realization
that this would never happen to him. Zhiekhill and Chaida might
be in an eternal struggle, neither ever gaining complete control,
but he was forever and for good or ill the Trapdoor Daemon. He
would never revert to his old self.

Then the drama caught him again, and he was tugged from his
own thoughts, gripped by the way Detlef retold the tale. In Tiodorov, the two sides of the protagonist were reflected by the two
women associated with them, Zhiekhill with his virtuous wife
and Chaida with a brazen slut of the streets. Detlef had taken
this tired cliché and replaced the stick figures with human beings.

Sonja Zhiekhill, played by Illona Horvathy, was a restless, pas-
sionate woman, bored enough with her husband to take a young
cossack as a lover and attracted, despite herself, to the twisted
and dangerous Mr Chaida. While Nita, the harlot, was played by
Eva Savinien as a lost child, willing to endure the brutal treatment
of Chaida because the monster at least pays her some attention.

The murder scene drew gasps from the auditorium, and the
ghost knew Detlef would, in order to increase the clamour for
tickets, spread around a rumour that ladies fainted by the dozen.
While Detlef's Chaida might be a triumph of the stage, the most
chilling depiction of pure evil he had ever seen, there was no
doubt that the revelation of the play was Eva Savinien's tragic
Nita. In *A Farce of the Fog*, Eva had taken and transformed the

dullest of parts – the faithful maidservant – and this was her first chance to graduate to anything like a leading role. Eva's glowing performance made the ghost's chest swell wet with pride, for she was currently his special interest.

Noticing her when she first came to the company, he had exerted his influence to help her along. Eva's triumph was also his. Her Nita quite outshone Illona Horvathy's higher-billed heroine, and the Trapdoor Daemon wondered whether there was anything of Genevieve Dieudonné in Detlef's writing of the part.

The scene was the low dive behind the temple of Shallya, where Chaida makes his lodging, and Chaida was trying to get rid of Nita. Earlier, he had arranged an assignation here with Sonja, believing his seduction of the wife he still believes virtuous will signify an utter triumph over the Zhiekhill half of his soul. The argument that led to murder was over the pettiest of things, a pair of shoes without which Nita refuses to go out into the snow-thick streets of Kislev. Gradually, a little fire came into Nita's complaints and, for the first time, she tried to stand up to her brutish protector. Finally, almost as an afterthought, Chaida struck the girl down with a mailed glove, landing a blow of such force that a splash of blood erupted from her skull like juice from a crushed orange.

Stage blood flew.

Then came the climax, as the young Kislevite cossack, played by the athletic and dynamic Reinhardt Jessner, having tracked Chaida down from his earlier crimes, bursts into the fiend's lodgings, accompanied by Zhiekhill's wife and brother, and puts an end to the monster during a swordfight. The Trapdoor Daemon had seen Detlef and Reinhardt duel before, at the climax of *The Treachery of Oswald*, but this was a far more impressive display. The combat went so far beyond performance he was sure some real enmity must exist between them. Offstage, Reinhardt was married to Illona Horvathy, to whom Detlef had made love in the company's last three productions. Also, Reinhardt was being hailed as the new matinee idol of the playhouse. His attractions for the young women of Altdorf were growing even as those of his genius employer diminished somewhat, although diminishing was certainly not what Detlef's stomach was doing with passing years of good food and better wine.

Detlef and Reinhardt fought in the persons of Chaida and the cossack, hacking away at each other until their faces were criss-crossed with bloody lines, and the stage set was a shambles. Slashing a curtain exposed the hastily-stuffed-away corpse of Nita, and Sonja Zhiekhill fainted in her brother-in-law's arms. Not a breath was let out in the auditorium. In Tiodorov's original, Chaida was defeated when Zhiekhill at last managed to exert himself and the monster dropped his sword. Skewered by the cossack's blade, Chaida turned back into Zhiekhill in death, declaiming in a dying speech that he had learned his lesson, that mortals should not tamper with the affairs of the Gods. Detlef had changed it around completely. At the point when the transformation began, the cossack made his death thrust, and Chaida parried it, striking with his killing glove and crushing the young hero's throat.

There was a shocked reaction in the house to this reversal of expectations. It had been Zhiekhill who had killed his wife's lover, not Chaida. This wasn't the story of the division between good and evil in a man's soul, but of an evil that drives out even the good. Throughout the third act, the ghost realized, Detlef had been blurring the differentiation between Zhiekhill and Chaida. Now, at the end, they were indistinguishable. He didn't need the potion any more. In a cruel final touch, Zhiekhill gave his bloody sword to his wife, of whose corruption he approves, and encouraged her to taste further the delights of evil by killing Zhiekhill's brother. Sonja, needing no potion to unloose the monster inside her, complied. With corpses all around, Zhiekhill then took his wife to Chaida's bed, and the curtain fell.

For a long moment, there was a stunned silence from the audience.

The ghost wondered how they would react. Looking across the dark, he saw again the red points of Genevieve's eyes, and wondered what emotion was hidden in them. *Dr Zhiekhill and Mr Chaida* was hard to like, but it was undoubtedly Detlef Sierck's dark masterpiece. No one who saw it would ever forget it, no matter how much they might wish to.

The applause began, and grew to a deafening storm. The Trapdoor Daemon joined his clamour with the rest.

II

The future emperor had been impressed with the play. Genevieve knew that would please Detlef. Elsewhere at the party, there was heated debate about the merits of *The Strange History of Dr Zhiekhill and Mr Chaida*. Mornan Tybalt, the thin-nosed Chancellor, quietly expressed extreme disapproval, while Graf Rudiger had apparently yawned throughout and glumly didn't see what all the fuss was about.

Two critics were on the point of blows, one proclaiming the piece an immortal masterpiece, the other reaching into the stable for his metaphors.

Guglielmo Pentangeli, Detlef's business manager and former cell-mate, was happy, predicting that whatever a person might think of *Dr Zhiekhill and Mr Chaida*, it would be impossible to venture out in society in the next year without having formed an opinion. And to form an opinion, it would be necessary to procure a ticket.

Genevieve felt watched, as she had all evening, but no one

23

talked to her about the play. That was to be expected. She was in a peculiar position, connected with Detlef and yet not with his work. Some might think it impolite to express an opinion to her or to solicit her own. She felt strange anyway, distanced from the play she'd seen, not quite able to connect it with the man whose bed she shared – if rarely using it at the same time he did – or else able to understand too well the sparks in Detlef that made him at once Dr Zhiekhill and Mr Chaida. Recently, Detlef had been darkening inside.

In the reception room of the Vargr Breughel, invited guests were drinking and picking at the buffet. Felix was conducting a quartet in a suite of pieces from the play, and Guglielmo was doing his best to be courteous to von Unheimlich, who was describing at length an error in Reinhardt's Kislevite swordsmanship. A courtier Genevieve had met – whom she had once bled in a private suite at the Crescent Moon tavern – complemented her on her dress, and she smiled back at him, able to remember his name but not his precise title. Even after nearly seven hundred years in and out of the courts of the Known World, she was confused by etiquette.

The players were still backstage, taking off make-up and costumes. Detlef would also be running through his notes to the other actors.

For him, every performance was a dress rehearsal for an ideal, perfect rendition of the drama that might, by some miracle, eventually transpire, but which never actually came to pass. He said that as soon as he stopped being disappointed in his work, he'd give up, not because he would have attained perfection but because he would have lost his mind.

The eating and drinking reminded Genevieve of her own need. Tonight, when the party was over, she'd tap Detlef. That would be the best way jointly to savour his triumph, to lick away the tiny scabs under his beardline and to sample his blood, still peppered with the excitement of the performance. She hoped he didn't drink to excess. Too much wine in the blood gave her a headache.

'Genevieve,' said Prince Luitpold, 'your teeth..'

She felt them, sharp against her lower lip, and bowed her head. The enamel shrank and her fangs slid back into their gumsheaths.

'Sorry,' she said.

'Don't be,' the prince said, almost laughing. 'It's not your fault, it's your nature.'

Genevieve realized Mornan Tybalt, who had no love for her, was watching closely, as if he expected her to tear out the throat of the heir to the Imperial crown and put her face into a gusher of royal blood. She had tasted royal blood and it was no different from a goatherd's. Since the fall of Arch-Lector Mikael Hasselstein, Mornan Tybalt had been the Emperor's closest advisor, and he was jealous of the position, afraid of anyone – no matter how insignificant or unlikely – who might win favour with the House of the Second Wilhelm.

Genevieve understood the ambitious Chancellor was not a well-liked man, especially with those whose hero was the Graf Rudiger, the old guard of the aristocracy, the electors and the barons. Genevieve took people as she found them, but had been involved enough with the great and the good not to want to pick sides in any factional conflicts of the Imperial court.

'Here's our genius,' the prince said.

Detlef made an entrance, transformed from the ragged monster of the play into an affable dandy, dressed as magnificently as the company costumier could manage, his embroidered doublet confining his stomach in a flattering manner. He bowed low to the prince and kissed the boy's ring.

Luitpold had the decency to be embarrassed, and Tybalt looked as if he expected another assassination attempt. Of course, the reason Detlef and Genevieve were allowed such intimacy with the Imperial presence was that, at Castle Drachenfels, they had thwarted such an attempt. If it were not for the play-actor and the bloodsucker, the Empire would now be ruled by a puppet of the Great Enchanter, and there would be a new Dark Age for all the races of the world.

A darker age, rather.

The prince complimented Detlef on the play, and the actor-playwright brushed aside the praise with extravagant modesty, simultaneously appearing humble, yet conveying how pleased he was to have his patron bestow approval.

The other actors were arriving. Reinhardt, a bandage around his head where Detlef had struck too hard in the final fight, was flanked by his wife Illona and the ingenue. Several artistically-inclined gallants crowded around Eva, and Genevieve detected a slight moue of jealousy from Illona. Prince Luitpold himself had asked if an introduction could be contrived to the young actress. Eva Savinien would have to be watched.

'Ulric, but that was a show,' Reinhardt said, as open as usual, rubbing his wound. 'The Trapdoor Daemon should be delighted.'

Genevieve laughed at his joke. The Trapdoor Daemon was a popular superstition in the Vargr Breughel.

Detlef was given wine, and held his own court.

'Gené, my love,' he said, kissing her cheek, 'you look wonderful.'

She shivered a little in his embrace, unconvinced by his warmth. He was always playing a part. It was his nature.

'It was a feast of horrors, Detlef,' the Prince said, 'I was never so frightened in my life. Well, maybe once...'

Detlef, briefly serious, acknowledged the comment.

Genevieve suppressed another shiver, and realized it had passed around the room. She could see momentarily haunted faces in the cheerful company. Detlef, Luitpold, Reinhardt, Illona, Felix.

Those who'd been at the performance in Castle Drachenfels would always be apart from the rest of the world. Everyone had been changed. And Detlef most of all. They all felt unseen eyes gazing down on them.

'We have had too many horrors in Altdorf,' Tybalt commented, a mutilated hand stroking his chin. 'The business five years ago with Drachenfels. Konrad the Hero's little skirmish with our green-skinned friends. The Beast murders. The riots stirred up by the revolutionist Kloszowski. Now, this business with the Warhawk..'

Several citizens had been slaughtered recently by a falconer who set a hunting bird on them. Captain Harald Kleindeinst, reputedly the hardest copper in the city, had vowed to bring the murderer to justice, but the killer was still at liberty, striking down those who took his fancy.

'It seems,' the Chancellor continued, 'we are knee-deep in blood and cruelty. Why did you feel the need to add to our burden of nightmares?'

Detlef was silent for a moment. Tybalt had asked a question many must have pondered during the evening. Genevieve didn't care for the man, but she admitted that, just this once, he might even have a point.

'Well, Sierck,' Tybalt insisted, pressing his argument beyond politeness, 'why dwell on terrors?'

The look came into Detlef's eyes that Genevieve had learned to recognize. The dark look that came whenever he remembered the fortress of Drachenfels. The Chaida look that eclipsed his Zhiekhill face.

'Chancellor,' he said. 'What makes you think I have a choice?'

III

Upon this peak in the Grey Mountains, there had once been a castle. It had stood against the sky, seven turrets like the talons of a deformed hand. This had been the fortress of Constant Drachenfels, the Great Enchanter. Now there was only a scattering of rubble that drifted like snow into the valley, spreading out for miles. Explosives had been placed throughout the structure, and detonated. The fortress of Drachenfels had shaken, and collapsed piece by piece.

Where once there had been a stronghold, there was now a ruin. The intention had been to destroy completely all trace of the master of the castle. Stone and slate could be smashed, but it was impossible to blow away like chaff the horrors that lay in memories.

Buried in the ruins for these five years was the Animus, a thinking creature with no true form. Just now, it resided in a mask. A plain oval like a large half-eggshell, wrought from light metal, so thin as to be almost transparent. It had features, but they were unformed, undefined. To gain character, the mask needed to be worn.

The Animus was not sure what it was. Constant Drachenfels had either created it or conjured it. A homunculus or a spirit, it owed its existence to the Great Enchanter. Drachenfels had worn the mask once, and left something of himself behind. That gave purpose to the Animus.

It had been left in the ruins when Drachenfels departed the world for one reason.

Revenge.

Genevieve Dieudonné. Detlef Sierck. The vampire and the play-actor. The thwarters of the great design. They had destroyed Drachenfels, and now they must themselves be destroyed.

The Animus was patient. Time passed, but it could wait. It would not die. It would not change. It could not be reasoned with. It could not be bought off. It could not be swayed from its purpose.

It sensed the disturbance in the ruins, and knew it was being brought closer to Genevieve and Detlef.

The Animus did not feel excitement, just as it did not feel hate, love, pain, pleasure, satisfaction, discomfort. The world was as it was, and there was nothing it could do to change that.

As the moons set, the disturbance neared the Animus.

As they made love, Genevieve licked the trickle of blood from old wounds in his throat. Over the years, her teeth had put permanent marks on him, a seal. Detlef had taken to wearing high collars, and all his shirts had tiny red stains where they rested against her bites.

His head sunk deep into the pillow, and he looked at the ceiling, vision going in and out of focus as she suckled his blood. His hand was on her neck, under her blonde curtain of hair. They were joined loin to loin, neck to mouth. They were one flesh, one blood.

He had tried to paint the experience with words, in one of his still-secret sonnets, but had never managed to his satisfaction to catch the butterfly feelings, pain and pleasure. In many ways his chosen tool – language – failed him.

Genevieve made him forget the actresses he sometimes took to his bed, and wondered if she too found this joining more special than her brief liaisons with young bloods. Their partnership wasn't conventional, hardly even convenient. But even as he felt the darkness gathering, this ancient girl was the candle-flame to which he must cling. Since Drachenfels, they had been together, sharing secrets.

A thrill shot through him, and he heard her gasp, blood bubbling in the back of her throat, knifepoint teeth scratching the leathered skin of his neck. They rolled over, together, and she clung to him as their bodies joined and parted. There was blood between them, and sweet sweat. He looked at her smiling face under his in the gloom, and saw her lick the red from her lips. He felt himself climaxing, first in the soles of his feet, then...

His heart hammered. Genevieve's eyes opened, and she shuddered, overlapping teeth bared and bloody. He propped himself above her, elbows rigid, and collapsed, trying to keep his weight off her. Their bodies slipped apart, and Genevieve eased herself forwards, almost clambering over his bulk, pressing her face to his cheek, her hair falling over his face, kissing him. He pulled the quilts up around them, and they nestled in a cocoon of warmth as the sun rose behind the curtains.

For once, their sleep came at the same time.

With the play and the party and their private embraces, they'd both been awake the night through. Detlef was exhausted, Genevieve in the grip of the vampire lassitude that came over her every few weeks.

His eyes closed, and he was alone in the dark of his mind.

He slept, but his thoughts still raced. He needed to work on

the swordfight to prevent more accidents. And he would have
to give thought to Illona, to balance the blossoming Eva's performance. And the second act could use delicate pruning. The
comic business with the Tsar's minister was just a tiresome leftover from Tiodorov.

He dreamed of changing faces.

This high in the Grey Mountains the air was as sharp as a razor;
as he inhaled, he felt its cutting pass in his lungs. Trying desperately not to wheeze and thus lose his habitual decorum, Bernabe
Scheydt completed his mid-morning devotions to the gods of Law:
Solkan, Arianka and Alluminas. At the dig, the first thing he had
ordered was the erection of a sundial. A fixed point on the world,
shadow revolving precisely with the inexorable movement of sun
and moons, the sundial was the perfect altar for worship of order.

'Master Scheydt,' said Brother Jacinto, touching his own forehead in a mark of respect, 'there was a subsidence in the night.
The ground has fallen in where we were digging yesterday.'

'Show me.'

The acolyte led him to the place. Scheydt was used to hop-
ping around the ruin, judging which lumps of rubble were sound
enough to be stepped on. It was important not to fall over. Every
time someone so much as tripped, two or three of the work-
force deserted in the night. The locals remembered Drachenfels
too well, and feared his return. Every slightest mishap was laid
to the lingering spirit of the Great Enchanter. Many more, and
the expedition would be reduced to Scheydt and the acolytes
the arch-lector had spared him. And acolytes dug a lot less well
than the mountain men.

The superstitious fever of the locals was nonsense. At the
beginning of the expedition, Scheydt had invoked the dread name
of Solkan and performed a rite of exorcism. If any trace of the
monster lingered, it was banished now to the Outer Darkness.

Order reigned where there had once been chaos. Still, there had been 'incidents.'

'Here,' said Jacinto.

Scheydt saw. A half-rotten wooden beam was balanced over a square pit. A few slabs angled into the edges, like the teeth of a giant. An earthy, shitty, dead thing smell fumed up from the hole.

'It must have been one of the cellars.'

'Yes,' Scheydt agreed.

The earliest-rising workmen stood around. Jacinto was the only one of the acolytes up from their comparatively comfortable village lodgings this morning. Brother Nachbar and the others were poring over and cataloguing the expedition's earlier finds. Back at the university in Altdorf, the arch-lector must be pleased with the success of this dig. The acquisition of knowledge, even knowledge of the evil and unholy, was one way in which the cult of Solkan imposed order upon chaos.

'We must pray,' Scheydt declared. 'To ensure our safety.'

He heard a suppressed groan. These peasants would rather be digging than praying. And they would rather be drinking than digging. They did not understand the Law, did not understand how important order and decorum were to the world. They were only here because they feared Solkan, master of vengeance, as much or more than they feared the ghosts of the castle.

Jacinto was down on his knees, and the others, grumbling, followed him. Scheydt read out the Blessing of Solkan.

'Free me from the desires of my body, guide me in the path of the Law, instruct me in the ways of seemliness, help me smite the enemies of order.'

Since he had embraced the cult, Scheydt had been rigid in his habits. Celibate, vegetarian, abstinent, ordered. Even his bowel movements were decided by the sundial. He wore the coarse robe of a cleric. He raised his hand to no one but the unrighteous. He prayed at perfectly defined intervals.

He was in balance with himself, and with the world as it should be.

The prayer concluded, Scheydt examined the hole in the ground.

The arch-lector had sent him to Drachenfels with orders to search out items of spiritual interest. The Great Enchanter had been a very evil man, but he'd had an unparalleled library, a vast collection of articles of power, a store of the most arcane secrets.

Only by understanding Chaos, could the cult of Solkan impose order. It was important to carry the battle to the enemy, to meet sorcery with cleansing fire, to root out and destroy the devotees of unclean gods.

Only the strongest in mind could qualify for this expedition, and Scheydt was honoured by his selection as its director.

'There's something down there,' Jacinto said, 'catching the light.'

The sun had risen, and was shining now into the cavity. An object reflected. It was the shape of a face.

'Get it,' Scheydt said.

The acolyte followed the order. Jacinto knew his place on the sundial. Two of the workmen lowered the young man into the cavity on a rope, and then hauled him back out. He handed the article he had taken from the floor of the pit to Scheydt.

It was a delicate metal mask.

'Is it anything?' Jacinto asked.

Scheydt was not sure. The object felt strange, warm to the touch as if it retained the heat of the sun. It was not heavy, and there was no place for a cord to bind it to a head.

His hands tingled as he held the mask up in front of him. He looked through the eyeholes. Beyond the mask, the acolyte's face was distorted. Jacinto seemed impossibly to be sneering at his master, tongue poked out, hands flapping by his ears, eyes crossed.

A flare of wrath went off in Scheydt's heart as he rested the mask against his skin. At once, something leaped into his skull, fastening on his brain. The mask was stuck to his face like a layer of paint. His cheeks convulsed, and he felt the metal move with his twitch.

He saw Jacinto truly now, stumbling back away from him.

He was still Bernabe Scheydt, cleric of Solkan. But he was something else too. He was the Animus.

His hands found the acolyte and lifted him up. With new strength, he held the struggling young man up high and tossed him into the pit. Jacinto crashed through the remaining beam and thumped, broken, against an unseen flagstone floor.

The workmen were running away. Some screamed, some prayed. He enjoyed their fear.

Scheydt, devotee of the Law, tried to claw the mask from his face, horrified at the disorder he'd wrought. But the Animus grew strong in a moment and stayed his hands.

The Animus burrowed into Scheydt, seeking out seeds of excess within his imprisoned heart, encouraging them to sprout. Scheydt wanted a woman, a roast pig, a barrel of wine. The Animus had found desires within its host and was prepared to help him slake them. Then, it would travel.

To Altdorf. To the vampire and the play-actor.

As the workmen tumbled and ran down the mountainside, Scheydt drew a huge breath and laughed like a daemon. The straight trees that poked through the rubble bent in the breeze of laughter.

IV

Detlef got to the theatre in the mid-afternoon, leaving Genevieve sleeping in their rooms on the other side of Temple Street. The rest of the company were there already, poring over the reviews. The *Altdorf Spieler*, which boasted a circulation in the hundreds, was stridently in favour of *The Strange History of Dr Zhiekhill and Mr Chaida*, and most of the lesser broadsheets followed its line. Felix Hubermann picked out phrases to be flagged across the posters, humming superlatives to himself as he underlined them, 'gripping... powerful... thought-provoking... spine-chilling... bowel-churning... will run and run...'

Guglielmo reported that the house was sold out for the next two months and heavily booked thereafter. The Vargr Breughel had another hit. On the set, Poppa Fritz, the stage-door keeper and an institution in the theatre, was on his knees, trying to scrub blood out of the carpet. Detlef had ordered buckets cooked up in anticipation of a long run. When he had burst the bladder in his glove as he seemed to strike Eva Savinien, the whole audience had been shocked. He recalled the spurt of feeling that came at that moment, as if his own Mr Chaida were gaining the ascendant, encouraging him to delight in horrors beyond imagining.

As he entered the rehearsal room, cast and company broke into congratulatory applause. He bowed, accepting the praise that meant the most to him. Then, he broke the cheer up by producing a scroll with 'a few more notes...'

When he was finished, and the girl who played the innkeeper's daughter had stopped crying, he was ready to consider the business matters Guglielmo Pentangeli thrust at him. He signed a few papers and contracts, including a letter of thanks to the Emperor for continuing his patronage of the Vargr Breughel.

'Does that hurt?' Guglielmo asked.

'What?'

'Your neck. You were scratching.'

It had become an unconscious habit. His bites weren't painful, but sometimes they itched. Occasionally, after Genevieve bled him, he felt tired and drained. But today he was refreshed, eager for tonight's performance.

'Did you know the Chancellor had condemned the play? In the strongest of terms.'

'He said as much last night.'

'It's here in the *Spieler*, look'

Detlef cast his eyes down the column of blocky print. Mornan Tybalt had branded *Dr Zhiekhill and Mr Chaida* an obscenity, and called for a ban on it. Apparently, the horrors of the play were an invitation to the feeble-minded to act in imitation.

Tybalt cited the thumb tax rioters, the Beast and the Warhawk as the logical results of a theatre exclusively concerned with the dark and the depraved, the violent and the vile.

Detlef snorted a laugh. 'I thought those riots were a logical result of the silly tax Tybalt himself devised.'

'He's still a powerful man at court.'

'A ban isn't likely, not with Prince Luitpold on our side.'

'Be cautious, Detlef,' advised Guglielmo. 'Don't trust patrons, remember...'

He did. Detlef and Guglielmo had met in debtors' prison, after the default of a previous patron. After Mundsen Keep, everything seemed like an unconvincing play. Sometimes he was certain the curtain would ring down and he would wake up back in his cell with the other stinking debtors and no hope of release.

Even a terrible death at the hand of Drachenfels would have been preferable to a life slowly dribbled away in the dark.

'Have Tybalt's comments engraved on a board, and hang them outside the theatre with all our good notices. There's nothing that increases queues like a demand something should be banned. Remember the houses they got after the Lector of Sigmar tried to suppress Bruno Malvoisin's *Seduced by Slaaneshi or: The Baneful Lusts of Diogo Briesach*?'

Guglielmo laughed.

'The Trapdoor Daemon is with us, you know,' Detlef said. 'I'm sure of it.'

'Box Seven has been cleaned out.'

'And...'

Guglielmo shrugged. 'The food was gone, of course.'

'It always goes.'

This was a recurring joke between them. Guglielmo claimed the offerings were taken away by the house-cleaners for their families, and that he should be allowed to put on sale tickets for Box Seven. It was only a question of five seats, but they were the most potentially expensive in the house. Guglielmo, like all ex-debtors, knew the value of a crown, and frequently mentioned how much the Vargr Breughel lost by not letting out Box Seven.

'Any other signs of spectral visitation?'

'That peculiar smell, Detlef. And some slimy stuff.'

'Hah,' Detlef exclaimed, delighted. 'You see.'

'Many places smell funny, and slime is easy to come by in this place. A good fumigation, and some new furniture and the box would be good as new.'

'We need our ghostly patron, Guglielmo.'

'Maybe.'

The Trapdoor Daemon heard Detlef and Guglielmo discuss him, and was amused. He knew the actor-manager only pretended belief as a pose. Still, there was an obvious kinship between them. Once, years ago, the ghost had been a playwright too. He was touched that Detlef remembered his work. Few others did.

From his space behind the walls, he observed everything, eyes to the peepholes concealed in the scrollwork of a tall cabinet no one ever opened. There were peepholes all over the house, and passageways behind every wall. The theatre had been built at a time when the reigning emperor alternately persecuted and patronised the players, necessitating the incorporation of multiple means of escape into the building. Actors who failed to please were able to get away without encountering the emperor's halberdiers, who then had a reputation as the harshest dramatic critics in the city.

Several players had got lost in the tunnels, and the ghost had found their skeletons, still in costume, strewn in nooks around the theatre's catacombs.

There was no formal rehearsal this afternoon. Everyone was elated from the night before, and eager to repeat the performance this evening. The test of a hit was its second night, the Trapdoor Daemon knew. Magic can sometimes strike once, and be lost forever. From now on, the company of *The Strange History of Dr Zhiekhill and Mr Chaida* would have to work to live up to their reputation.

Poppa Fritz, who had been with the house almost as long as the ghost, handed out mugs of coffee and flirted with the chorus

girls. If anyone was responsible for the endurance of the legend of
the Trapdoor Daemon it was Poppa Fritz. The stage-door keeper
had encountered him on more than one occasion, usually when
in his cups, and always embroidered and elaborated when he
told of these incidents.

According to Poppa Fritz, the ghost was twenty feet tall and
glowed in the dark, with bright red skulls in the pupils of his
huge eyes, and a cloak woven from the hair of slaughtered
actresses.

Detlef did what the Trapdoor Daemon would have done, and
concentrated on Illona Horvathy and Eva Savinien. They had
few scenes together, but the contrast between them was vital
to the piece, and last night Eva had outshone Illona to the det-
riment of the play. The trick was to bring the one up without
taking the other down.

Illona was not in a good mood, but tried hard, listening intently
to Detlef and following his instructions to the letter. She was
intently aware of her position. Having had twins a few years ago,
Illona was constantly struggling to keep her figure. Last night she
must have realized that in the next Vargr Breughel production,
Eva Savinien would be the leading lady and she'd be playing
somebody's mother. Reinhardt Jessner, on hand merely to read
his lines, gave his wife support, but was careful not to tread in
the director's way.

Eva, however, was quietly firm, displaying a backbone of
steel in her willowy body. She might step from ingenue to star
on the strength of Nita, and was even more careful than Illona.
She was not a flirt exactly, but she knew how to flatter without seeming to, to ingratiate without being unctuous, to further
herself without displaying a hint of ambition. In the end, Eva
would be a great star, an extraordinary presence. The Trapdoor
Daemon had seen that from the first, when she had had the
merest walk-on as a dancer in *The Treachery of Oswald*. Since

then, she'd grown inside. He felt pride in her achievements, but also nagging doubts.

Just now, while Illona and Detlef were playing the scene in which Sonja first meets and is attracted to Chaida, Eva sat on a table, hugging her knees, watching intently, and Reinhardt Jessner was in a huddle with her, massaging an ache in her back.

Before scaling the mountain, you first conquer the foothills, and the gossip was that Eva would doubtless seduce Reinhardt away from Illona before she tackled Detlef. The Trapdoor Daemon discounted this rumour, for he knew the girl better, understood her more finely. She wouldn't have a personal life until her position was assured.

Then, Detlef was working with Eva, restaging their final argument, smiling encouragement when he wasn't spitting hateful lines at her. After their dialogue was over, Detlef lightly tapped Eva on the skull and she fell down as if mightily smitten. The company applauded, and Reinhardt helped her up. The ghost saw Illona watching her husband intently, chewing a corner of her lip. Eva, without cruelty or encouragement, pushed Reinhardt away, and paid attention to what Detlef told her about her performance, nodding agreement at his points, taking them in.

The Trapdoor Daemon realized he'd not misjudged Eva Savinien. The girl didn't need to bestow any favours. She would advance on talent alone. And yet, despite the affection he felt for her, he could not but realize there was something chilling about the girl. Like some great performers, there might not be any real person inside the roles.

'All right,' Detlef concluded. 'I'm happy. Let's go out there tonight and kill 'em.'

V

The mountain whore was snoring, eyes swollen shut, as Scheydt chewed his tough meat, washing the chunks down with bitter wine. He'd returned to his room and made his wishes known to the innkeeper in language blunter than the dolt was used to hearing from a cleric of the Law. The Animus rested inside his head as Scheydt fulfilled the desires that had been revealed to him. The mask was a part of him now, and he could open its mouth to eat, to speak, to gobble...

Scratching himself, he stood over the shrine he had erected in the corner of the room when he first came to the inn. It was perfectly laid out, balanced and symmetrical, the symbol of the strength of order over Chaos, an arrangement of metal rods and wooden panels around a central sundial, engraved with the sayings of the Law, decorated with preserved leaves. He hiked up his robe and relieved himself on the shrine, washing away the leaves with his powerful flow of urine.

The noise woke up the whore, and she rolled away, her head

to the wall, sobbing. After years of self-denial, Scheydt hadn't been a gentle lover.

There was a knocking at the door.

'What is it?' Scheydt grunted.

The door opened, and an acolyte ventured in. They must all be chattering about him.

'Brother Nachbar?'

The acolyte goggled at Scheydt, appalled at what he saw. He made the sign of the Law, and Scheydt turned around, the last of his flow making a quarter-circle on the floorboards.

Scheydt let his robes fall.

Nachbar could not speak.

The Animus told Scheydt he did not have to put up with fools like this for much longer.

'Get me a horse,' he ordered. 'I'm leaving this pest-hole.'

Nachbar nodded and retreated. The fool was so brain-blasted by the Law that he would carry out Scheydt's orders even if the cleric told him to consume his own excrement or slide a long sword into his scrawny belly. Perhaps, as a parting gesture, he would so order the brother, and tidy up a loose end. No, there was enough tidiness in the world. Let the end stay loose for someone to trip over.

Scheydt washed his foul-tasting mouth out with the last of the wine, and tossed the bottle out of the window, ignoring the shattering crash below. He hoped someone with bare feet would chance by.

Since the Animus and Scheydt had come to an agreement in their shared body, Drachenfels's creature could afford to slumber a little. It wasn't so much a question of taking over as it was of allowing the host to do what he always had wanted to do. The host was not a slave. Rather, the Animus set him free from himself, from the conventions that restricted his desires. Considering the grey grimness of Scheydt's life, the Animus was doing him a favour.

It would take Nachbar a while to get the horse organised. Scheydt hawked and spat at the steaming ruin of the altar. He slipped back into bed, roughly turning the whore over, thumping her fully awake. He ripped her tattered garment, and forced himself onto her, grunting like a hog.

The moons were up and Genevieve was about. She had wakened to an awareness of her own strength. Having fed well, she wouldn't feel the red thirst for days.

Temple Street was busy, crowds hustling to the Vargr Breughel for the evening performance. She was amused by the excerpted reviews emblazoned upon the boards above the doors.

A broadsheet-seller was exchanging papers for coins, shouting about another Warhawk murder. Obviously, atrocity sold well. Everyone in the city was looking up at the sky half the time, expecting the huge bird to swoop, talons first, out of the dark.

The night tasted fine. The first of a fog lingered around her ankles. In the gutter, an old woman was bent double, scooping up dog turds with her ungloved fingers, dropping them in a sack. She was a pure-gatherer, and would sell her crap-crop to a tannery for use in the curing of hides. The woman shrank away instinctively from Genevieve. A vampire-hater, naturally. Some people didn't object to picking up shit, but couldn't abide the presence of the undead.

Poppa Fritz recognized Genevieve and, with a bow, admitted her to the Vargr Breughel by the stage door.

'The Trapdoor Daemon is about tonight, Mam'selle Dieudonné'

She had listened to the old man's spook tales for years. Fond of him, she'd become fond of his ghost.

'Does our spectre care for the drama?' she asked.

Poppa Fritz cackled. 'Oh yes. *Dr Zhiekhill and Mr Chaida* is definitely to his taste. Anything with blood in it.'

She showed him her teeth in a friendly way.

'Begging your pardon, mam'selle.'

'That's quite all right.'

Inside, everyone was busy. Tonight, she would watch the play from the wings. Later, Detlef would quiz her in detail, asking her honest advice. In an open space, Reinhardt Jessner was practising his sword moves, bare-chested and sweating, muscles gliding gracefully under his skin. He saluted her with his foil, and continued to fence with his shadow.

She caught the theatre smell in her nostrils. Wood and smoke and incense and paint and people.

A rope dangled beside her, and Detlef came down it from the gods, breathing a little heavily. His belly might be swelling but his arms were still hard muscle. He clumped onto the stage, and hugged her.

'Gené, dear, just in time...'

He had a dozen things to ask her, but he was called away by Guglielmo with some tiresome business matters.

'I'll see you later, before the performance,' he said, dashing off. 'Stay out of trouble.'

Genevieve wandered, trying not to get in the way. Master Stempel was mixing up stage blood in a cauldron, cooking the ingredients over a slow flame like Dr Zhiekhill preparing his potion. He dipped a stick into the pot, and brought it up to the light.

'Too scarlet, don't you think?' he said, turning to her.

She shrugged. It didn't smell like blood, didn't have the shine that excited her thirst. But it would pass for non-vampires.

She went to the ladies' dressing rooms, passing a pile of flowers outside Eva Savinien's cramped quarters and stepping into the largest suite on the corridor. Illona was painting her face meticulously, peering into a mirror. Genevieve cast no reflection, but the actress sensed her presence and looked around, trying to smile without disturbing the drying paint.

Illona was another veteran of Drachenfels. They didn't need to talk to communicate.

'Have you seen the notices?' Illona asked.

Genevieve nodded. She knew what must be bothering her friend.

'"A new star shines"?' Illona quoted.

'Eva was good.'

'Yes, very good.'

'So were you.'

'Hmm, maybe. I'll just have to be better.'

The actress was working on the lines around her mouth and eyes, powdering them over, smoothing them into a mask of flour and cochineal. Illona Horvathy was a beautiful woman. But she was thirty-four. And Eva Savinien was twenty-two.

'She'll be in this room next time, you know?' Illona said. 'She radiates. Even from the stage, even in rehearsal, you can see it.'

'It's a good part.'

'Yes, and it's the making of her. But she has to fill it, she has to be there.'

Illona began to comb her hair. The first strands of grey were there already.

'Do you remember Lilli Nissen?' she asked. 'The great star?'

'How could I forget? She was to play me, and I ended up playing her. My one moment in the limelight.'

'Yes. Five years ago, I looked at Lilli Nissen and thought she was a fool, clinging to a past she should have let go, still insisting she play roles ten or twenty years younger than she was. I even said she should be glad to play mothers. There are good parts for mothers.'

'You were right.'

'Yes, I know. That's why it's so painful.'

'It happens, Illona. Everyone gets older.'

'Not everyone, Gené. Not you.'

'I get older. Inside, where it counts, I am very old.'

'Inside is not where it counts in the theatre. It's all out here,' she gestured in front of her face, 'all outside.'

There was nothing Genevieve could say that would really help Illona

'Good luck for tonight,' she tried, feebly.

'Thank you, Gené.'

Illona looked back into the mirror, and Genevieve turned away from the empty stretch of glass where her image was not. She had the feeling there were eyes behind the mirror, where hers might have been reflected, looking at her curiously.

The Trapdoor Daemon squeezed through the passage behind the ladies' dressing rooms, looking through the one-way mirrors like a patron in an aquarium examining the fish. The vampire Genevieve was with Illona Horvathy, talking about Eva Savinien. Everyone would be talking about Eva today, tonight, and for a long time...

In the next room, the chorus girls were getting into their costumes. Hilde was shaving her long legs with a straight blade and rough soap, and Wilhelmina was stuffing her bosom with kerchiefs. He retained enough of his maleness to linger, watching the fragile young women, feeling arousal and guilt.

He liked to think himself a guardian spirit, not a peeper.

He pulled himself away, and passed to the next mirror. The passage was narrow, and his back scraped against the wall as he pushed on, feeling pressure on his rough hide.

Beyond the glass, Eva Savinien was already in costume. She sat before her mirror, hands in her lap, looking emptily at herself. Alone, she was like a stored mannequin, waiting for the puppeteer's fingers to come and bring her life.

And what life she would have.

The Trapdoor Daemon gazed at Eva's perfect face, conscious

of his own shadow on the glass. He was glad the mirror was not silvered on this side, throwing his hideousness back at him.

'Eva,' he breathed.

The girl looked around, and smiled at the mirror.

The first time, during the run of *A Farce of the Fog*, the actress hadn't been sure what she'd heard.

'Eva,' he had repeated.

She was calm then, certain there was a voice.

'Who's there?'

'Just... just a spirit, child.'

The actress had been instantly suspicious.

'Reinhardt, is that you? Master Sierck?'

'I'm a spirit of the theatre. You'll be a great star, Eva. If you have the nerve, if you have the application..'

Eva had looked down, and pulled her robe around her against a chill.

'Listen,' he'd said. 'I can help you...'

He had been coming to her dressing room mirror for months, giving her advice, passing comment on each nuance of her performance, encouraging her to stretch her instrument.

Now he'd helped her as much as he could. Soon her future would be her own responsibility.

'In the fourth act,' he said, 'when you fall, you are falling away from the audience. You should take them with you as you die.'

Eva nodded, paying close attention.

VI

The horse died under him just before dawn. Thereafter, the Animus kept Scheydt running through the twilight, almost matching the pace of the animal it had driven to a foamy death.

If there was a record time for the trip from the Grey Mountains to Altdorf, Scheydt would beat it. No Imperial mess-enger could best his stamina, his resolve, his purpose.

Scheydt's feet were bleeding in his boots and his joints popped with each step, but the Animus ignored its host's pain. As long as Scheydt's skeleton and musculature were mostly intact, it could keep going. If the cleric of Solkan wore out, the Animus would just find another host.

The road passed under his pounding feet as the sun rose. Scheydt was lagging behind the Animus, ceding control of the body, slumping into occasional dozes during which his conscious-ness would shrink, giving the creature inside him a clearer hold on the world, a more acute vision of the things around. They were already out of the mountains and into the Reikwald Forest.

The road ran straight, bounded by tall evergreens. Scheydt's feet struck holes in the ground-mist. His footbeats and laboured breathing were the only sounds in earshot.

Ahead, the Animus saw a small figure, set side-saddle on a pony, proceeding slowly down the road. It was a plump, middle-aged woman in the robes of a priestess of Shallya. In the country-side, priestesses often passed from village to village, exercising the healing arts, delivering babies, ministering to the sick.

Scheydt caught up with the pony, and pulled the priestess from her perch. She struggled, and he snapped a right-angle into her spine, tossing her into a roadside ditch. The pony bent under his unaccustomed weight, and he dug in his heels like spurs. The animal wouldn't last the morning, but would give him speed.

'My shoes,' the girl said.

'Shoes?'

'It's snowing. I can't go into the streets without my fur shoes.' The girl stood up to him, growing in stature, unbending her body, squaring her shoulders. There was a dab of red paint on her cheek, a graze from earlier.

He made and unmade fists, then slipped one meaty hand into his studded metal glove. It was an impressive prop.

'Hurry away, Nita, my dove,' he sneered, the false teeth bulging and deforming his mouth. 'Your Mr Chaida has an important appointment. We can't have trash like you lying about while we entertain a lady.'

'My shoes.'

It was the third night. Eva Savinien was even better than in the last two performances. Illona was much improved, but she was still outshone. It was almost eerie. This didn't come from him, Detlef knew. It was something inside the girl, blossoming like a flower.

She moved on the stage, towards the lights. He hadn't directed her in that. In her position, the audience's attention would be focused. He was pushed into the shadows behind if he was to hit his mark and strike his blow.

Clever girl.

'I'll give you shoes,' he said, following her, raising his glove.

He wondered if anyone had been teaching little Eva how to steal a stage. She was becoming an adept thief.

Squeezing the bladder of stage blood, he brought his hand down, thumping her from behind, bursting the sac.

She fell, not to the boards but to her knees. Seeing an opportunity, she was seizing it. Blood dribbling down her beautiful face, she looked out into the audience for a long, silent moment, then fell on her face.

Now that was over, he'd have to take back the scene.

From Box Seven, the Trapdoor Daemon saw his pupil perform, and was pleased. Through Eva, he could reach an audience again, could make them feel joy, despair, love, hate...

He hadn't been so excited by a discovery for many seasons.

Her new death scene was masterly, an unforgettable moment. Now the scene was Nita's, not Chaida's. The audience would remember the play as the story of a street girl's downfall, not of a cleric's double nature.

He was too rapt to join the applause that exploded from the house when Eva Savinien came to take her curtain call. Flowers were conveyed to the stage. The company joined the applause. Even Detlef Sierck tipped a salute to her. She was modest, bowing only slightly.

Exhausted by the performance, she had no more to give. She'd discharged her obligation to the audience, and knew how to take its praise.

She'd have to be cultivated properly. A play would have to

be found for her, a suitable vehicle. She might need a patron as well as a tutor.

When they hailed her, they would be doing the Trapdoor Daemon honour.

The girl brushed past Genevieve on the way to her dressing room, an attendant carrying her flowers behind her. Eva Savinien had never spoken with her beyond the demands of conventional pleasantry. Genevieve assumed she was wary of vampires.

'That's a fine creature,' Detlef said, wiping his paint-smeared face. 'A fine creature indeed.'

She nodded agreement.

'She took that scene from me as you'd take a toy from a toddler. It's a long time since anyone's done that.'

'How do you think Illona feels?'

Detlef was pensive, his knit frown dislodging the slabs of make-up that made Chaida's brows beetle. Eva was back in her dressing room now, alone.

'She spends a lot of time in her room, doesn't she? Do you think Eva has a jealous lover?'

He considered the point, and spat out Chaida's false teeth into his hand.

'No. I think she's a devout worshipper at the shrine of self, Gené. She spends her spare time improving herself.'

'Is she improved?'

'In herself, yes. I don't know if the company will be happy to work with her much longer.'

'I understand she has had other offers. There were flowers tonight from Lutze at the Imperial Tarradasch Players.'

Detlef shrugged.

'Of course. The theatre is a nest of vultures. Eva is a tasty morsel.'

'Very,' she said, a twinge of red thirst in her tongue.

'Gené,' Detlef scolded.

'Don't worry,' she said. 'She'd have thin blood, I think'

'Lutze won't get her. She'd have to apprentice for years to get anywhere near a lead. I'll find something for her after *Dr Zhiekhill and Mr Chaida* concludes its run.'

'She'll stay?'

'If she's as clever as I think. A jewel needs a setting, and this is the best company in Altdorf. She won't want to be Lilli Nissen, surrounded by fifth-rate hams to make her look good. She needs the challenge of an excellence that forces her to rise.'

'Detlef, do you like her?'

'She's the best young actress in seasons.'

'But do you like her?'

His shoulders shifted. 'She's an actress, Gené. A good one, possibly a great one. That's all. You don't have to like her to see that.'

A stifled sob caught Genevieve's attention. By the stage door, Reinhardt was shaking Illona. They were arguing, and Illona was in distress. It was easy to deduce the subject of their dispute. Poppa Fritz shoved past the couple, bowed under the weight of a vast basket of flowers.

Reinhardt pulled Illona to him, and tried to calm her crying with a hug.

'It's this play,' Detlef said. 'It's making us find out things about ourselves we might prefer not to know.'

The darkness was in his eyes.

VII

After three days on the road, Scheydt was approaching Altdorf on foot. The Animus was quiet now, and he recalled the details of his trip as if trying to piece together a vivid but fast-fading nightmare. Animals had died, and people too. Pain was a constant thing with him, now. But it didn't matter. It was as if the pain were someone else's, not connected to his soul, to his heart. His boots would have to be peeled from his feet, blood congealing in them. His left arm was broken, and flapped awkwardly. His robes were ragged and filthy with the dust of travel. His face was frozen, immobile, the replica of the mask fused with it. Unconscious of the hurt, Scheydt walked on, one foot in front of the other, trudging in the deep wheelruts of the back road.

The gates of the city were ahead. People clustered around, queuing with their wares to be passed by the Imperial customs. There were watchmen about, doubtless looking for felons and murderers. And soldiers were taking their tithes from the merchants who came to Altdorf with perishable goods, silks, jewels or weapons.

Two young whores joked with the watchmen. A donkey was defecating spectacularly in the road, causing a commotion of people away from its rear end and a heated argument between the beast's owner and various bystanders. Scheydt joined a group of foot travellers, and waited to be passed. At the gate, an officer of the watch was checking purses. Anyone with less than five crowns was refused entry to the city. Altdorf had enough beggars.

A sweetmeat vendor with a tray of pastries was passed through. Then, it came to be Scheydt's turn. The officer laughed.

'You've no hope, ragamuffin.'

The Animus came awake in Scheydt's head and fixed its gaze on the officer. The laughter died.

'I am a cleric of Solkan. The university of Altdorf will vouch for me,' Scheydt explained.

The officer looked at him in disbelief.

'A tramp from a midden, more like.'

'Let me pass.'

'Let's have your purse then.'

Scheydt had none. It must have fallen away during his journey, gone with his hat and cloak. The officer turned to the next man in the queue, a mariner on his way back to his ship at the Altdorf docks, and started examining his papers.

'Let me pass,' Scheydt said again.

The officer ignored him, and he was rudely shoved out of the way.

Scheydt stumbled away some twenty paces, feet not quite working properly. Then he took a run at the gate, head down. His skull punched between the mariner and the officer, and his shoulders slammed both men back against the iron grille of the gate. A crossbow twanged and a bolt struck his back.

His hands went between the bars, and he swept them aside as if they were curtains. He heard oaths from the soldiers and the rest of the crowd. Iron buckled and broke. On the other side of the gate, the sweetmeat vendor looked on in panic, spilling cakes from his tray.

The mariner was in his way. Scheydt made a fist and put it through the sailor boy's head, punching his nose out through the back of his skull. Pulling his bloody hand loose, he heard a squelch as if he were extracting his fist from a bowl of thick, half-set gruel.

A soldier slashed at him with a short sword, and Scheydt held up his broken arm to parry. The blade bit into his forearm, lodging in the cracked bone. Scheydt pressed forwards with his arm, driving the sword's edge into the face of its owner. The split-headed soldier fell out of the way. There was a hole in the gate. Scheydt walked through it, a sword still stuck in his arm.

'Stop in the name of the Emperor!' shouted the officer.

He felt a blast at his back and was pushed forwards. Without losing his footing, he turned to see the officer through a cloud of smoke. The man was holding a flintlock pistol. Scheydt felt clean air on his exposed shoulderblades. The ball had burst and spread, ripping away his robe and his skin. The officer emptied powder from his horn into the gun, and reached for his sack of lead balls.

Scheydt strode to the officer and, with his good hand, took away his works. He emptied white gunpowder from the horn over the man's face, and held the pistol by its barrel, his finger through the trigger guard. The lock was fixed back.

The officer's eyes widened with panic as he choked.

With his elbow, Scheydt smashed the officer's throat apple, driving him back against the stones. He held the pistol near the officer's clown-powdered face, and worked the trigger with his knuckle. A flint-spark danced from the breech into the officer's eyes. The man's head caught fire in a puff, and Scheydt walked away. As he hurried from the gates, his forearm came off and fell into the gutter.

* * *

He needed to practise the transformation. Not the make-up tricks –
the palmed teeth, the extensible wig, the greasepaint lines that
only appeared under a certain light – but the rest of it. Anyone
could make himself into a monster on the outside. To be convincing, Detlef's Chaida had to come from inside.

He sat alone in the theatre's bar, staring at the pitted wooden
top of a table, trying to find the darkness in his heart. In the
hearts of his audience.

He remembered the eyes of Drachenfels. He remembered his
months in Mundsen Keep. Some monsters are born, not made.
But hunger and cruelty could drive a man to any lengths. What
could turn him – Detlef Sierck – into something as prodigiously
evil as Constant Drachenfels? The Great Enchanter had been
shaped by centuries, millennia. Sorcery and sin, temptation and
terror, ambition and agony. Did men become Chaidas a little at
a time, like sands dropping in an hourglass, or was the transformation instant, as it appeared on the stage?

He made fists, and imagined them landing blows. He imagined skulls being crushed.

Eva Savinien's skull.

A black hand clutched at his heart, and slowly squeezed. His
fists tightened into knots, and his lips drew back from his teeth.

The darkness throbbed in his mind.

Mr Chaida grew in him, and his shoulders slumped as his body
bent into the shape of the monster.

An animal mind expanded inside his own.

There was such pleasure in evil. Such ease and comfort. Such
freedom. The space between desire and fulfilment was an instant.
There was a fiery simplicity to the savage.

At last, Detlef understood.

'Detlef Sierck,' said a voice, cutting through his thoughts, 'I am
Viktor Rasselas, steward and advisor to Mornan Tybalt, Chancellor of the Empire, patron of the Imperial bank of Altdorf.'

Detlef looked up at the man, eyes coming into focus.

He was a reedy character, dressed in smart grey, and he had a scroll in his gloved hands. The seal of the Imperial counting house was his cap-badge.

'I am here to present to you this petition,' droned Rasselas, 'demanding that you cease performance of *The Strange History of Dr Zhiekhill and Mr Chaida*. It has been signed by over one hundred of the foremost citizens of the Empire. We allege that your drama inflames the violent tendencies of the audiences and, in these bloody times, such an inflammation is...'

Rasselas gulped as Detlef's hand closed on his throat.

He looked at the man's fearstruck face and gripped tighter, relishing the squirming feel of the neck muscles trapped under his fingers. Rasselas's face changed colour several times.

Detlef rammed the steward's head against the wall. That felt good. He did it again.

'What are you doing?'

He barely heard the voice. He slipped his thumb under Rasselas's ear, and pressed hard on the pulsing vein there, his nail digging into the skin.

A few seconds more pressure, and the pulse would be stilled.

'Detlef!'

Hands pulled his shoulder. It was Genevieve.

The darkness in his mind fogged, and was whipped apart. He found he was in pain, teeth locked together, an ache in his head, bones grinding in his hand. He dropped the choking steward, and staggered into Genevieve's arms. She supported his weight with ease, and slipped him into a chair.

Rasselas scrambled to his feet and loosened his collar, angry red marks on his skin. He fled, leaving his petition behind.

'What were you thinking of?' Genevieve asked.

He didn't know.

VIII

The pupil was learning faster than the Trapdoor Daemon had expected. She was like a flirtatious vampire, delicately sucking him dry of all his experience, all his skill. She took rapid little sips at him.

Soon, he'd be empty. All gone.

In her room beyond the glass, Eva sobbed uncontrollably, her face a cameo of grief. Then, as one might snuff out a candle, she dropped the emotion completely.

'Good,' he said.

She accepted his approval modestly. The exercises were over.

'You have refused Lutze's offer?' he asked.

'Of course.'

'It was the right thing to do. Later, there will be more offers. You will take one, eventually. The right one.'

Eva was pensive, briefly. He could not read her mood.

'What troubles you, child?'

'When I accept an offer, I shall have to go to another theatre.'

'Naturally.'

'Will you come with me?'

He said nothing.

'Spirit?'

'Child, you will not need me forever.'

'No,' she stamped her feet. 'I shall never leave you. You have done so much for me. These flowers, these notices. They are as much yours as mine.'

Eva wasn't being sincere. It was ironic; off the stage, she was a poor dissembler. Truly, she thought she'd outgrown him already, but she wasn't sure whether she was strong enough to proceed the next few steps without her familiar crutch. And, at the back of her mind, she feared competition, and assumed he would find another pupil.

'I am just a conscientious gardener, child. I have cultivated your bloom, but that does no credit to me.'

Eva didn't know, but she was the first he had instructed. She'd be the last.

Eva Savinien came along only once in a lifetime, even a life as extended as the Trapdoor Daemon's.

The girl sat at her mirror again, looking at her reflection. Was she trying to see beyond, to see him? The thought gave him a spasm of horror. His hide crawled, and he heard the drip of his thick secretion.

'Spirit, why can I never see you?'

She'd asked that before. He had no answer.

'Have you no body to see?'

He almost laughed but his throat couldn't make the sound any more. He wished what she suggested were true.

'Who are you?'

'Just a Trapdoor Daemon. I was a playwright once, a director too. But that was long ago. Before you were born. Before your mother was born.'

'What is your name?'

'I have no name. Not any more.'

'What was your name?'

'It wouldn't mean anything to you.'

'Your voice is so beautiful, I'm sure you are comely. A handsome ghost like the apparition in *A Farce of the Fog*.'

'No, child.'

The Trapdoor Daemon was uncomfortable. Since the play opened, Eva had been pressing him about himself. Before, all her questions had been about herself. About how she could improve herself. Now, uncharacteristically, she was being consumed by curiosity. It was something she'd discovered inside, and was letting grow.

She was wandering about her room now, back to him. A bouquet had arrived from the palace every day since the first night. Eva had made a conquest of Prince Luitpold. She took yesterday's stiff blossoms from their vase and piled them with the others.

'I love you, spirit,' she said, lying.

'No, child. But I shall teach you to show love.'

She whirled around, the heavy vase in her hand, and smashed the mirror. The noise of the shattering glass was like an explosion in the confined space of the passage. Light poured in, smiting his shrinking eyes like a rain of fire. Shards pattered against his chest, sticking to the damp patches.

Eva stepped back, glass tinkling under her feet.

She saw him. Unfeigned, unforced horror burst out of her in a screech, and her lovely face twisted with fear, disgust, loathing, instinctive hate.

It was no less than he had expected.

There was an urgent knocking at Eva's door. Shouts outside the dressing room.

He was gone through his own trapdoor before anyone could intervene, pulling himself through the catacombs on his tentacles, driving himself deeper into the heart of the theatre, determined to flee from the light, to hide himself from wounded eyes, to bury himself in the unexplored depths of the building. He knew his way in the dark, knew each turn and junction of the passageways. At the heart of the labyrinth was the lagoon that had been his home since he first changed.

More than a mirror was broken.

She broke the lock and pulled the door open. Eva Savinien was having hysterics, tearing up her dressing room. At last, Genevieve thought rather cattily, a genuine emotion. It was the first time Eva had suggested offstage that she might have feelings. The mirror was smashed, the air full of petals from shredded bouquets.

The actress flinched as Genevieve stepped into the room, others crowding in behind her. Like a trapped animal, Eva backed into a corner, as far away as possible from the broken mirror.

There was an aperture behind the looking glass.

'What is it?' Illona asked the younger woman.

Eva shook her head, and tore at her hair.

'She's having a fit,' someone said.

'No,' said Genevieve. 'She's had a fright. She's just afraid.'

She held out her hands, and tried to make calming gestures. It was no good. Eva was as afraid of Genevieve as she was of whatever had thrown such a scare into her.

'There's a passage here,' said Poppa Fritz from near the mirror. 'It goes back into the wall.'

'What happened?' asked Reinhardt.

Detlef shouldered his way into the room, and Eva threw herself at him, pressing her face to his shirt, her body racked with sobs. Detlef, astonished, looked at Genevieve as he patted Eva's back, trying to quiet her down. Being the director made him stand-in father for everyone in the company, but he was not used to this sort of behaviour. Especially not from Eva.

The actress broke away from Detlef suddenly and, darting between the people crowding the room, ran through the door, down the passageway, out of the theatre. Detlef called after her. There was a performance tonight, and she could not run out.

Genevieve was examining the hole where the mirror had been. A cool breeze was coming from it. And a peculiar smell. She thought she heard something moving far away.

'Look, there's some sort of liquid,' Reinhardt said, dipping his finger into a slimy substance that clung to a jagged edge of glass. It was green and thick.

'What is going on here?' Detlef asked. 'What's got into Eva?'

Poppa Fritz leaned into the cavity and sucked a whiff into his nostrils.

'It's the Box Seven smell,' Reinhardt said.

Poppa Fritz nodded sagely. 'The Trapdoor Daemon,' he said, tapping his nose.

Detlef threw up his hands in exasperation.

Bernabe Scheydt had found the theatre easily. It was on Temple Street, one of the city's main thoroughfares. But, by the time he reached the place, Scheydt was not much more use to the Animus. Although he'd bound his stump as best he could with rags torn from his robes, he had lost a lot of blood. He was leaking badly through the hole in his back, and he still had the head of a crossbow quarrel lodged in his spine. This host was dying under the Animus, just as the horses that had brought him to Altdorf had died under Scheydt.

He managed to haul himself into the alley beside the Vargr Breughel Memorial Playhouse, and slumped across from the stage door. As he lurched into the recess a passing woman pressed a coin into his hand, and gave him the blessing of Shallya.

Gripping the coin in his remaining fist, he let the wall support him. He was aware of the slow trickle of blood from his many wounds, but he felt little. Suddenly, the stage door clattered open, and a girl came running out. She must be from the company. She was young, with a stream of dark hair.

The Animus made Scheydt stand up on weary legs, and totter towards the girl, blocking her path. She dodged, but the alley was narrow. He collapsed against her, bearing her towards the wall, dragging her down. She struggled, but did not scream. Already in the grip of panic, she had no more fear.

As he fell on her, Scheydt's leg bent the wrong way and snapped, a sharp end of broken bone spearing through muscle and flesh below the knee. With his hand, he grabbed the girl's hair, and pulled himself up to her face.

The girl began screaming. The Animus guided its host forwards. Scheydt pressed his face close to the pretty girl's, and it peeled off, sliding down between them.

Suddenly, he was free, and pain poured into his body. He shrieked as the full agony of his wounds fell on him like a cloak of lightning.

Without the Animus, he was lost, abandoned.

The girl, calming, stood up, heaving him off.

He could not stop shaking, and liquid was spewing from his mouth. He curled into a ball of pain, his limbs ending in ragged edges of agony. Looking up, he saw the girl feeling her face. The mask was in place, but not joined to her yet. The white metal caught the moonlight, and glowed like a lantern.

She was not screaming any more. But Scheydt was, letting out a tearing, dying, jagged howl from the depths of his disordered soul.

Detlef examined the hole, and was glad nobody suggested he explore the passage. It would have been hard for him to get through the mirror-sized gap, and there was something about the dark beyond that reminded him of the corridors of Castle Drachenfels.

'They must go back for miles,' he said.

Guglielmo was by his side, with a sheaf of floor-plans and diagrams, shaking his head.

'Nothing is marked, but we've always known these were approximate at best. The building has been remodelled, knocked down, rebuilt, refitted a dozen times.'

Genevieve was nearby, waiting. She was in one of her siege moods, as if she expected a surprise attack at any moment. Stage-hands were out looking for Eva.

Illona was trying to look concerned for the girl.

'And this part of the city is rotten through with secret tunnels and passageways from the wars.'

Detlef was worried about tonight's performance. The audience was already arriving. And they were expecting to see the discovery of the season, Eva Savinien.

There was no time to deal with this.

IX

The new host stood up, the Animus settling on her face. Scheydt was writhing at her feet, scrabbling with his hand at her leg, trying to pull himself up.

'Give it back,' he shouted through his pain.

It was easy to shake him off.

The Animus was intrigued by the cool, purposeful mind of Eva Savinien, and by the recent blot of panic that had been scrawled across the hitherto perfect page of her thoughts. This was the vehicle which would get it close to Genevieve and Detlef. Close to its purpose. It would have to be more circumspect now.

Like Scheydt, this host had her needs and desires. The Animus thought it could help assuage them.

She spread and fisted her fingers, feeling the pull and push of her muscles as far up as her elbows, her shoulders. The Animus was conscious of the perfection of her young body. Her back was as supple as a fine longbow, and her slender limbs as well-proportioned as an idealized statue. She spread her arms, heaving her shoulders, stretching apart her breasts.

The screaming man at her feet was attracting attention. There were crowds in the street, and they passed comment. Soon, someone would intervene.

Scheydt had denied himself everything, and, with the Animus in his mind, had exploded. Eva was more in accord with herself, but there were still things the Animus could do for her. And she welcomed its presence, feeding it the information it needed to proceed towards its purpose.

Detlef and Genevieve were both in the building, but it would stay its killing blow for the moment. The revenge had to be complete. It would be cautious not to wear out this host as fast as it had Scheydt.

'Eva,' said a male voice.

The Animus allowed Eva to turn to the man. It was Reinhardt Jessner, standing in the doorway. He was an actor in Detlef's company, a buffoon but a decent one. He could be of use.

'What's wrong?'

'Nothing,' she said. 'Stage fright.'

Reinhardt looked unsure. 'That's not like you.'

'No, but one shouldn't be like oneself all the time, don't you think?'

She eased past him into the theatre, and darted up a small, hungry kiss at his bewildered mouth. After only a moment, he responded, and the Animus tasted the actor's soul.

The kiss broke, and Reinhardt looked down at Scheydt.

'Who's this?'

'A beggar,' she explained. 'Overdoing his act somewhat.'

'His leg is broken. You can see the bone.'

Eva laughed. 'You should know the tricks that can be done with make-up, Reinhardt.'

She shut the door on the still-kicking cleric of Solkan, and let Reinhardt take her back to the stage.

'I'm perfectly all right,' she kept saying. 'It was just stage fright... just an accident... just a panic...'

'Curtain up in half an hour,' Poppa Fritz announced.

Eva left Reinhardt, and made her way back to her dressing room. The Animus remembered the thing the host had seen beyond the mirror. There was no time to take account of it.

'Poppa,' she told the hireling. 'Get me a new mirror, and whip my costumier into action.'

Below the Vargr Breughel, underneath even the fifth level of the basements, there was a saltwater lagoon. A hundred years ago, it had served as a smugglers' den. It had been abandoned in haste; chests of rotted silks and dusty jewels stood stacked haphazardly on the shores. This was the Trapdoor Daemon's lair. His books swelled up with the damp like leavened bread, but the water was good for him. He could drink brine, and needed to immerse his body every few hours. If his hide dried out, it cracked and became painful.

But not as painful as the heartache he now felt.

He had known how it would end. There could be no other outcome. As a dramatist, he must have understood that.

But...

Collapsed on the sandy slope, his bulbous head in the water, its ruff of tentacles floating around it, he was alone with his despair.

Everything had been a futile attempt to put off the despair.

He heard the constant drip of water down the walls of this dungeon, and saw the rippling reflection of his lanterns on the water's surface.

Sometimes, he wondered if he should just cast himself off, and let his body wash through the tunnels to the Reik, and then to the sea. If he were to throw away the last of his humanity, perhaps he might find contentment in the limitless oceans.

No.

He sat up, head breaking the water, and crawled away, leaving a damp trail behind him.

He was the Trapdoor Daemon. Not a spirit of the sea.

There were age-eaten wooden statues of gods and goddesses around the walls – of Verena and Manann, Myrmidia and Sigmar, Morr and Taal. They had been ship's figureheads. Now, their faces were vertically lined where the grain of the wood had cracked, and greened with masks of moss. Slowly, they became less human. When the Trapdoor Daemon had first found this place – the marks of his own change barely apparent to anyone else – the faces had been plain, recognizable, inspiring. As he had become monstrous, so had they. Yet they retained their human faces underneath.

Underneath his skin, he was still a man.

The Trapdoor Daemon stood up. On two legs, like a man. The water had washed away some of his pain.

Lanterns burned eternally in his lair. It was as richly appointed as a palace, albeit with furniture rescued from the scenery dock.

The boatlike bed where he slept looked like a priceless antique from the Age of the Three Emperors, but was in fact a sturdy replica constructed for a forgotten production of *The Loves of Ottokar and Myrmidia*. Nothing was what it seemed.

Somewhere above, the company would be preparing for the curtain. He had not missed a performance yet. And he wouldn't break his habit tonight. Not for something as inconsequential as a heartless actress.

From a hook, he hauled down a cloak intended to be worn by a mechanical giant in one of the old melodramas.

He wrapped himself up, and slithered towards his trapdoor.

The crowds outside the theatre treated him as a madman, and kicked him into the street. The newly broken bone in his leg sawed through his flesh. On his knees, his hand pressed to his stump, he threw back his head and screamed.

The world spun around him. There was no such thing as a fixed point. A sundial is only useful if the sun is out.

Clouds gathered in the night sky, obscuring the moons.

Bernabe Scheydt yelled, and people hurried away from him. His face had been torn away, and he felt as if he were smothered with a mask of hungry ants, a million tiny mandibles dripping poison into his flayed flesh.

Up in the sky, a speck appeared. A black, flapping speck.

His scream ran out, and he just let the pain run through his whole body. His throat was torn and bleeding inside.

The speck became a bird, and he fixed his eyes on it.

An officer of the watch came near, his club out, and he stood over Scheydt, prodding him with a polished boot.

'Move on,' the watchman said. 'This is a respectable district, and we can't be having the likes of you.'

The bird was coming down like a rocket, beak-first, its wings fixed as if it were a missile.

'I... am... a cleric of the law.'

The copper spat, and kicked him in the knee, sending a jolt of pain through his body.

The bird still came. The watchman heard the whoosh as the hawk sliced like a throwing knife through the air, and turned around. He raised his club, and fell backwards, away from Scheydt, stifling his own yell.

The hawk fastened on Scheydt's head, beak gouging for his eyes, talons fixing about his ears. The bird had razor-edged metal spurs fixed to its ankles, and it had been trained in their use.

There was screaming all around.

'Warhawk, warhawk!'

The beak prised Scheydt's skull open and dug in expertly. It didn't feed, it rent apart. A gush of warmth expelled from the cleric's head, and dribbled down his face.

Then the pain was gone, and the bird was flying away.

Scheydt collapsed in the street, an unrecognizable, torn, broken mess. The clouds passed, and moonlight streamed down on the corpse.

X

'There's been a murder,' Guglielmo announced. 'Outside in the street.'

'What!'

Every new development was like a punch to his head. Detlef couldn't keep up.

Eva was in a corner, trying to reassure everyone that she was all right, that she could go on tonight. She was dressed and made up for Act One, turned into the bedraggled, painted Nita.

Guglielmo had a burly guard placed in Eva's dressing room, but the actress didn't want protection. She'd changed completely, and Detlef wondered if her earlier panic had been an act. If so, she'd fooled him completely. And he couldn't think of any reason for the performance. His own dresser draped Zhiekhill's robes around him, pinning them up. Cindy, the make-up assistant, set the trick wig under his cap. He felt like a baby, fussed over but ignored, an object not a person.

If a play lives through the first week, it can run for an age.

Detlef wondered if the players could live through this first week of *The Strange History of Dr Zhiekhill and Mr Chaida*.

Poppa Fritz reported that there were protesters outside. They'd been hired by Mornan Tybalt, and come to picket the lines of theatre-goers. Now, having come to stop a play and stayed to witness a murder, they were on the point of rioting.

'It was another Warhawk killing.'

Detlef couldn't move his face to react as the special grease-paint was laid on.

The watch were on their way.

He had lost track of Genevieve, but could trust her to look after herself. He hoped he could trust her to look after him too.

'It has nothing to do with us,' Guglielmo said. 'A beggar was the victim.'

In her dressing room, Illona Horvathy was loudly filling a bucket with her dinner, as she'd done before every performance of every play she'd ever been in. Cindy stood back and judged her handiwork passable. Outside, he was Zhiekhill. Inside, he didn't know...

He heard the first notes of Felix Hubermann's overture.

'Places, everyone,' Detlef shouted.

Feeling the cold, she made her way down the narrow passage, knowing the floor was likely to give way under her. It was dark, but she was at home in darkness.

Genevieve knew the Vargr Breughel was connected with the labyrinth of tunnels that criss-crossed under the city. Altdorf had suffered too many wars, sieges, revolutions and riots not to be worm-holed through with secret ways. There was a drip of slime from somewhere, and the Box Seven smell was strong in the confined space. It was a surprise, however, to find the body of the building itself so extensively undermined, as if the theatre was a stage set, backed not by solid walls but by painted canvas.

From the passageway behind the ladies' dressing rooms – to which, equipped as they were with one-way mirrors, the management could have charged admission and secured quite a substantial income from the city's wealthier devotees of female flesh – she'd passed into a hub-like space, from which tunnels led off to all the points of the compass. There were also trapdoors in the ceiling and floor, so she supposed this knot was one of the secret junctions, a nodal point in the labyrinth.

There were few cobwebs, which suggested these paths were travelled often. In an alcove in the wall at the junction, a small bowl of matter burned, giving off a glow and a smell. It was longbane, a wood known to burn slowly, sometimes for up to a year.

This was an inhabited lair.

'Anyone home?' she asked, the passages throwing back echoes at her. There was no other answer.

She remembered the dark hallways of Drachenfels, and the unease that had set into her soul when she entered that castle. Even before anything had happened, she'd known that had been an evil place, the haunt of monsters and madness. This was different.

Reflecting upon her emotions, she realized she was depressed, not afraid. Whatever walked here, walked alone, lived alone. It hid away in the dark not from malice but from shame, fear, self-disgust.

She opened a door, and a stench enveloped her.

Her sense of smell was keener than a human's, and she had to hold her nose until the first wave had dissipated. Her stomach convulsed, and she would have vomited if there'd been any food in her. She didn't need to eat, but sometimes did so to be sociable or to sample a taste. But she hadn't taken anything solid for weeks. The nausea spasms were like blows to her abdomen.

Standing up, she looked into the cupboard.

It was something's larder, well-stocked with pale sewerfish, dog-size rats, various small altered creatures. The meat animals of the labyrinth all bore the taint of warpstone: the fish were eyeless or possessed of rudimentary forelimbs, the rats had heads out of proportion with their thin-furred bodies, other beasts were unidentifiable as what they had formerly been. They'd all been killed by something strong that broke necks or took large bites from its prey. Evidently, the epicure would not touch meat that was not yet a few days rotten, and these morsels had been left to putrefy a little, until they were fit to serve the larder-keeper's taste.

'Gods,' Genevieve swore, 'what a way to live!'

Moving on, she came to a drop that fell away into the depths of the city like a cliff. It was covered with what looked like a ship's rigging, a net of thick ropes, sturdy if tattered. It would be comparatively easy to climb down, but she thought that adventure could wait for another night.

Down below, she heard water lapping.

Turning away, she confidently expected to be able to retrace her steps. Within fifty paces, she was in new territory, lost.

She thought she was still on the same level as the theatre, and if she held still she could even hear the distant sounds of Felix's overture. She could not have gone that far into the labyrinth. There were trapdoors all over the place. Some must lead back to the public ways of the house.

Trying another promising door, she found herself surrounded by books and papers, stuffed into floor-to-ceiling shelves. There was a longbane taper burning, giving the room a woody, pleasant smell.

Longbane was known as Scholar's Ruin, because its fumes were mildly euphoric, mildly addictive.

This was a fairly ordinary theatre library. There were much-used and scribbled-on copies of standard works. A full set of the plays of Tarradasch, actors' and directors' copies of other repertory warhorses, some basic texts on stagecraft, a bundled collection of playbills, scrolled posters. A bound folio of Detlef Sierck was upside-down among the other books.

Genevieve looked about, wondering if any unusual book might turn up here, some grimoire of power bound in human skin and holding the key to a vast magical design. There was nothing of the sort.

What she did find was a whole case given over to books by someone of whom she had barely heard, a playwright of the previous century named Bruno Malvoisin. He was the author of *Seduced by Slaaneshi*, which she remembered as a scandalous piece in its day. Apart from that, he'd contributed nothing which still lived in the repertoire. She read the titles of plays from the elegant spines of the books: *The Tragedy of Magritta, The Seventh Voyage of Sigmar, Bold Benvolio, An Estalian's Treachery, Vengeance of Vaumont, The Rape of Rachael.* A whole life was wrapped up between these covers, a life spent and forgotten. Evidently, Bruno Malvoisin meant something to the inhabitant of the labyrinth. That might help solve the puzzle. She must ask Detlef if he knew anything about the man. Or, more usefully, Poppa Fritz: the stage-door keeper was an inexhaustible fount of theatrical lore.

She stepped back into the passageway, and tried the next trapdoor. It led to a small space that smelled of bread and belched a pocket of warm air at her. Genevieve almost passed it by, but then recognized that the back of the space was a door as well. She pulled herself into the recess, and pushed the door – a heavy, iron flap but unlocked – open.

Slipping out of one of the ovens, she found herself in the kitchens of the Vargr Breughel Memorial Playhouse. A chef turned, gasped, and dropped a tray of intermission pastries.

'Sorry,' she said. 'I thought I was cooked through.'

XI

Throughout the play, the Animus observed Detlef Sierck. In their scenes together, Eva was close to him, and the Animus could see through the filter of her mind. The actor was a huge man, almost swollen, physically strong, a powerful projector. This host wouldn't formerly have been able to best him in a struggle. Even with the Animus guiding her, taking away any restraints of pain or conscience, she might take a long time to overcome him. And Eva knew that, frail as she might seem, the vampire would be even more resilient.

With the rider in her mind, Eva lived the role of Nita as never before, wrestling the piece away from Detlef and the other players. The second act curtain was hers, as she returned on her knees to Chaida, lifting her scarf away from her bruises and throwing herself upon his mercy. The tableau was thunderously applauded.

Once the curtain was rung down, Detlef said, 'Good work, Eva, but, perhaps, from now on, less is more...'

As she stood up, the scene shifters working around them to change the stage set, Detlef looked at her. Sweat was pouring from him, beads glistening through his monster face-paint. His role was exhausting.

Reinhardt swarmed around, and kissed her on the cheek.

'Magnificent,' he said, 'a revelation...'

Detlef frowned, his Chaida brows moving together ferociously.

'She gets better and better, don't you think?'

'Of course,' the actor-manager nodded.

'You're a star,' Reinhardt said, touching her chin with his thumb.

The Animus knew that Reinhardt Jessner wanted sexual congress with its host. From Bernabe Scheydt, it understood lust.

'Just remember,' Detlef said, 'at the end of the play, I kill you.'

Eva smiled and nodded humbly. The Animus sampled the complicated emotions that ticked over inside the host's head. She was more ordered in her thoughts than Scheydt, the supposed devotee of the Law, had been. In her single-mindedness, she was very like the Animus itself. In the near distance she had purposes, and every step she took brought her nearer their achievement. Surprised, the Animus found itself in sympathy with Eva Savinien.

Coolly, professionally, the host stood to one side of the stage, allowing her dresser to change her shawl, and a make-up artist to dab stage blood and blue bruising onto her face.

'More flowers,' said an old man Eva knew as Poppa Fritz. 'Flowers from the palace.'

The Animus allowed Eva a tight smile. She thought the admiration of influential men a distraction. Despite everything, despite her resolve, despite her calculation, her life was for the theatre. She thought of taking lovers, patrons, a place in society. But they were just underpinnings. Her purpose was out in the limelight, out on the stage. Eva understood she was different, and didn't expect to be loved by individuals. Only the audience counted, that collective heart which was hers to win.

'And a special bouquet,' Poppa Fritz continued, 'from a kind spirit...'

A chill struck Eva, surprising the Animus.

Poppa Fritz held out a card, upon which was written, 'From the Occupant of Box Seven.'

'That's the Trapdoor Daemon's perch,' he explained.

A panic grew inside Eva, but the Animus soothed it away. Sampling the girl's memory, it understood her instinctive fears, understood the tangle into which she'd got herself. It could help her overcome these untidy emotions, and so it did.

The Animus was beginning to lose its sense of a distinct identity. It had started to think of itself as herself. Its former existence was a dream. Now, it was Eva Savinien. She was Eva.

Her name was called, and without a thought she took up her place on the dark stage. The curtains parted, and the light came up.

Nita lived.

Eva was different tonight. Of course, the Trapdoor Daemon had expected that. After the shock she'd had, most actresses would not even have gone on this evening.

He couldn't understand, though, how she could be so magnificent. She was a different person onstage. The screaming girl in the dressing room was left behind somewhere, and all the audience could see was Nita. He wondered how much of the luminousness of her playing was down to fear, down to the memory of the thing she had seen.

Having confronted a monster in her real life, was she better able to understand Mr Chaida's mistress? Later, would she come back to her guiding spirit just as the Kislevite drab persistently crawled to her abusive lover?

The ghost was almost frightened. He understood Eva the actress, but he couldn't begin to fathom out Eva the woman. He didn't even really believe there was such a person.

In Box Seven, he was racked with sobs, stifling the noise, feeling the tears leaking from his huge eyes.

On the stage, Nita cringed under a torrent of abuse from Chaida. The monster took a willow-switch to her back, and poured forth a stream of obscenities, insults, taunts.

The Trapdoor Daemon, like the rest of the audience, was held horrorstruck.

Detlef Sierck's Chaida capered like an ape, almost dancing with glee as he inflicted hurt upon hurt. As Eva's performance grew in strength, so she pushed her co-star to greater lengths.

Evil was in the Vargr Breughel Theatre. Concentrated under the lights, shining for all to see. Detlef's Zhiekhill and Chaida would be remembered as one of his great roles. It went beyond make-up. It was as if the playwright were truly living out the duality, the heights of nobility, the depths of depravity. Some might fear for the performer's sanity and assume he had gone the way of the notorious Laszlo Lowenstein, the horrors of his stage roles overwhelming his real life until man and monster became indistinguishable.

On stage, Mr Chaida clumped with heavy boots over the prone form of the innkeeper's child, gleefully stomping the life out of her.

Listening from his hiding places, the Trapdoor Daemon had learned that tickets for *Dr Zhiekhill and Mr Chaida* were changing hands at ten times their face value. Every night, masked dignitaries were cramming into the boxes, unable to bear not having seen the piece. More seats were being squeezed into the stalls and circle, and commoners were paying a week's wage to stand by the walls, just to wonder at the spectacle, to be a part of the occasion.

The audience screamed as the innkeeper's daughter's head came off, and Chaida booted it into the wings.

It was magical. And fragile. No one knew how long the spell

would last. Eventually, the play might fall into a set pattern, and become a routine entertainment, and those lucky enough to see it early would look with pity upon those who came later in the run.

The scene changed. Nita was alone now, singing her song, trying to beg from unseen passers-by the kopecks she needed to bribe the gate-keeper to let her out of the city. Away from Chaida, she might have a chance. Back in her village, she could find a life.

Half the audience was trying to hide their tears.

Her hands out, she felt the buffeting of the uncaring Kislevites. Her song ended, and she slipped to the stage, fluttering scraps of paper drifting about her to signify the famous Kislev snows. In her ragged clothes, Nita shivered, hugging herself.

Then the shadow of Chaida fell upon her. And her doom was sealed.

XII

It was taking Detlef longer to recover after each performance. There were three major fights, four violent love scenes and six murders in the script, plus the physically gruelling transformation scenes. He was picking up as many bruises as a pit-fighter. He must be sweating off pounds, although that didn't seem to be affecting his gut.

Tonight, he'd barely been able to stand up for the curtain calls. Once the piece was over, the weight of weariness fell on him from a great height. They were all calling for Eva, anyway. He could easily fade into the scenery.

Once the curtain was down for the last time, Reinhardt had to help him off the stage, choosing a path between the ropes and flats.

There was a pile of floral offerings the size of an ox-cart heaped up by the ladies' dressing rooms. All for Eva.

Scraping at his face, pulling off his Chaida deformities, he staggered to his own dressing room, and collapsed on a divan, head pounding like a blacksmith's anvil. He was sure Reinhardt had stabbed him during the fight, but had so many pains that he couldn't isolate any individual wound. His dresser soaked a cloth, and dropped it on his forehead. Detlef garbled out a thanks.

He was still shaking, still in the grips of Mr Chaida.

When he shut his eyes, he saw Eva Savinien mutilated and dismembered. He saw rivulets of blood in the streets of Altdorf. He saw children thrown into open fires. Human bodies rent apart, entrails strewn in the dirt, eyes pecked by ravens, tongues pulled out.

He woke out of his doze, horrors still vivid in his mind.

Guglielmo was there, with the broadsheets. They were full of the latest Warhawk murder.

'The watch don't know who the beggar was,' Guglielmo said. 'The regular beggars in Temple Street claim never to have seen him, although he doesn't exactly have a face you could identify. He wore an amulet of Solkan, but the assumption is that he stole it. There's no connection with the other victims. No connection with the theatre.'

Detlef could imagine the hawk's spiked feet latching onto human flesh, the beak gouging skin, hammering at bone.

'I've ordered an extra patrol of the night guard on the street, and I'm putting a few bruisers in the building tonight. This whole thing stinks of trouble. What with Eva's broken mirror and the Warhawk death, I think we might have the beginnings of a curse here.'

Detlef sat up, his back and arms aching. Poppa Fritz was in the room too, looking solemn.

'This house has had curses before,' the old man said. '*Strange Flower*. It seems the Trapdoor Daemon took against it. The production never got to the first night. Illnesses, accidents, mishaps, assaults, disagreements. The whole thing.'

'There is no curse,' Detlef said. '*Dr Zhiekhill and Mr Chaida* is a success.'

'There've been cursed successes.'

Detlef snorted. But he couldn't summon up the contempt for superstition that would once have burst forth unasked when anyone talked of curses on plays. Actors were quite capable of fouling up a production without supernatural intervention.

'Tybalt's called for us to be shut down again,' said Guglielmo. 'I don't know what's got into him. Some moral crusade or other marched up and down outside all evening. Rotten fruit was thrown at the front of the theatre, and a couple of heavies tried to rough up the ticket takers.'

Genevieve appeared.

'Gené,' he said. 'A voice of sanity.'

'Maybe,' she replied, kissing his cheek. She smelled, peculiarly, of fresh bread.

'Where've you been?'

She did not answer him, but asked a question of her own. 'Who was Bruno Malvoisin?'

'Author of *Seduced by Slaaneshi*? That Bruno Malvoisin?'

'Yes, him.'

'An old playwright. Bretonnian, originally, but he wrote in Reikspiel so he must have been an Imperial citizen.'

'That's all?'

'That's all I know,' Detlef said, not understanding. 'He must have died fifty years ago.'

Poppa Fritz shook his head. 'No, sir. Malvoisin didn't die, exactly.'

Genevieve turned to the old man.

'You know about him?'

'What is all this, Gené,' Detlef asked.

'A mystery,' she said. 'Poppa Fritz?'

'Yes, mam'selle. I know about Bruno Malvoisin. I've been in

the theatre a long time. I've seen them come, and I've seen them go. All the greats, all the failures. When I was a young man, Malvoisin was a famous playwright. A director, too.'

'Here in Altdorf?'

'Here in this house. When I was an usher's apprentice, he was resident playwright. He suffered under a curse. Some of his works were banned, suppressed. The emperor of the day branded *Seduced by Slaaneshi* obscene...'

'That, I know about,' Detlef interjected. 'It's pretty filthy, although has a certain style. We might revive it one season, suitably amended and updated.'

'He was a brooding man, obsessed, hard to work with. He fought a duel with the manager of the theatre. Hacked his head half off for cutting a curtain speech.'

'A likable fellow, then?'

'A genius, sir. You have to make allowances for genius.'

'Yes,' Detlef said. 'Of course.'

'What happened to him?' Genevieve asked.

'He began to alter. Warpstone must have got into him. They said *Seduced by Slaaneshi* offended the Chaos gods, and Tzeentch took a terrible revenge on him. His face changed, and he began to turn into... into something not human. He wrote furiously. Dark, delirious, difficult stuff. Mad plays that could never be staged. He wrote an epic verse romance, alleging that the emperor had made a mistress of a she-goat. It was published anonymously, but the watch traced him as the author. He was hardly human, then. Finally, shunned by all, Malvoisin disappeared mysteriously, slipped away into the night.'

Detlef nodded. 'Just the thing Malvoisin would do. His plays never have disappearances that aren't mysterious, and no one in them ever slips away into the afternoon. What has all this nonsense about an old hack got to do with anything?'

Everyone looked at Genevieve.

She thought a while before saying anything. At last, she came out with it.

'I think Bruno Malvoisin is our Trapdoor Daemon.'

XIII

With Bernabe Scheydt and the nameless mountain whore, the act of sexual congress had been a simple thing the Animus had been able to understand. Scheydt had offered money for pleasure, and then promised not to give the girl pain if she acceded to his wishes. Actually, Scheydt had reneged; he had neither passed over coin nor refrained from hurting her. The abuse of the girl, terrorising her even after she proved compliant, had been part of the cleric's desire. It had been as important, or more so, than the simple physical gratification.

With Eva Savinien and Reinhardt Jessner, the act was the same, but the meaning was different. The Animus found itself caught up in Eva's thoughts as she admitted Reinhardt into her body, as she let the actor see in her the fulfilment of his desires. She felt pleasure, genuine pleasure, but exaggerated it for his benefit.

The Animus was an amateur in these matters, and let itself be guided by Eva. The congress was better for the actress than it had been for the cleric, perhaps because she expected less of it.

He had willingly come with her, escorting her home after the performance. She rented a bare garret in the theatre district of Altdorf, one of many identical rooms in the area. Later, she'd have a house, luxuries, many clothes. Now, this was just a place to sleep when she was not at the Vargr Breughel. She'd brought other lovers here – her first acting tutor, one of Hubermann's musicians – but the liaisons had never outlasted her partner's professional usefulness. She had no shrine in her room, no pictures on the walls. Aside from the bed, the main item of furniture was a desk at which she studied her parts, a shelf above it weighed down with reading copies of the plays in the Vargr Breughel's repertoire, with her roles underlined and annotated.

After their companionable, fairly affectionate love-making, Reinhardt was overwhelmed. The Animus was puzzled but Eva understood.

Shaking by her, Reinhardt was thinking of his wife and children. He sat up, the quilt falling away from his chest, and reached for the wine bottle on the stand by the bed. Eva propped herself up on a pillow, and watched her lover gulp down drink. Moonlight shone on his damp skin, making him pale as a ghost. He was bruised from his nightly duel with Detlef Sierck.

She cuddled next to him, and pulled him back down, stroking his hair, quieting his shivers. She couldn't stop his guilts, but she could ignore them. Eva's mind was racing. The carnal warmth had passed from her heart and she was calculating. She'd been able to make Reinhardt want her, but could she make the man love her?

The Animus didn't understand her distinction.

She thought on, pondering the success and implications of her latest move. The Animus wasn't capable of being taken by surprise, but it noted that, for a moment, Eva had gained control of their shared mind.

The host dared be impatient with it, dared assume its purpose was subordinate to her own.

Eva had won Reinhardt as an ally. As things stood, she could cajole and blackmail him to her cause with further favours or a threat of exposure. But he'd be a stronger partisan if he loved her outright, if he was bound to her by ties stronger than lust or fear.

She found something inside herself that brought tears to her eyes. She lay still, not overdoing it, letting the tears well and flow. Tensing, she gave the impression that she was fighting against a burst of emotion. She waited for Reinhardt to take notice.

He reared over her, and touched a wet cheek.

'Eva,' he said, 'what is it?'

'I was thinking,' she said, 'thinking of your wife...'

Her words were like a dagger in Reinhardt's throat. The Animus savoured the small hurt.

'What a lucky woman she must be,' Eva said, seeming to be bravely trying to smile. 'People like Illona, she'll always be popular. I know what people think of me. It isn't easy being me and I can't change...'

He was comforting her now, his own doubts forgotten. Deep inside, they were satisfied. The Animus felt the warmth of her achievement.

'Don't cry,' he said, 'my love...'

Eva had him.

'Gené, why do I feel vast schemes are being laid against me?'

She had no answer beyond, 'Because maybe there are,' and had the wit not to say that.

It was late and they were still at the theatre, on the couch in Detlef's dressing room. Captain Kleindienst had wanted to ask them questions about the Warhawk killing but they had honestly not been able to help him. However, the icechip eyes of the watchman – famous as the man who had exposed the Beast – had made Genevieve uncomfortable. He seemed like another vampire-hater.

And his pet scryer, a red-headed young woman named Rosanna Ophuls, had been confused by the tangle of leftover emotions and impressions that clung to the Vargr Breughel. She'd not been able to stand being in the theatre more than a few minutes, and Kleindeinst had allowed her to wait outside in his carriage.

'They'll catch the Warhawk, Detlef.'

'Like they caught Yefimovich? Or the revolutionist Kloszowski?'

Both felons were still at large, on the run. The Empire was overrun with murderers and anarchists.

'Maybe they won't catch him. But it will end. Everything ends.'

'Everything?'

He looked piercingly at her. She remembered Illona Horvathy's similar look when Genevieve had told her everyone grew old.

'I'm thirty-six, Gené, and everyone takes me for ten or fifteen years older. You're, what... ?'

'Six hundred and sixty-eight.'

He smiled, and touched her face with a pawlike trembling hand.

'People think you're my daughter.'

He stood up and wandered to his mirror. Detlef was beginning to frighten her. His shoulders were slumped, and when he walked around the room it was in Chaida's distinctive lope. He always had his dark look now. He examined his face in the glass, pulling actorish expressions, baring his teeth like an animal.

She was at her most awake in the height of the night. She could keenly sense the darkness inside him. It was a cold, sharp dark. She wondered if it were the theatre itself that had disconcerted Rosanna, or Detlef.

Even though there'd been no chance of identification, Detlef had insisted Kleindeinst let him look at the corpse of the Warhawk's latest victim. Genevieve had stood by him while the oilskin sheet was drawn back from the skinless, eyeless face. The repulsive stench of dead blood, spoiled for her, poured off the man in the street. And Detlef had been fascinated, excited, drawn to the horror. Kleindeinst's scryer had certainly noticed this unhealthy interest and been sickened by it. Genevieve felt for her.

'Detlef,' she asked. 'What's wrong?'

He threw up his hands, a typically theatrical gesture. It made people in the back of the stalls feel they knew what he was thinking.

But someone close, someone as close as Genevieve, could see the imposture. The mask was loose, and she was glimpsing something behind. Something that reminded her horribly of Mr Chaida.

'Sometimes,' he said, struggling with something inside him, 'I think of Drachenfels...'

She held his hand, slim strong fingers around his. She too remembered the castle in the Grey Mountains. She'd been there before Detlef.

In truth, she'd suffered more within its walls, had lost more than him.

'It might have been better if we'd been killed,' he said. 'Then, we'd be the ghosts. We wouldn't have to carry on.'

She held him in her arms, and wondered when she had ceased to understand what went on inside him.

Suddenly, he was enthused. 'I think I've found a subject for my next play. It will something Eva can play the heart out of.'

'A comedy,' she suggested, hoping. 'Something light?'

He ignored her. 'There's never been anything good about the Tsarina Kattarin.'

The name scraped Genevieve's spine.

'What do you think,' Detlef said, smiling, 'Eva as the Vampire Empress? You could be a technical advisor.'

Genevieve nodded, non-committal.

'It would be a fine horror to follow *Zhiekhill and Chaida*. Kattarin was a real fiend, I understand.'

'I knew her.'

Detlef was surprised, then brushed it away. 'Of course, you must have. I never made the connection.'

Genevieve remembered the Tsarina. Their association was a part of her life she preferred not to think of too often. There was too much blood in those years, too many hurts, too many betrayals.

'In a sense, we were sisters. We had the same father-in-darkness. We were both Chandagnac's get.'

'Was she...?'

Genevieve knew what he was thinking. 'A monster? Yes, as far as anyone is.'

He nodded, satisfied.

Genevieve thought of the rivers of blood Kattarin had let loose. Her long life had had more than its complement of horrors. And she didn't feel an inclination to conjure them up again. Not to supply an audience hungry for sensation and atrocity.

'There are enough nightmares, Detlef.'

His head rested on her shoulder, and she could see the scabbed-over marks she'd left on his neck. She wanted to taste him, and yet she was afraid of what might be in his blood, what she might catch from him...

How much of his darkness had he caught from her? In his Kattarin play, did he intend to take the role of Vladislav Dvor-jetski, the Empress's poet lover? Eva would be perfect casting for the monster queen.

Perhaps she was condemning Detlef too easily. It could be that she was as dark in her soul as he was in his obsessions. His work had only teemed with the macabre and monstrous since he had been with her. Bleeding a man sometimes meant taking things from him other than blood. Maybe Genevieve was a truer sister-in-darkness to Kattarin the Great than she liked to think.

'Never enough nightmares, Gené,' he murmured.

She kissed Detlef's neck, but did not break the skin. He was exhausted, but not asleep. They stayed locked together for a long time, not moving, not talking. Another day crept up on them.

XIV

Last night, the Trapdoor Daemon had heard Detlef and Genevieve talking about him. Poppa Fritz had reminisced about the days before he began to alter.

The days when he'd been Bruno Malvoisin.

The playwright he had been seemed now like another person, a role he had cast off with his human flesh.

In the passage behind the rehearsal rooms, where he was able to look in on the company at work, he stretched his major tentacles to their utmost length. Usually he wrapped himself in a cloak and held the centre of his body high, imagining a belly and two human legs below his chest. Today he let himself flop naturally, six tentacles spreading like the pad of a waterlily, the clump of his other external organs and the hard blades of his beak, protected by the leathery tent of his body.

There was very little of Malvoisin left.

In the rehearsal room, Detlef was reading notes to the company. This morning, he had few comments, distracted by the swirl of events around the play rather than fully involved in the drama itself.

The Trapdoor Daemon was puzzled by Eva.

His protégée sat aside as usual, Reinhardt hovering guiltily while paying overdone attentions to Illona. Eva was calm and in control again, different from last night. It was as if she'd never seen his true form. Or maybe she'd found the strength in herself to accept what she had seen? Whatever the case, she wasn't concerned this morning with the monster she had met last night.

A few of the chorus girls had been prattling about a murder outside the theatre. The Trapdoor Daemon knew nothing of that, except that he'd eventually be blamed.

As Malvoisin, he had written about evil, about how attractive it could be, how seductive a path. When he began to change, he had thought that he had himself succumbed to Salli's temptations, as Diogo Briesach in *Seduced by Slaaneshi* had to his own private daemons. Then, as he became less bound by human thinking, he came to recognize there was no more evil in him when his shape changed than there had been before.

In a sense, he'd been freed by his mutation. Perhaps that was the laugh line of Tzeentch's jest at his expense, that he could only be aware of his humanity once his human form was buried in a morass of squiddy altered flesh. Still, he realized that for others warpstone was a polluter of the soul as well as the body.

Watching Genevieve, who was herself watching Detlef with a new attentitiveness, the Trapdoor Daemon wondered whether a warpstone shard had been shot into his protégée.

Eva Savinien had changed, and she was changing still.

He had allowed the company to break up for lunch, and told them they did not have to come back until the evening's performance. *The Strange History of Dr Zhiekhill and Mr Chaida* was rolling of its own accord now, and Detlef was almost at the point when, even if everything else were not falling apart, he would have been prepared to let it alone. Long run shows develop by themselves, finding ways to stay alive. He was even grateful to Eva Savinien, whose unpredictable luminescence was prodding everyone in the company in unexpected directions.

Illona, for instance, was suggesting that she might have the makings of a tragic heroine as she slipped into the age range for roles like the Empress Magritta or Ottokar's Wife.

In Poppa Fritz's rooms, he found Genevieve surrounded by unscrolled maps, weighted down at the corners with books and small objects. She was with the stage-door keeper and Guglielmo, trying to make sense of the diagrams of the tunnels under the theatre.

'So,' she said, 'we're agreed? This one is a deliberate fraud, to be found by the enemies of someone taking refuge.'

The older-looking men nodded.

'It's too clearly marked,' Guglielmo said. 'Obviously, it's designed to get anyone who relies on it hopelessly lost. Possibly even to lead them into traps.'

'What are you three conspirators up to?' Detlef asked. 'Plotting to join Prince Kloszowski's revolutionist movement?'

'I'm going to try to find him,' Genevieve said.

She was dressed in clothes Detlef had not seen her wear in years. In Altdorf, she was usually found in subdued but elegant finery: white silks and embroidered Cathayan robes. Now she wore a leather hunting jacket and boots, with sturdy cloth trews and a man's shirt. She looked like Violetta, disguised as her twin brother in Tarradasch's *Hexenachtabend*.

'Him?'

'Malvoisin.'

'The Trapdoor Daemon,' Poppa Fritz explained. In the gloom, the old man looked like a crumpled parchment himself.

'Gené, why?'

'I think he's suffering.'

'The whole world is suffering.'

'I can't do anything about the whole world.'

'What can you do for this creature, even if he is Bruno Malvoisin?'

'Talk to him, find out if he needs anything. I think he was as frightened as Eva by what happened.'

Poppa Fritz rolled up the fake map, and slipped it into its tube, coughing in the dust that belched from it.

'He's some kind of altered, Gené. His mind must be gone. He could be dangerous.'

'Like Vargr was dangerous, Detlef?'

Vargr Breughel had been Detlef's stage manager and assistant. A dwarf born of normal parents, he'd been with the actor-playwright-director since the beginning of his career. In the end, he'd turned out to be an altered thing of Chaos and had killed himself rather than be tortured by a stupid man.

'Like you were dangerous?'

Detlef had been born with six toes on one foot. His merchant father had remedied the defect in early childhood with a meatcleaver.

'Like I am dangerous?'

She opened her sharp-toothed mouth wide and made play-claws of her hands. Then, she dropped her monster face.

'You know as well as I do that warpstone sometimes just makes a monster of you on the outside.'

'Very well, but take some of our bruisers with you.'

Genevieve laughed, and crushed a prop candlestick into a squeezed ball of metal.

'I'd only have to look after them, Detlef.'

'It's your life, Gené,' he said, wearied. 'You do what you want with it.'

'I certainly intend to. Poppa Fritz, I'll go in here,' tapping a chart, 'from the stalls. We'll have to break open this old trapdoor.'

'Gené,' he said, laying a hand on her shoulder. A child sometimes, she was also ancient. She kissed him, quickly.

'I'll be careful,' she said.

Reinhardt Jessner knew he was being a fool, but couldn't help
himself. He knew he was hurting Illona, and would be hurting
their twins, Erzbet and Rudi. In the end, he was hurting himself most of all.

But there was something about Eva.

She was in his blood like snakepoison, and it couldn't be
sucked out with a simple bite. Since the first night of *Dr Zhiekhill and Mr Chaida*, the bane was creeping through him. He had
known it at the party afterwards. One or other of them was
always going to make a move. It had been her, but it could as
easily have been him.

He felt physically sick when he was away from her, unable to
think of anything, of anyone, else. And when he was with her,
there was a different kind of pain, a gnawing guilt, a self-disgust,
an awareness of his own foolishness.

The more he loved Eva, the more certain he was the girl would
leave him. He could do nothing more for her. He was a stepping
stone, half-sunk in the stream. There were larger, sturdier stones
ahead. Eva would go on to them.

They had snatched a few hours together away from the theatre
in the afternoon, rutting in the hot dark behind the drawn
curtains of her upstairs room. She had already outpaced and out-
worn him, slipping into an easeful sleep while he, exhausted,
lay awake next to her in her narrow bed, mind crowded and
uncomfortable.

This was not the first time, but it was the worst. Before, Illona
had known but been able to bear it. The other girls had not
lasted, could not last.

He had half-thought Illona had encouraged him to be unfaithful, and they had been better together afterwards than before. Theatrical marriages were difficult and usually foundered. Little diversions gave them strength to carry on.

Now, Illona was in tears all the time. At home, the twins were forever fighting and demanding. He spent as little time there as possible, preferring either to be with Eva or at the Temple Street gymnasium fencing and lifting weights.

Eva shifted beside him, and the covers fell away from her sleeping face. Daylight dotted in through the rough weave of the curtains, and Reinhardt looked down at the girl.

An ice-kiss touched him.

As she slept, Eva looked strange, as if there were a layer of thin glass stretched over her face. Reinhardt caught strange almost-reflections in the surface.

He touched her cheek, and found it hard, like a statue.

As his fingertips pressed, the quality of her skin changed, becoming yielding, warm. Her eyes opened, and she took his wrist in a surprisingly strong grip.

He was truly afraid of her now.

Eva sat up, pushing him back against the plastered wall, her warm body against his, her face empty of expression.

'Reinhardt,' she said, 'there are things you must do for me...'

XV

The labyrinth was different here. While the passages behind the dressing rooms were cramped, these were almost spacious, the underground equivalents of thoroughfares. Odd items had drifted down from the world above. One corridor was lined with flats from various productions, laid end to end so mountain scenery gave way to Darklands jungle, then to the plasterboard flagstones and painted bloodstains of a dungeon, then to a storm-whipped seascape on springs so it would roll behind a stage ship, then to the corpse-littered Chaos Wastes. Genevieve tried to remember which plays went with each canvas.

She sensed her quarry was close. The Box Seven smell lingered faintly, and she had better nostrils than true humans. Some of the painted scenes had dried-slime smudges on them, indicating that the Trapdoor Daemon used this path. She wondered if she should call out, or if that would drive Malvoisin further into hiding.

Having spent so many of her years penned up in one way

or another, she could imagine what kind of life the Trapdoor Daemon had down here. What she couldn't imagine was him finding any other kind of life. Humans barely tolerated her, and were invariably hostile to any of her kind who shapechanged. It wasn't an unfounded prejudice, but it was also not entirely just.

The passageway angled down, and ended in a curtained chamber. She looked around for the trapdoor, and found it, disguised as the top of a large barrel.

Originally the tunnel had had a ladder for human use, but that had mainly been scraped away, replaced by a set of protuberances that gave Genevieve an idea of what Malvoisin must look like. The smell was very strong, a whiff of dead fish and saltwater rising from the depths.

For now, she left the tunnel alone, replacing the barrel-top. Today she was going to search only the uppermost levels. She suspected Malvoisin might choose to loiter near the surface. She'd found many of his peepholes, and been amused by the private rooms into which they afforded a view.

Obviously, the Trapdoor Daemon alleviated his solitude by taking an interest in the company of the Vargr Breughel Memorial Playhouse.

She wondered how many of her own private moments had been overseen. From a peephole accessible if she stood on the barrel, she could see into a stockroom where, among the dusty wigstands and tins of facepowder, she had once bled Detlef intimately.

The red thirst had come upon her during a reception, and she had dragged her lover to this forgotten corner of the theatre, taking mouthfuls of his flesh and gently puncturing his excited skin, gorging herself until he was dangerously weak, a half-dozen new wounds opened on his body. Had once-human eyes witnessed her lustful gluttony?

Retracing her footsteps to the last horizontal junction, she explored a new fork. Nearby, there was a rapid slithering, and she darted in its direction, her nightsight enabling her not to slam into a wall. She didn't call out. Something large was moving fast.

The slithering turned a corner and she followed it. There was no movement of air, so she guessed this was a closed space. She came to a wall, and stopped. She couldn't hear anything now. Looking back, she realized she'd been fooled. They didn't call Malvoisin the Trapdoor Daemon lightly. Somehow, he'd slipped into the walls, ceiling or floor, and escaped her.

However, she was canny. And she had time.

The Animus let Eva guide it to the theatre, with Reinhardt as thoroughly in tow as if he were a pig led by a brass ring through his nose. From Eva, it had learned that destroying Detlef and Genevieve wasn't enough for its purpose. Before they died, they must be broken apart, the bond forged at the fortress of Drachenfels sundered completely. That way, they'd die knowing nothing lasting had come of their triumph. The Animus was grateful for the new insight, realizing at last that it hadn't been prepared to do its master's bidding until it joined with its current host. The Great Enchanter must have foreseen this when he forged the Animus, realizing his creature wouldn't be whole until it was partially human.

It was gathering about itself the tools it needed. Eva, of course, was the key, but others – Reinhardt, Illona, the Trapdoor Daemon, even Detlef and Genevieve themselves – must play their parts. For Eva, the Animus was very like Detlef, conceiving a drama and then guiding his company through their parts. The Animus was not above being flattered by the comparison. Created as a cold intellect, it bore the vampire and the play-actor no malice. It just knew that their destruction was its purpose. From Eva, it had learned a considerable respect for Detlef Sierck's prowess as a man of the theatre.

Eva left Reinhardt at the Temple Street gymnasium for his afternoon exercises, knowing he would come when needed. The host had her own purpose, distinct from that of the Animus.

For the moment, their ambitions meshed neatly. If a conflict ever arose, each was confident of victory over the other.

The Animus let Eva go on thinking she was in control.

Outside the theatre, there were three distinct crowds. The largest was an unruly queue at the box office, demanding seats for *The Strange History of Dr Zhiekhill and Mr Chaida*. A few well-known touts were preying on these, charging unbelievable prices for genuine tickets, and slightly more credible coin for badly-forged imitations which would never pass Guglielmo Pentangeli's ushers. Competing with the eager would-be patrons was a line of placard-waving petitioners, mostly well-dressed matrons and thin young men in shabby clothes, protesting against the play.

One placard was a vivid poster of Detlef as Mr Chaida, showing him as a giant trampling over the murdered citizens of Altdorf. Since the last host's death, the protests had increased fourfold.

As Eva neared, the third crowd were aroused to activity. These, she was gradually becoming used to. There were liveried footmen with floral offerings and billets douces and formal invitations, and well-dressed young men keen to pursue their suits in person. Besides romantic overtures, Eva Savinien was daily pestered by professional offers, from all over the Empire and as far off as Bretonnia and Kislev. There could be no doubt that the young actress was the toast of Altdorf.

Graciously accepting flowers, invitations and letters, Eva passed through the crowd, politely fending off the more persistent suitors. Slipping through the front door, she immediately dumped her crop of tributes into the arms of Poppa Fritz, who staggered under the burden. She would go through the letters later.

'You should start sending your flowers to the Retreat of Shallya,' a voice said.

It was Illona. Eva turned, squashing a mouse of irritation in her mind. She didn't want this distraction now.

'That's what I did in the last century, when I was in your position. Flowers move you out of your dressing room and are no real use. The patients at the hospital will at least get something out of them.'

'A good idea,' Eva agreed. 'Thank you, Illona.'

'We should talk, Eva,' the older woman said.

'Not now.'

Illona looked sharply at Eva, eyes penetrating. It was as if she knew something, saw something. The Animus knew this was not possible. Not now.

'Take care, Eva. You've charted a dangerous course. Lots of squalls and shallows, rocks and whirlpools.'

Eva shrugged. This was most tiresome. Illona had fixed her with a look, making a strong-link chain between them.

'I was your age once, you know.'

'Naturally. Most people were.'

'And one day, you'll be my age.'

'The gods willing, yes.'

'That's right. The gods willing.'

The chain between them broke, and Eva bowed slightly.

'This has been most enlightening,' Eva said. 'But if you'll excuse me...'

She left Illona in the foyer, and went in search of Detlef. The Animus could taste the nearness of its purpose.

XVI

The vampire had invaded his world. The Trapdoor Daemon didn't yet know how he felt about that. He'd been alone so long. Alone except for Eva. And she was now lost to him.

From the ceiling, where he could cling to the holds he'd carved, he angled his eyes down, and watched Genevieve as she carefully made her way down the main passage.

The Trapdoor Daemon understood Genevieve Dieudonné had been an actress. Once. He admired her courage, and her caution. The labyrinth had its dangers, but she evaded them with skill. She was used to prowling corridors in the dark. Eventually, the red glints of her eyes would find him.

His heart pulsated inside his shroud of darkness.

Once, Bruno Malvoisin had loved an actress, Salli Spaak. No, not an actress, but a courtesan who used the stage to give her respectability. She had rejoiced in her celebrity, as the crowds came to gawp at her rather than see the play. Salli had been the mistress of the then-emperor's youngest brother, Prince Nikol.

The fortunes of the theatre had ebbed and flowed with her patron's feelings for his lady.

Genevieve reminded the Trapdoor Daemon of the long-dead temptress. So did Eva, although Salli had never been as gifted on the stage as Malvoisin's recent protégée.

When Salli and the Imperial Brother quarrelled, laws were passed against the theatre and halberdiers came to bar the house's doors. And when she pleased Nikol, gifts and favours were showered upon the whole company.

Salli had made a conquest of Bruno Malvoisin as she had made conquests of many others. She enjoyed the fear that spread whenever she bestowed her favours on another. It was not a good idea to sleep with the mistress of Nikol of the House of the Second Wilhelm. The prince had publicly duelled and dispatched several of Salli's admirers, and Malvoisin knew a man who won a duel with Prince Nikol wouldn't escape with his life.

Genevieve looked up, and the Trapdoor Daemon retreated a little in his cloud of artificial shadow. She didn't seem to see him. He didn't know if he was disappointed, whether he wanted to be found or not.

Behind Salli's beautiful face, there had been a terrible corruption. And Malvoisin had caught it. Like Genevieve – like Eva, even – she had not been entirely human. Prince Nikol had ultimately committed suicide after being lured into taking part in an unholy rite of the Proscribed Cult of Tzeentch, and Salli had been driven out of Altdorf by a mob. By then, Malvoisin was shambling through backstreets in a heavy cloak, trying in vain to disguise his increasingly obvious deformities. By night, he'd written reams, pouring out words as if he knew he had to discharge the entire rest of his life's worth of work within weeks. The day his swelling head shrugged off his nose, he'd gone underground.

Shaking her head, Genevieve continued down the passage.

Eventually, she'd solve all the puzzles of the labyrinth. Then the Trapdoor Daemon would have to consider her as a problem.

Salli had believed in warpstone the way a weirdroot addict believes in dreamjuice. At great expense, she acquired the deadly material and added it to her food, to the food of her lovers. Malvoisin had not been the only one to change. The marks had been on the prince when he was found hanging from Three Toll Bridge.

He was, however, the only one to survive.

Salli had been a secret worshipper of Tzeentch, had enjoyed spreading corruption around her. She'd been the chosen instrument of the Chaos god, and had struck him down. In *Seduced by Slaaneshi*, he had dared to present on the stage things never intended for human audiences. His sins had been registered in the darkness, stirring into action powers from which there was no escape.

When Genevieve had passed, the Trapdoor Daemon let himself down from the roof, and settled on the flagstones. He pushed tentacles against two tiltstones in the wall – spaced far enough apart that no one ordinary man could reach them both – and dropped soundlessly into the slide that appeared in the floor.

He descended several levels, and slid into the comforting cold of the black waters beneath the theatre.

Detlef sat on the stage, in Dr Zhiekhill's chair, alone with himself in the auditorium. There was a lantern on the set, amid the doctor's retorts and cauldrons, but otherwise the huge space was dark. He looked out into the empty black, knowing in his mind the precise dimensions of the hall. Dimly, he could see the velvet of the expensive seats. In his island of light, he might have been alone in the entire building, the entire universe.

Still drained from last night, he wasn't sure whether he'd have the energy for tonight's performance. It always came at the last moment. At least, it always had so far. The bite on his neck was irritating him, and he wondered if it might have become infected. Perhaps, he and Gené should stay away from each other for a while.

Their last time together, after the first night, had been bloodier than usual. The red thirst had been strong in her. Occasionally, through the years, he'd had cause to fear that he might not survive their love-making. In the heat, neither man nor vampire really had any self-control. That, he supposed, was the whole point of the heat. If she wounded him too deeply, he supposed she would feel obliged to let him suckle her blood, to become her son-in-darkness, to cheat death and become a vampire himself.

The prospect, always between them but never discussed, excited and frightened him. Vampire couples had a bad reputation, even among other vampires.

At this time in the afternoon, the theatre was asleep, the actors and the audience hours away. Like Genevieve, the Vargr Breughel was only really alive after nightfall.

Genevieve had been made a vampire almost as a child, before she'd settled on her personality; if it came to it, Detlef would change while a fully-formed human being. 'Vampires can't have children,' his lover had once told him, 'not in the natural way. And we don't write plays.' It was true: Detlef could not think of a single great contribution to the arts – or to much else, besides bloodshed – that had been made by one of the undead. To live possibly forever was an attractive, intriguing prospect, but the coldness that came with it frightened him.

The coldness that could make a Kattarin.

Vampire couples were the worst, becoming more dependent upon each other with the passing centuries, more contemptuous of the rest of the world, more callous, more murderous. Each became the only real thing in the other's world. Eventually, Genevieve told him, they became one creature in two bodies, a berserk feeding beast that had to be stopped with silver and hawthorn.

A hand touched his neck and slipped around his throat with catlike ease. His heart stuttered, thinking the Trapdoor Daemon, angered by Gené's intrusion into his lair, had come to lay a death-squeezing tentacle on him.

He turned and, in the light of the lantern, saw Eva's face, a mask-like oval in repose, worn and expressionless like the bas-relief on a much-used coin.

Her touch was odd, neither warm nor chill.

She smiled, and her face came alive. After all, she was on stage. Detlef wondered what scene Eva was playing.

Lifting her hand and his head with it, she made him stand up. Eva was tall enough to look him in the eye. Tall enough – like Illona and very few others, and unlike Genevieve – to play love scenes with him that looked good from the most remote box in the house.

He expected the kiss, but it was a long time coming.

Genevieve had been working her way up a peculiar network of stairs and ladders which, she realized, must exist inside the thick walls of the Vargr Breughel. Complicated joists and beams provided support for the thinnest shell of stone. By her reckoning, she was heading for an egress somewhere on the roof of the theatre, between the huge comic and tragic masks carved in stone on the eaves.

Perhaps the laughing or crying mouths and eyes were doorways.

She came to a trapdoor that was thick with dried slime, suggesting repeated use. As she touched the latch, she had one of her rare flashes of precognition. With the dark kiss, Chandagnac had given her a touch of the scrying ability. Now, she knew opening this door would solve mysteries, but that she wouldn't like the solutions. Her hand stayed, fingers on the latch, and she knew that if she left the door closed, her life would continue as it was now. If she pushed, everything would change. Again.

She made a fist of her hand, and held it to her chest. In the close space, her breathing was loud. Unlike the Truly Dead vampires, she still breathed. That made her nearly human. And so did her curiosity, her need to know.

Working the latch and pushing through the trapdoor, she wondered briefly if she'd have been happier in herself if her father-in-darkness had killed her before making a vampire of her. Then, she would have been completely apart from the living. Free from the tangles that wound around her heart.

The Box Seven smell was stronger here than anywhere else she'd been in the labyrinth. And no wonder, for this was Box Seven.

Beyond the curtains of the box, there was a light. It must be down on the stage. She stood up, stretching herself to work the cramps out of her arms and legs. Then, she parted the curtains.

On the stage, Detlef was rehearsing with Eva.

This must be the Act Three curtain, where Nita appeals to Zhiekhill for help, not knowing that the kindly man who has offered her protection is actually her monstrous tormentor. The poor girl tries to persuade Zhiekhill to give her money by making pathetic advances, and, in his arousal, he transforms into Chaida, battering her back onto the divan in Zhiekhill's study for a tableau highly suggestive of the action which must come between acts in the minds of the audience.

Watching them kiss, Genevieve waited for the transformation. One came, but not the one she was expecting.

XVII

The Animus was pressed against Detlef Sierck's face, and picked up his confusion, his desire, his pain. Also the growing cancer of darkness. It was the darkness the Animus needed to touch. It would be a simple matter to have Eva seduce him carnally, as she had Reinhardt Jessner. But what would be the point? Sex was not the thing that would break Detlef away from Genevieve. It was the darkness, the Chaida inside Detlef's Zhiekhill, the suppressed impulse to brute degradation.

Eva gripped Detlef's throat hard, exerting pressure as they kissed, almost choking him.

'Hurt me,' she whispered.

Detlef froze in her embrace.

'No,' she said. 'It's what I need, what I want...'

She was almost, but not quite, quoting from *The Strange History of Dr Zhiekhill and Mr Chaida*. Nita had been hurt so much, the text implied, that she had developed a perverse taste for pain. And Nita came as much from the pen and mind of Detlef Sierck as from the performance of Eva Savinien. He had written about the thrill of hurting and being hurt, and the Animus knew he'd found those feelings, like so much, inside himself, and spread them out on the stage. That experiment would be the destruction of him, just as Zhiekhill's dabbling eventually led to his own obliteration.

Eva's grip grew stronger, her thumb-knuckles digging into the soft pouch of flesh beneath Detlef's beardline.

'Hurt me,' she repeated, darting kisses at his face, 'badly.'

His eyes caught the light, and the Animus saw in them that it had reached inside him to dredge up the wish to inflict pain that had always been a part of the genius. It had been one of the things that gave him the surprising strength he needed to help best the Great Enchanter. It was one of the things that made him attracted to the vampire girl.

A part of Detlef Sierck was obsessed with pain, with blood, with evil. And obsession was so close to love as to be sometimes indistinguishable.

Eva took one of her hands from Detlef's throat, and made a claw of her nails, angling to rake the playwright's face.

He struck her hand aside.

His face was a mask of anger, his features conforming exactly to the actors' textbook image of rage, projecting an emotion he couldn't fully feel.

Detlef gripped the hand at his throat, and broke it away. He hit her, hard knuckles colliding with her cheek, raising an instant bruise.

The Animus was pleased.

Eva taunted Detlef, cajoling and insulting, pleading and prodding. She invited punishment, tempted him to become Chaida.

She slapped his face, and he punched her chest. Thanks to the Animus she felt no pain, but was enough of an actress to present a counterfeit that was better than the real thing.

In the struggle, their clothes were loosened, torn. Between blows, they exchanged hungry caresses.

Eva took a prop retort from the stage table, and smashed it against her face. It was sugar glass, but the sticky shards stuck to her, grinding between them as they kissed, grazing their faces. They scratched each other, drawing lines of blood.

Detlef punched her in the stomach, hard. She doubled over, and he threw her down onto Zhiekhill's divan.

This was the Third Act Curtain.

Eva experienced a surge of doubt, but the Animus washed it away. Everything was fine. Detlef tore at her clothes, rendering her smart dress as ragged as Nita's costume.

Detlef fell on Eva, and the curtains did not close.

Genevieve was horrorstruck, her blood on fire. Her canine teeth slid from their gumsheaths. And her fingernails were talon-shaped diamonds. What she saw on the stage made her want blood.

She didn't understand the unnatural love scene being played out below, but she hated herself for being aroused to the red thirst by it. What was coming out of Detlef had always been inside him, she realized. Perhaps this was no more perverse than their own love-making, a blend of human and vampire embrace that always involved the spilling of blood if not the giving of pain. But here Eva was leading Detlef, tugging at him as Mr Chaida tugged in the finale at Sonja Zhiekhill, trying to awake the monster inside her leading man.

She stood in Box Seven, the sea-stench all around her, and looked down, frozen. She was a typical vampire, she thought. Unable to do anything, but watching all the time, waiting for the scraps to fall from the table.

Then, with a dizzying lurch inside her mind, she had another flash of precognition, a scryer's insight that changed everything.

This was not a private moment she'd happened to oversee.

This was a puppet show. Somewhere, somehow, something was working the strings, jerking Eva and Detlef to an obscene dance that was at least partly for her benefit. What her lover and the actress were doing on the stage looked more convincing than it should. They were acting, exaggerating so their violent love-making would register all over the house.

Frightened, Genevieve looked around. There was a playwright, a director. A drama was being played out, and she was a part of it too.

She was in the audience now, but she knew she would be called soon to play a part.

Again, everything was beyond her control.

In the Temple Street gymnasium, Reinhardt Jessner pushed his body up and down, spine a rigid bar, thick arms like pump handles. His nose touched the hardwood floor again and again. His mind was racing so fast he needed to tire his body to catch up.

Arne the Body, his instructor, advised him to slow down, but he could not. Throughout his career, he had taken care of his body, his instrument. If the script were thrown away, Reinhardt could outfight Detlef Sierck in the finale of *Dr Zhiekhill and Mr Chaida* and hardly bring a sweat to his brow.

Now, he swung a heavy weight about, feeling the burn in his forearms and shoulders.

Eva. It was all her fault.

He stood to lose everything. His family, his career, his self-respect. And all for Eva, who was already preparing to throw him away, her eye set on Detlef.

He hoisted the weight repeatedly, muscles thick in his arms and neck, teeth grit together. His back and chest were damp with perspiration, and he felt trickles in his close-cropped hair and beard.

Good luck to Eva and Detlef, he thought.

If it weren't for Detlef, Reinhardt would be a leading man

himself. He was certainly drawing more attention as the actor-manager grew flabbier and crankier. Especially if a production afforded him a chance to take his shirt off. Perhaps he should take Illona and found his own company. A touring troupe maybe. Away from the stink of the city, there'd be less glamour, less acclaim, less money. But maybe there'd be a life worth living.

Eva.

He had to end it now. For Illona, for the twins. For himself.

He dropped the weight, and stood back. Arne grinned at him, and made his bicep inflate like a pig's bladder, the veins standing out on it like thick worms.

He would go to the theatre, and end it with Eva.

Then things would come together.

XVIII

'No,' said Detlef, quietly. Having touched something inside himself, he was now letting it go, leaving it well alone, pushing it back into the depths.

Eva stilled, staying her hand from the blow.

'What?'

'No,' he said, firmer now. 'I won't.'

He was ashamed of himself, and uneasy. He stood back, hands by his sides. He didn't want to touch her again.

Eva looked real fury at him, and, leaping from the divan, went for his face. He grabbed her wrists, and held her fast, keeping her away from him, pushing her back.

He felt his bruises, but also a strength inside him. He had resisted temptation. He had not become Mr Chaida.

'Hurt meee,' Eva screeched.

There was something wrong with her face, as if there were a layer of thin steel over it. She had foam on her lips, and was fighting seriously now. Her attacks were not in the least playful.

'What are you?' he asked.

'Hurt me, wound me, bite me...'

He pushed her off, and backed away from her, shaking his head.

From the darkness, a pair of hands clapped, the sound reverberating around the auditorium, turning into a thunder of applause.

The Animus had lost. It knew the fact with a gem-bright certainty. The beast in Detlef Sierck hadn't been strong enough to take over his heart completely. He was as much Zhiekhill as Chaida. He could be tainted and taunted, but not destroyed that way. There was too much else in his spirit, too much light in the darkness.

The host was shaking with the trauma of defeat. She was near the end of her usefulness. If the Animus couldn't destroy Detlef's soul, it would have to make do with ending his life.

Eva pressed her hands to her face, trying to keep the loose mask from coming free. As the Animus faded from her mind, she felt her pain, her shame, her rage.

Her hands were wet with tears. She huddled, sorry for herself, wrapping what was left of her clothes about her. Detlef was stern, uncomforting. She didn't understand what she'd found inside her.

She had thought the Animus a blessing, but it turned out a curse.

The Animus slowly withdrew its tendrils from Eva, detaching itself at every point from her mind and body, cutting off her feelings, relinquishing its degree of control over her.

Only the purpose remained.

Still applauding, Genevieve latched onto her pride in Detlef. He had defeated something as invisible and beastly as Mr Chaida She hoped she might have been able to do the same, but doubted herself.

'It's me,' she shouted, 'Gené'

Detlef shaded his eyes and peered into the darkness. He could never see her like that. He did not have vampire eyes.

He was suddenly self-conscious.

'There's something wrong,' he tried to explain. 'We weren't responsible.'

Eva was sobbing quietly, forgotten, abandoned.

'I know. There's something here, something evil.'

She tried to sense another presence, but her scrying was gone. It was only an occasional thing.

'Gené,' he said. 'Where...'

'I'm in Box Seven. There's a secret passageway.'

She turned to check the open trapdoor, and saw something huge and wet squeezing through it.

The back of her hand covered her still-wide, still-sharp mouth, but she did not scream.

She was beyond screaming.

'It's all right,' the Trapdoor Daemon tried to say.

He knew how he must look.

The vampire dropped her hand, and her eyes shone red in the dark. She swallowed and straightened up. Trying not to be revulsed, she couldn't keep the pity out of her face.

'Bruno Malvoisin?'

'No,' he said, the word long and low from his flesh-concealed mouth. 'Not any more.'

She put out her sharp-nailed hand.

'I'm Genevieve,' she said. 'Genevieve Dieudonné.'

He nodded, his huge lump of a head wobbling. 'I know.'

'What's going on?' Detlef shouted from the stage.

'We have a visitor,' Genevieve said over her shoulder.

It was over with and he was out in the open. The Trapdoor Daemon felt a strange relief. There would be pain, but he didn't have to hide any more.

Poppa Fritz was snoring in his cubby-hole when Reinhardt went in through the stage-door.

His resolve was strong inside him.

'Eva!' he shouted.

He blundered through the backstage dark. In the afternoons, all the lights were down, as Guglielmo tried to save crowns on candlewax and lanternwick. But there was a light somewhere. Out on the stage, perhaps.

'Eva!'

'Up here,' said a voice, not Eva's. It was Detlef.

Reinhardt made an entrance, his heavy boots clumping on the stage. He recognized the tableau. It was Act Four, when the cossack found Chaida in Zhiekhill's study with the beaten and bruised Nita.

Detlef was out of his make-up, but he had blood on his face and his clothes were a mess. Eva was on her knees in her spot, face in her hands. It was hard not to follow the script and take his own place, where the girl would throw herself into his embrace, and plead for him to rescue her from the monster.

But this was not a rehearsal or a performance.

'Reinhardt,' Detlef said, 'send Poppa Fritz for a doctor. Eva needs help.'

'What happened?'

Detlef shook his head.

'Things are complicated just now.'

Reinhardt looked about him.

Eva was really distraught, which was outside his experience of her. Suddenly, her hands still to her face, she stood up, and ran to him. He held out his hands to ward her off, and she slipped between his arms, shoving her head close to his.

'What is it?'

He took her wrists, and prised her hands away from her face.

Genevieve's attention was torn. She was beginning to be able to make out the Trapdoor Daemon properly. He carried his own darkness with him, she realized, like a shroud. His head projected up above a ring of thick tentacles, and had to angle back, huge eyes swivelling forwards, so he could speak through the beak-like mouth in the centre of what must be his chest. The marks of his alteration were unmistakable, giving him some of the aspects of Tzeentch, the Changer of the Ways. His eyes were what she saw most, liquid and human.

But the drama on the stage was not played out. The Trapdoor Daemon had slithered forwards, all his appendages in motion as he pulled himself to the balcony of the box. They both looked down at the tableau.

Eva was with Reinhardt, and Detlef was looking at them, then out into the dark.

Experimentally, she touched the Trapdoor Daemon's wet hide. He shrank away, but relaxed, and let her fingers press his skin.

'Beautiful, huh?' he commented.

'I've seen worse.'

Suddenly, the tableau moved.

XIX

Reinhardt dropped Eva on the stage, and she sprawled at his feet like the stuffed dummies who stood in for corpses in the play. It was as if all the life had seeped out of her.

'She was... sick, I think,' Detlef explained.

Reinhardt was just beyond the island of light, but Detlef could see there was something strange about his face. He was wearing a mask.

'Reinhardt?'

The actor stepped into the light, and Detlef felt a hand of dread fall on his shoulder. Reinhardt seemed taller, broader, his bunched muscles straining his clothes. And his face was a terrible, calm blank, silverwhite and dead. He moved like an automaton, but slowly his motion became easier, more fluid, as if the rust in his joints were being oiled away.

'Play-actor,' Reinhardt said, his voice different.

Reinhardt looked around, head moving like a giant lizard's, and strode briefly into the dark. He returned with a background prop in his hand.

A war-axe from Chaida's collection of weapons.

'In the name of the Great Enchanter, Constant Drachenfels,' Reinhardt said, hefting the axe, 'you must...'

The axe jumped forwards, blade whistling.

'...die!'

The axe-edge slammed against Detlef's forehead, all Reinhardt's strength behind it.

He could hear Gené screaming.

The screech died in her throat as Detlef staggered under the blow. Reinhardt's axe was a ruin, its painted wooden blade crushed against Detlef's hard head. With a snarl of rage, the young actor slammed the heavy handle of the prop against the playwright's neck, knocking him out of the circle of light.

Genevieve was looking for a quick way out of Box Seven. The Trapdoor Daemon was thinking with her, and stretched out a tentacle to pull loose a curtain. There was a chandelier in the auditorium, fixed by a long chain that ran through strong eye-hooks across the ceiling and down one wall so the chandelier could be lowered and lit. Malvoisin took hold of the chain, and twined the end of his tentacle around it.

Reinhardt was gone beyond humanity, white face impassive as he stumped towards Detlef on heavy feet.

The Trapdoor Daemon yanked the chandelier chain, and it came loose of its eyehooks. The chandelier was unsteady, dropping the stubs of last night's candles into the stalls as Malvoisin hauled on the chain. It was fixed to the ceiling by only the central hook, and plaster dust was powdering out from its mooring as the chandelier crowded up close, anchoring the chain.

Reinhardt had his hands on Detlef, and had lifted him up, ready for a throw.

'Quick,' the Trapdoor Daemon hissed, giving her the chain.

She was over the side like a sailor, and hurtling through the

air, booted feet first. There was a whistle in her ears as her hair
streamed out, and she swayed unsteadily as she tried to aim for
Reinhardt's expanse of chest.

She heard herself shouting.

The Animus was settled immediately.

The host had been in an excited state when the attachment
was made. His confused feelings for Eva were easy to convert
into feelings against Detlef.

Detlef had always been in the younger actor's way, keeping
him from the leading roles. Years of losing fights and fair maid-
ens and applause to Detlef Sierck had bitten deep into the good
humour and big heart of Reinhardt Jessner.

The axe had come apart in his hands, a pretend weapon with
no real use, but Detlef was stunned.

Feeling the host's muscles pumping, the Animus lifted Detlef
high, preparing to toss him forever from the stage, to break his
back on the rows of chairs in the stalls.

A cannonball blow struck Reinhardt in the chest, and he staggered back, dropping Detlef.

The girl who had shot out of the dark on a chain rolled across
the stage like an acrobat, and stood up. She had her teeth and
claws out.

This was perfect. The Animus could achieve its purpose. Detlef
and Genevieve were both here.

Detlef stood up. The Animus slammed Reinhardt's heavy elbow
into his face, smashing his nose, knocking him back against the
canvas wall of Dr Zhiekhill's laboratory. He shook his head,
spreading blood around him like a dog drying itself, and tried
to stand up.

The vampire came for him, and met a fist which sent even
her reeling. Reinhardt had been strong, but with the Animus in
his mind he was a superman.

Doors were opening in the auditorium, as people were alarmed by the noise. The company was arriving, and crowds were building up outside.

Genevieve scratched through his britches, drawing blood but doing no hurt.

The Animus brought up Reinhardt's knee against the vampire's chin, and shoved her across the stage.

Lights were streaming in.

The Animus came down hard on Genevieve, knee pinning her body. Reinhardt's hands went around her head.

Only silver or fire or a stake through the heart could truly kill a vampire. But having her head wrenched off wouldn't do her health any good.

The Animus twisted, feeling the vampire's strong neck muscles stretch, her bones draw apart. She had her overlapping teeth clenched but her lips drawn back. Her eyes were dots of fire.

Detlef was hammering on his shoulders, as pointlessly as a gnat might bother an ox.

The vampire's head would come off in a moment.

Detlef stepped back, giving the Animus the room to do his bloody business. Genevieve hissed through her teeth, and spat hate up at Reinhardt's mask.

'For the Great Enchanter,' the Animus said, 'Constant...'

Something huge and heavy fell on Reinhardt, ropy limbs twisting around his body, hauling him backwards.

XX

The Trapdoor Daemon had made his way across the ceiling, and dropped down onto the stage.

Reinhardt Jessner had gone mad. The way Eva Savinien had gone mad. Malvoisin did not understand, but he realized there was more to the story of *Dr Zhiekhill and Mr Chaida* than an old Kislevite fable. In a sense it was literally true. Something could bring out the Chaida in all men, and that something had afflicted Eva, and now Reinhardt.

He found uses for the limbs of his altered body, constricting Reinhardt's wrists to break his grip on Genevieve's neck. The vampire had shown him a moment of consideration and, for that, he owed her his loyalty.

Reinhardt left Genevieve and stood, turning around in the Trapdoor Daemon's grasp, chopping with his hands at the bases of his tentacles, thumping for the nerves.

The actor was strong, but his body was only human.

Out in the auditorium people were shouting.

A firebrand hurtled through the air, and landed nearby on the stage. Detlef was stamping it out, protesting.

'Look,' someone shouted. 'A monster.'

Yes, the Trapdoor Daemon thought, a monster. Help me fight the monster.

Reinhardt struggled furiously, cold like a machine, methodically trying to throw off Malvoisin.

'Kill the monster,' someone shouted.

A missile bounced off his hide, and Malvoisin realized who the shouters thought was the monster.

'Kill!'

Detlef was confused. Reinhardt had gone mad, and some creature of the depths was wrestling with him all over the stage.

He picked up Genevieve, and tried to get her to run. She was confused, but finally picked up her feet as they descended the steps into the auditorium.

There were actors there, and an officer of the watch, and strangers in from the street. Everyone was shouting. No one knew what was going on. Poppa Fritz was waving a lantern and shouting at the top of his voice.

Genevieve stumbled, but started pulling Detlef away from the stage, towards the exit. She wanted them to run.

Detlef looked back. Reinhardt wore the monster like a cloak now, but was free of its grip. With a flex of his shoulders, the actor shrugged the thing off, and threw it away. It landed with a wet thump, spreading out, and some people cheered.

Reinhardt walked forwards, and stepped off the stage, falling six feet but landing perfectly. He stood up straight, and kept walking, wading through bolted-to-the-floor seats as if the stalls were a wheatfield.

The people started quieting down as Reinhardt's legs crushed through solid wood and upholstery.

The watchman was in the way. Reinhardt smashed his chest with a sideswipe, and bloody foam came from his mouth and nose as he went down, coughing.

Gené was tugging him.

'It's after us,' she said, 'and it won't give up.'

Reinhardt had said something about Drachenfels.

'Is it him? Come back?'

Genevieve spat. 'No, he's in Hell. But he sent something back to fetch us there.'

'Ulric's teeth!'

Reinhardt tore the arm off a man, and tossed it aside, walking calmly through the fountain of blood. He was turned into a golem of force, unstoppable, single-minded, unreasoning, unmerciful.

Detlef and Genevieve ran into the foyer, and found a crowd pressing in. Ticket-holders mostly. The seeds of panic were sprouting. They had to fight forwards.

Reinhardt exploded through the double doors, and everyone started screaming at once. Windows were smashed out in the rush as the crowds tried to back away, and furniture was trampled underfoot.

Detlef and Genevieve were caught by the crowd, and pulled away. Reinhardt just fixed his cold eyes on them, and began killing his way towards them, breaking the backs and necks of the people in his way as if he were a poulterer processing chickens. The foul smells of death – blood, shit and fear – hung in the air.

They were out in the street now, and night was gathering. The crowd was running this way and that. Detlef collided with a matronly woman wearing a Moral Crusade sash and carrying a 'DOWN WITH DETLEF SIERCK' placard. She screamed at his bloody face and fainted. He picked up the placard, and held it like a weapon.

He heard a rattle of hooves and wheels. Some kind of help was coming. Gené still had his hand.

'This won't do any good,' she said. 'We've got to keep running.'

The Animus stood on the pavement, dead bodies all around.

The vampire and the play-actor were scurrying, but they wouldn't escape it.

A carriage got between it and its prey, and men in armour piled out, weapons ready. The Animus recognized the Imperial militia.

'By the order of the Emperor Karl-Franz,' began an officer. 'I demand–'

The Animus took off the officer's head, and squeezed it between flat hands until it burst like a pumpkin.

A subordinate gulped, and ordered an attack.

Crossbow bolts struck the Animus's head but it ignored them. Swords slashed its chest, cutting to the bone. It didn't care.

The vampire and the play-actor were still in its sight. They were scrabbling back into the theatre.

The Animus turned around.

'Fire!'

Pistol balls slammed into its body, making it stagger. It picked up the headless officer's heavy sabre.

Reinhardt Jessner had been a great swordsman.

Whirling the blade about it, lopping off everything that got in the way, it strode towards the Vargr Breughel Memorial Playhouse, intent on the attainment of its purpose.

A pistolier threw his weapon at the Animus, and it spanged off the flying blade. With a lunge, the Animus split the pistolier's neck, opening a gap under his chin. Drawing the sword out of the already-dead man, it passed the blade across the face of a Moral Crusade protester, making a blood-edged crease of his eyes and the bridge of his nose.

Detlef Sierck was closing the doors of the theatre, drawing the night-bolts. The Animus punched two holes in the doors, where the bolts were, and then kicked its way back into the foyer.

It stepped over the earlier dead.

The prey were not in sight. It fixed its eyes on one side of the room, and then raked its vision across to the other. It was looking for the slightest trace of the fleeing couple.

A trapdoor on the floor was slightly askew, the corner of a carpet flapped around it. Disguised as a flagstone, it would normally not have been noticeable.

It bent down, and pulled up the trapdoor, wrenching it off its hinges.

A gallon bottle, wrapped in rush matting, was lobbed from one side of the foyer, and smashed against its chest, stabbing the skin with tiny shards of glass. A thick, sweet liquid sloshed all over it, soaking the tatters of its clothes, clogging in its hair and beard.

A thin, elderly man was the culprit.

From Reinhardt's memory, the Animus recognized Guglielmo Pentangeli.

The Tilean business manager had a lamp in his hands, a naked flame with the glass off it.

'Brandy?' he asked.

Guglielmo tossed the lamp at the Animus.

There was an explosion, and the Animus was in the middle of a man-shaped statue of flame.

XXI

As people kicked him with heavy boots, shouting, 'Death to the monster,' Malvoisin remembered why he'd spent all these years in his catacombs. Reaching across the stage, the Trapdoor Daemon hauled itself away from his persecutors, shrinking from the light, shrieking through his beak.

He knew where the nearest trapdoor was, and slid through it, feeling a burst of relief as the wood slammed behind him, cutting him off from the chaos out in the upperworld.

The slide took him down towards the waters.

He needed to get his hide wet and he needed to sleep. Here in the dark – in his dark – there was peace.

But he could hear footsteps. And shouts. And fire.

Even here, they came for him. There'd be no peace now, ever.

Genevieve kept running, Detlef at her heels. There were miles of tunnels down here. The thing in Reinhardt might not be able to follow them. They were in one of the main passageways, heading down towards the Trapdoor Daemon's domain. When they found a bolt-hole, they would rest, and think out what to do.

She should have died thirty years ago, on her first wander in the fortress of Drachenfels. That would have saved a lot of trouble, a lot of bloodshed.

Detlef was babbling, but she didn't have time to listen. She could feel a great deal of heat. There was a fire down here. A fire that was growing closer.

A curtain fell in front of them, and she knocked it aside. It was a dusty cobweb, and came apart, leaving filthy scraggles of sticky stuff on her face and clothes. Small animals and large insects scuttled around their feet.

The fire was behind them, back near the trapdoor they'd come through.

She was back to being an animal again, pure instinct and bloodlust, running from a bigger cat, crushing smaller things underfoot. That was her Mr Chaida, the cruel heart beating inside, ever ready to take over.

They slammed into a wall. Looking round, she realized they were in a magazine. A rack on one wall was loaded with swords and daggers, all angled dangerously outward. They were lucky not to have run straight into them.

She shouldn't have forgotten there were likely to be traps throughout the labyrinth.

'In the floor,' Detlef said, indicating a manhole cover. She was on her knees, tugging at a ring. They heard footsteps, and she pulled harder. The ring came off, with a screech of protest.

'It's bolted from the underside.'

'There must be a trick.'

The footsteps were huge, thumping the ground like giant fists. The tunnels shook. She could smell smoke, and her eyes were watering. In the dark, distant flame flickered.

'It's iron,' she said. 'It leads into the sewers.'

'So? We're in the shit already.'

She shrugged and made awls of her fingers, piercing the metal with agonising slowness. She made fists, and pulled. Pain came alive in her shoulders and elbows.

A walking furnace squeezed into the chamber. A walking furnace with Reinhardt Jessner's face.

Genevieve pulled and heard the bolts breaking. The manhole burst free, and she choked on a gasp of truly foul air. Then, they were all in the middle of an explosion.

Detlef realized that pulling the manhole had let out a cloud of sewer gas. He felt a liquid heat on his face – beard and eyebrows singeing – and was thrown against a hard wall. Even with his eyes screwed shut, the light was brighter than the sun.

He knew something was broken inside him.

Trying to stand up, he realized his left leg wasn't working. He opened his eyes, and saw the explosion had blown itself out. Scraps of cobwebs and detritus were burning, but most of the fire was gone.

Reinhardt had been smashed against a rack of old weapons. His body was blackened with soot and burns, but bright blades shone where they pierced him. Three swordblades stood out of his chest, points glinting. He'd been cooked alive, and now he was spitted. The stench of burned human meat was bitter in Detlef's mouth and nostrils.

Apart from anything else, Reinhardt's head hung wrongly, his neck broken.

Genevieve was on her feet. Her face was sooty, and her clothes were ruined. But she was all right. She was in a better shape than him.

'It's gone,' she said.

She took him in her arms, and checked his wounds. When she touched his knee, pain shot through him.

'How... bad?'

She shook her head.

'I don't know. I think it's just a clean break.'

'Sigmar's holy hammer.'

'You can say that again.'

He touched her face, wiping the black grease away from her girl's skin. Her teeth were receding, and the red spark in her irises was dying.

'It's all right,' she said.

Behind her, Reinhardt Jessner's eyes opened wide in his black face, and he lurched forwards, pulling the rack of swords that pierced him away from the wall.

He roared, and Genevieve hugged Detlef hopelessly.

If Reinhardt fell on them, they'd be transfixed many times. All three would die down here.

XXII

Malvoisin launched himself at Reinhardt for the second time, bearing him away from Detlef and Genevieve, crashing him against a smoke-smeared wall. Reinhardt broke in several places, and swords tore through his flesh, revealing angry red gashes in his burned-black body.

He had his tentacles around the madman, and was squeezing. The body was already a corpse, but it clung to life. Malvoisin squeezed desperately, using his altered body as he'd never done before. He had grown strong in his lair, he realized. He'd wasted himself loitering in the depths of his own dark

In the sea, he might have had a chance.

Reinhardt's face came off, and stuck to his own.

The Animus left its ruined host, and latched onto Bruno Malvoisin, burrowing into his altered body, seeking his still-human brain. He must have a core which could be soured, turned against the Animus's prey. A core of bitterness, self-hate, misery.

This would be the final, and most powerful host.

It rose from Reinhardt's body, and stretched out its tentacles, reaching for Genevieve.

The vampire girl stood, wide-eyed. 'Malvoisin?'

The Animus was about to tell her 'no.' But the Trapdoor Daemon said, 'Yes, I'm still here.'

Angry, the Animus prepared for its final, fatal blows.

The monster came for them, and Detlef offered up his final prayers. He thought of all the parts he'd never take, the plays he'd never right, the actresses he'd never kiss...

Tentacles slipped around his broken leg, and latched onto his burned clothes, creeping up his body. Genevieve was entwined too. The Trapdoor Daemon was all around them.

In the centre of its head was a blank white face.

Then the monster froze like an ice statue.

Genevieve gasped, unwanted red tears on her cheeks.

She reached for the mask, but it seemed to elude her fingers, sinking into Malvoisin's hide as if it were disappearing under the surface of a still pond.

The mask was swallowed.

Inside his mind, Malvoisin wrestled the Animus, swallowing the creature of Drachenfels at a gulp.

It was hot inside, and he knew he would not last.

'Salli,' he said, remembering...

He had been altered by warpstone, but he had never truly been the Trapdoor Daemon. That was just a theatre superst-ition. Where it counted, he'd always been Bruno Malvoisin.

He had changed as much as he was going to in his lifetime.

And the Animus wasn't going to change him more.

The Animus didn't even regret its failure as it died. It was a tool that had been broken. That was all.

Malvoisin slumped, the fire burning inside him.

A white tunnel opened in the dark, and a figure appeared. It was Salli Spaak, not old and bent as she'd been when she died, but young again, ripe and beckoning.

'Bruno,' she purred, 'it was always you I loved, always you...'

The white tunnel grew and grew until it was all he saw.

Genevieve left Detlef and crawled over to Malvoisin. He was shaking, but he was dead. The thing had gone, forever.

Something about him was changed. The bulk of his body was still the sea creature he had become, but his head was shrunken, whiter. Where the mask-thing had touched was a face. It must have been his original face. It was in repose.

The mask was like Dr Zhiekhill's potion. It brought out what was inside people, buried in their deeps. In Eva and Reinhardt, it had brought out cruelty, viciousness, evil. In Bruno Malvoisin, none of those things had mattered, and it had only brought out the goodness and beauty he'd left behind.

'Is it dead?' Detlef asked.

'Yes,' she said. 'He is.'

'Blessings of Sigmar,' he breathed, not understanding.

She knew now what she must do. It was the only thing that could save the both of them. Crawling over to him, she made sure he was comfortable and in no immediate danger.

'What was it?'

'A man. Malvoisin.'

'I thought so.'

She stroked the burned stubble of his scalp.

'I suppose we'll have to take the play off... for a while.'

She tried to find the strength.

'Detlef,' she said. 'I'm leaving...'

He knew at once what she meant, but still had to prod her. 'Leaving? Leaving me?'

She nodded. 'And this city.'

He was quiet, eyes alive in his blackened face.

'We're no good to each other. When we're together, this is what happens...'

'Gené, I love you.'

'And I love you,' she said, a thick tear brushing the corner of her mouth. 'But I can't be with you.'

She licked away her tear, relishing the salt tang of her own blood.

'We're like Drachenfels's thing, or Dr Zhiekhill's potion, bringing out the worst in each other. Without me, you won't be obsessed with morbid things. Maybe you'll be a better writer, without me to anchor you in darkness.'

She was nearly sobbing. Usually, she only felt this way when a lover died, old and decrepit while she remained unaged, their youth flown in a mayfly moment, leaving her behind.

'We always knew it couldn't last.'

'Gené..'

'I'm sorry if it hurts, Detlef.'

She kissed him, and left the chamber. There must be a way out of this sewer.

XXIII

In the dark with his hurts and a dead thing that had been a man, Detlef overcame his urge to cry.

He was a genius, not a poltroon. His love would not die. Nothing he could do would stifle that. He would end up expending millions of words on it, and still never be able to snuff it out. His sonnet cycle, *To My Unchanging Lady*, was not complete, and this parting would inspire the third group of poems. It would spur him perhaps to his greatest work.

The smell was terrible. It was the smell of death. The familiar smell of death. Detlef felt a kinship with the dead playwright.

'Bruno,' he said, 'I'll revive all your plays. You've earned that much of me. Your name will live again. I swear it.'

The dead thing didn't answer, but he'd not expected him to.

'Of course, I might make some revisions, bring your work up to date just a little...'

Genevieve was gone, and she would never come back. The loss was worse than any wound he'd sustained.

He tried to think of something – anything – that would make the hurt go away, would make it better.

Finally, he spoke again, 'Bruno, I'm reminded of something Poppa Fritz told me. It's a story about a young actor visiting Tarradasch himself, when he was producing his own plays in Altdorf, running the old Beloved of Ulric theatre across the road, although I've also heard it about a young minstrel visiting the great Orfeo...'

His breathing was stronger now, and the pain in his leg was going away. Soon, they'd come for him. Gené would send people back for him. Guglielmo wouldn't let him lie broken for long.

'Anyway, Bruno, here's the story. A young actor from the country comes to the big city in search of fame and fortune on the stage. He can sing, he can dance, he can juggle, and he was a star in his university players' company. The young blood gains an audition with Tarradasch, and the great man is quite impressed. But not impressed enough to offer a place in his company. "You're good," Tarradasch says, "you've got a lot of talent, you've got the looks of a leading man, you've got the strength of an acrobat, and you've the grace of a dancer. You've learned your audition pieces very prettily. But there's one thing you haven't got. You haven't got experience. You're not yet eighteen, and you know nothing of life. You've not loved, you've not lived. Before you can be a great player, and not just a talented mannequin, you must go out and live life to the full. Come back to me in six months, and tell me how you've fared."'

Detlef's face was wet with tears, but his trained voice didn't break.

'So, Bruno, the lad leaves the theatre, Tarradasch's advice going round and round in his head. Six months later, he comes back, and he has a new story. "You were so right, master," he tells the great man, "I've been out there in the city, living for myself, experiencing everything. I've met this girl and she's shown me things about myself I could never have imagined. This has never happened before. We're in love, and everything in my life dances like blossom on a spring breeze."'

Detlef looked at the slumped bulk of the man who'd been the Trapdoor Daemon.

'"That's perfect," Tarradasch says, "now if only she would leave you..."'

Part Two

The Cold Stark House

I

Lying in his bed, he heard music from far away. To him, the music seemed to fill the endless rooms and passageways of Udolpho like a sweet-scented but poisonous gas, drifting with invisible malevolence through the towers and turrets, suites and stables, garrets and gables of the immense, rambling, mostly derelict estate. Down in the great hall, the harpsichord was being played, not well but with a sorcerer's enthusiasm. Christabel, dark daughter of Ravaglioli and Flaminea, with her supple hands and sinister smile, was practising. It was a dramatic piece, expressing violent emotions.

Melmoth Udolpho understood violent emotions. Thanks to Dr Valdemar's potions and infusions, he was a prisoner in his own shrunken body, his brain a spark of life in an already rotting corpse. But he still had violent emotions.

He thought again of his will. Poor Genevieve must come out, or she would hold up the succession forever. She was fresh now, but – like him – she would live long, too long. Pintaldi must be recognized as Melmoth's grandchild, in order to pass the fortune on to his current favourites, the twins. Young Melmoth was the purest Udolpho of the lot of them, and Flora would make a grand consort for him when he grew up and took his position in the world. Only the long-gone Montoni, whose bastard Pintaldi claimed to be, could possibly have matched him.

A few nights ago, Young Melmoth and Flora had surprised Mira, one of the maids, and tied her up. They had placed a mouse on her stomach, and then clapped a cup over the animal, fixing it in place with a scarf. After an hour, the mouse had got hungry, and tried to eat the soft floor of its cell. Young Melmoth thought that a fine experiment, and had kissed Flora on the lips to celebrate its success. They were of Montoni's line, undoubtedly; although Ulric alone knew what their mother had been.

The will must reflect the purity of Udolpho blood. Several times in past centuries, brothers had married sisters, cousins married cousins, simply to keep the blood pure.

Old Melmoth was nearly blind, but he hadn't left his bed in perhaps thirty years and didn't need his sight. He knew where the curtains hung around him, and where his tray was placed each day.

He could no longer taste food, and his sense of smell was also completely gone. He couldn't lift his limbs more than an inch or two and only then with great effort, or even raise his head from its deeply-grooved pillow. But he could still hear. If anything, his hearing was sharper than it had been when he was younger.

He heard everything that went on within the walls of Udolpho.

In the ruined west wing, where the roofs were gone and the exquisite mosaic floors designed by his mad great-uncle Gesualdo were open to the elements, wolves sometimes came to root around. In the stables, flies still buzzed around the neglected and dying horses. In the cellars, rats scratched against old oak doors, wriggling between the bones of forgotten prisoners. And, in her rooms, poor Mathilda, her swollen head almost insupportable, sometimes raged against her fate, smashing the furniture and attacking the servants with an energy Old Melmoth could only envy. There must be provision in the will for Mathilda So long as she remained human, she would be a beneficiary.

In the darkness that was forever before his face, a light appeared. It was small at first, but it grew. The light was blue and sickly, and there was a face in it. A familiar face. A long nose, and sunken hollows where eyes had been.

Old Melmoth recognized the features of his eldest son. 'Montoni,' he gasped, his papery throat spitting out the name like a hairball. The rightful heir to the House of Udolpho, vanished into stormy night sixty years earlier, looked down at the ruin of his father, and his empty eyesockets filled with pity.

Old Melmoth's face cracked as he smiled. His gums hurt. Not yet. He wasn't ready yet. He clung to his bedclothes as he clung to life. There was more to be done, more to be changed. He was not ready to die.

II

Prince Kloszowski prayed to gods in which he no longer professed to believe that none of his travelling companions had died of the Yellow Ague. He guessed most of them had succumbed to simple malnutrition or the ministrations of an overenthusiastic torturer, but one of Marino Zeluco's permanent guests might have carried disease enough to provide a swift escape of the duce's dungeons. As the cart trundled along the rough road towards the marshes, he felt several of the bodies leaking onto him, and clamped his hand tighter over his mouth and nostrils. This close, he could taste the stench of the corpses. Breathing was becoming a problem. Naturally, Kloszowski was at the bottom of the pile, and the press of bodies was becoming insupportable. He could no longer feel his legs and feet, and his elbows burned every time he tried to move his arms. The darkness was hot, and getting hotter with every uncomfortable mile.

The duce had told him the only way out of the dungeons of Zeluco was in a corpse-cart, and here he was proving the parasite right. Unless the ordeal were to end soon, Kloszowski would sadly not be alive to benefit from the irony. His mother, the Dowager Princess, wouldn't have approved of his current situation. But his mother hadn't approved of any of his situations since early infancy, so that was hardly a novelty. He needed to cough but the weight on his back was too much. He could only choke feebly, grinding thinly-fleshed ribs against the rough wooden planks of the cart.

Of all his daring escapes, this was the least enjoyable. Through the cracks between the planks, he sucked cold, clean air, and occasionally caught glimpses of reflected light from puddles in the road. The novice of Morr, comfortable on his padded driver's seat, was humming a gloomy melody to himself as he transported human waste to the marsh that served the dungeons as a markerless graveyard. There were things in the marsh the Zelucos liked to keep well-fed, in the hope of dissuading them from forsaking watery homes in search of live meat. Tileans were like that, keener to come to an accommodation with the creatures of Chaos than on crusading against the filthy monstrosities.

Zeluco had too cosy a life extorting from the peasants to bother much with good works. He was a typical parasite, the fruit of ten generations of inbreeding, oppression and perfumed privilege. Come the revolution, Kloszowski swore, things would be different...

The weather was unpredictable in this benighted land where marsh met forest, and Kloszowski had several times heard the patter of rain on the canvas cart-cover. He was sure the occasional rumble of thunder stirred in with the steady creaking of cartwheels. This was flash-flood country. Most of the roads were little better than ill-maintained causeways.

Kloszowski rebuked himself again. His predicament was, as usual, his own fault. Along the road to revolution, there were always distractions, and too often he let himself be tempted. He had first preached the cause to Donna Isabella Zeluco, impressing upon her, between more conventional attentions, the justice of his struggle. She had seemed convinced the rule of the aristocracy was an obscenity that should be wiped, through violent revolution, from the face of the world. However, it proved unwise to proceed from his philosophical and amorous conquest of the duce's wife to pursue, in rapid succession, both of his daughters, Olympia and Julietta. The girls had been eager to learn of the revolution and of the casting-off of chains, especially when Kloszowski had demonstrated that the outmoded and hypocritical chastity fostered by their parents' class would be swept away along with any notions of rank and title. But as the sisters' enthusiasm rose, with enormously satisfying results, so that of their mother abated.

The cart bumped over a stone in the road and someone's protruding bone stabbed into his side. He definitely heard thunder. The superstitious said thunderclaps were tokens of the anger of Ulric, god of battle, wolves and winter. Kloszowski, who knew gods were fictions invented by the parasite clergy to excuse their position over the toiling masses, prayed to Ulric for delivery from the bottom of this corpse-pile. A flash of lightning lit up the crack beneath his eye, and he saw the mud of the road, a tuft of grass white in the instant's lightburst. Very close, thunder drum-rolled again. There must be a storm coming.

One night, emerging in disarray from a tryst with one or other of the girls, he'd found himself seized by men-at-arms and hauled up before the duce for a lengthy lecture on the rights and duties of inherited wealth. Donna Isabella, her conversion forgotten, stood dutifully beside her gross and wealthy husband, nodding at every point as if his speech were not the self-interested prattle of an ape-brained idiot. After Zeluco had concluded his address, failing to give Kloszowski adequate opportunity to refute his infantile arguments through reasoned debate, he had ordered that the revolutionist be confined to the depths of the dungeons of Zeluco for the remainder of his life. The duce had introduced the prisoner to Tancredi, a hooded minion reputed to be the most exquisitely skilled torturer in all Tilea, and assured him, Kloszowski, that their acquaintance would deepen into a full and mutually entertaining relationship that would provide him, Zeluco, with many enjoyable hours. The duce was looking forwards to screams of agony, retractions of deeply-held political convictions and heart-rending, though futile, apologies, offers of restitution and pleas for mercy.

The bone broke his skin and cut deeper. The pain was good. It made Kloszowski aware he could still feel. His blood trickled and clogged under him. The fog that had been creeping into his brain dissipated. The cart was speeding up, as the novice tried to get his unpleasant task over with before the storm broke.

Were it not for the warmth, generosity and sympathy of Phoebe, the jailer's comely and impressionable daughter, Kloszowski would be in the dungeon still, stapled to the wall, waiting for Tancredi to heat up his branding irons, dust off his knuckle-cracking screws, and start leafing through anatomies for inspiration.

He might yet fail in this escape, if the breath were crushed out of him by the other corpses. He fought to draw in a double lungful of air, and held it inside as long as he could, exhaling in a steady, agonising, stream. Then, he fought for the next breath. Fires of pain were burning up and down his back. He could feel his feet now, as if they were being pierced by a thousand tiny knives. He tried to move, to shift the weight of the dead from his spine.

He vowed, if he survived, to write *The Epic of Phoebe*, which would celebrate the jailer's daughter as a heroine of the revolution, worthy of comparison with the martyred Ulrike Blumenschein. But he recalled that he had frequently vowed to write epics, and invariably lost impetus after fewer than a score of pages had been filled. As a poet, he was more successful with more concise pieces, like the six stanzas of his well-remembered *The Ashes of Shame*. He tried to frame the first canto of *The Ballad of Phoebe*, planning a mere dozen or so verses. Nothing much came of it, and he wondered whether *Phoebe: A Sonnet* would suffice to repay his debt of gratitude.

The cart was slowing. Kloszowski wondered what was bothering the novice.

These were bad days for the revolution. In the dungeons, he realized he had not written a word of poetry since his flight from Altdorf, shortly after the Great Fog Riots. Once, verse had spewed from his mind like liquor from a stabbed wineskin, carrying his passion to those who heard him recite or read his pamphlets, stirring up suppressed dissent wherever it reached. Now, there was rarely anything. The revolutionist leaders were scattered, imprisoned or dead, but the cause lived on. The fire might be dwindled to a flame, but so long as there was breath in him, he would fan that flame, confident that it would eventually burn away the loathed worldwide conspiracy of titled thieves and murderers.

The cart halted, and Prince Kloszowski heard voices.

He could speak the elegant Tilean of the parasitical classes, the dowager having ensured his complete education, but he found it hard to follow the coarser argot of the oppressed masses. That had proved an embarrassment during his stay in Miragliano, where he had hoped to seed a revolt but found himself mainly ignored by potential revolutionists unable to understand his courtly speech. In the end, he had left the city when the Yellow Ague began to spread, and people started frothing yolky dribble in the streets. Tilea had more diseases going round than there were ticks on a waterfront dog.

Three different voices were engaged in a spirited conversation. One was the novice of Morr, the others men he had encountered on the road. The men were on foot and the cart was being drawn by two adequate horses from the duce's stables. The men obviously saw the inequity as an injustice, and were arguing that it should be rectified at once. Any other time, Kloszowski would have supported their just cause, but if this trip were extended any further, there was quite a chance that his absence from the dungeons of Zeluco would be noted, and a cadre of men-at-arms sent in pursuit.

The duce was not one to forgive a man who had, he alleged, wronged his wife and daughters, let alone spread sedition throughout his estates, suggesting his tenant farmers be allowed to retain the greater part of their produce for themselves rather than turning over nine-tenths to the castle granaries. And Donna Isabella was unlikely to look favourably upon a lover who had, she claimed, deserted him in favour of greener olives, no matter how much he had told her that fidelity was merely another of the chains society used to confine the true revolutionist into a dungeon of conformity.

The novice of Morr was insistent. He would not give up the horses, and be stranded on an open road with a cartload of fast-spoiling bodies.

Suddenly, the novice changed his mind. There were other voices. Other men, not on foot, had come out of a copse at the side of the road, and were insisting the novice turn over the duce's horses to their comrades, whose own mounts had been killed. There were voices all around and Kloszowski heard horses snorting as they drew near. The cart was surrounded. One of the horsemen spoke surprisingly well, addressing the novice in cultivated Old Worlder. He claimed his men had been unhorsed during a bloody battle with a band of foul skaven, the ratmen who were such a problem in the Blighted Marshes, and that the novice should be proud to help out such heroes.

The novice at least pretended to believe the man, and the horses were unharnessed. The foot-weary travellers strapped their saddles to new mounts, and the whole band rode off, hooves thumping against the soggy road.

'Banditti,' spat the novice when the party was out of earshot.

Kloszowski wondered if his back had snapped under the strain. If he tried to stand up, would he find his bones turned to knives, carving inside his flesh like Tancredi's white-hot skewers. Certainly, the pain was spreading.

The cart wasn't going any further. Thunder sounded again.

He moved his arms, testing their strength, hoping his spell in the dungeons had not sapped him too much. Then, he pressed against the bottom of the cart, pushing his back upwards. It was an agony, but he felt bodies parting as he fought his way up through the pile. His head pushed against the canvas sheet that had been tethered over the corpses. It was leashed tight, but the fabric was old and rotten. Making a fist, he punched upwards, and felt the material give. He stood up, the canvas tearing as he forced his way through the hole he had made. There was a sigh of escaping corpse-gas, which fast dispersed, leaving only a vile taste in the back of his throat.

It was evening, night not quite fallen. In early spring, the swamp insects were already active, although not the murderous nuisance they would be at the height of summer.

He breathed clean air, and stretched out his arms in triumph. He was not broken inside.

The novice, a very young man with his hood down around his shoulders, screamed and fainted dead away, slumping in the road.

Kloszowski laughed. He could imagine what he looked like, exploding from among the dead.

The sky was thick with irritated clouds, and neither moon was visible. The last of the sunset spilled blood on the horizon, and scattered orange across the marshlands to the south. A light rainfall began, speckling Kloszowski's shirt. After the heat and the grime, it was pleasant, and he looked up at the sky, taking the rain on his face, feeling the water run down into his beard. It began seriously raining, and he looked down, shaking his head. The rain was purer water than he had tasted in weeks, but it felt like just-melted chips of ice, freezing him to the bone in a minute.

The poet-revolutionist clambered down from the cart, wondering where he was and what he should do next.

To the south were the Blighted Marshes, currently agitated by the downpour of pebble-sized drops. To the north was a thin, scrubby forest and a thick mountain range that ran along the Bretonnian border. Neither direction was particularly inviting, but he'd heard especially vile stories about the marshes. It was sound sense to stay away from anything that announced itself on the map as being blighted.

In the distance, he heard horsemen. Coming this way. They would be in pursuit of the banditti, but they wouldn't be averse to recapturing an escaped prisoner. His decision was made for him.

III

The library of Udolpho was one of the largest privately-owned collections in the Old World. And the most neglected. Genevieve stepped into the huge central gallery, and held up her lantern. She stood on an island of light in an ocean of shadows.

Where were Ravaglioli and Pintaldi?

There was dust thick on the floor, recently disturbed. Ravaglioli and Pintaldi were in the book-walled labyrinth somewhere. Genevieve paused, and tried to listen. Her ears were abnormally sensitive. Ravaglioli often said there was something strange about her.

She could hear the rainwater blowing against the five thirty foot high windows at the end of the gallery. She knew there was going to be a daemon of a storm. Often, storms raged around Udolpho, besieging the mountain fastness as surely as a hostile army. When the rains fell thick, the passes became gushing culverts, and there was no leaving the estate.

Somewhere in the library, a wind blew through a hole in

the walls, producing a strange, flutelike keening. It was tuneless, but fascinating. Vathek claimed the cries were those of the Spectre Bride, murdered four centuries previously by her jealous brother-lover on the eve of her wedding to Melmoth Udolpho's great-great-grandfather Smarra. Genevieve believed few of Vathek's ghost stories. According to the family lawyer, every stone of Udolpho, every square foot of the estate, was triply haunted by the ghost of some ancient murdered innocent. If he were to be taken on trust, the estates would still be knee-deep in blood.

Blood. The thought of blood made Genevieve's heart race. Her mouth was dry. She'd been off her food lately. She imagined nearly-raw beef, bleeding in a tureen.

She was walled in by ceiling-high cases, weighted down with more books than were imaginable. Most of the volumes had been undisturbed for centuries. Vathek was always rooting around in the library, searching for some long-lost deed or long-forgotten ghost story. The cases were the walls of a maze no one could completely map. There was no order, no filing system. Trying to find a particular book would be as futile as trying to find a particular leaf in the Forest of Loren.

'Uncle Guido!' she shouted, tiny voice bouncing between bookcases. 'Signor Pintaldi?'

Her ears picked up the clatter of sword on sword. She had found the eternal duellists. A cloud of dust descended around her. She held her breath. Between the tinkling clashes, she heard the grunts of men locked in combat.

'Uncle Guido?'

She held up her lantern and looked towards the ceiling. The cases were equipped with ladders to provide access to the upper shelves, and there were walkways strung between them, twenty feet above the flagstone floor.

There were lights above, and shadows struggled around her.

She could see the duellists now, clinging to the bookcases, lashing out with their blades.

Guido Ravaglioli, her mother's brother-in-law, was hanging by one arm from a ladder, leaning into the aisle. Genevieve saw his bristle beard above his tight white ruff, and the white splits in his doublet where Pintaldi's swordpoint had parted the material. Pintaldi, who claimed to be the illegitimate offspring of Old Melmoth's vanished son Montoni, was younger and stronger, leaping from case to case with spiderlike dexterity, but her uncle was the more skilled blademan. They were evenly matched, and their duels usually resulted in a tie.

Very rarely, one would kill the other. No one could remember what their initial argument had been.

Genevieve called to the duellists, begging them to stop. Sometimes, she felt her only position in Udolpho was as family peacemaker.

Ravaglioli hurled an armload of heavy books at his unacknowledged cousin-by-marriage. Pintaldi swatted them out of the way, and they fell, spines breaking, to the floor. Genevieve had to step back. Ravaglioli thrust, and his swordpoint jabbed into Pintaldi's shoulder, drawing blood. Pintaldi slashed back, scribing a line across Ravaglioli's forehead, but he was badly thrown by the wound and his hand couldn't grip the sword properly.

'Uncle, stop it!'

There were too many duels in Udolpho. The family was too close to get along. And with Old Melmoth still on his deathbed, nobody could bear to leave for fear they'd be cut out of the will.

The fortune, she understood, had been founded by Smarra Udolpho's father, a plunder-happy pirate who had ravaged the coast with his galleass, the *Black Cygnet*. Down through the centuries, the money had been compounded by a wide variety of brigandry, honest endeavour and arranged marriages. There was enough for everyone but everyone wanted more than enough. And, despite the visible fortune, there were forever rumours that the Black Cygnet had concealed the greater part of his treasure in a secret location about the estate, prompting many persistent but fruitless searches for buried gold.

At least, this was what she understood. Details were often hazy. Sometimes, she was unsure even of who she was. She remembered only Udolpho, one day much like the last. But she did not remember ever being younger than her sixteen summers. Life in this house was unchanging, and sometimes she wondered if she had lived here all her life or merely for a moment. Could this be a dream? Dreamed by some other Genevieve, intruding into an entirely different life, forgotten entirely when the dreamer was awake?

Pintaldi staggered across a walkway. Its ropes strained, and Ravaglioli hacked through the support ties, laughing madly.

Her possible second cousin fell to his knees. He was bleeding badly, the red standing out against the white of his open-necked shirt. Pintaldi had finely-trimmed moustaches and, understandably, a face lined with old sword scars.

Shouting with triumph, Ravaglioli used his sword like an axe, parting another thick rope.

The walkway fell apart, wooden planks tumbling to the floor, one single rope remaining. Pintaldi fell, his unwounded arm bent around the rope, and dangled in mid-air. He cried out. His sword plunged down, and stabbed into a fallen book.

Ravaglioli was sagging against one of the shelves, squeezed against a row of huge, thick books. He didn't look triumphant now. There was blood in his eyes.

Pintaldi tried to get a firmer hold on the rope, reaching up with his hurt arm. But his fingers wouldn't make a gripping fist. Her uncle wiped his face off, and made the last cut, parting the rope. Genevieve gasped. Pintaldi swung heavily into the book-case, bones breaking, and fell badly before her. His head was at an unhealthy angle to his body.

There was nothing she could do but wait.

Wearily, Ravaglioli descended from his perch. He'd been hurt himself during the duel, and was bleeding into his clothes. He couldn't get up the energy to hawk enough phlegm to spit on his slain opponent.

Genevieve looked at him, not needing to restate her complaint. He already knew this family feuding was pointless, but couldn't stop fighting any more than she could stop peacemaking. That was the way of Udolpho.

Why did the blood seeping from his shallow headwound excite her so? She could smell it, taste it. It glistened as it trickled. She felt a thirst she didn't understand.

A forked spear of lightning struck the ground beyond the win-dows, filling the library with a painful flash. The thunder sounded instantly, shaking the whole edifice of Udolpho.

She supported Ravaglioli, helping him to a couch, and sitting him down. He would need sleep.

Later, she would have to give a full report to Vathek, and he would take it up with Old Melmoth. The will, a much-discussed secret between the patriarch and his lawyer, might have to be altered. The will, the main topic of conversation in the halls of Udolpho, was always being altered, unknown clauses being added, taken out, restored, substituted, reworded or rethought. Nobody but Melmoth and Vathek knew what was in the will, but everyone thought they could guess...

She walked to the window, and looked out into the night. The library was the heart of the southern wing of Udolpho, a man-sion built like a vast cross on its plateau, and from its windows there was a view of the slopes which descended towards the plains. When the weather was clear, admittedly a rare occasion, you could see as far as Miragliano and the sea. Now there was only a spectacular cloudscape, and a fascinating pattern of rain splatters. One of the sickly trees by the ruined Chapel of Manaan had been struck by the lightning blast, and was burning like a lamp, a tattered flame amid the dark, fighting lashing sheets of rainwater. Its flickering light made the stones of the chapel seem to dance, animated, Vathek would have claimed, by the souls of the victims Smarra's pirate father had sent to the bottom of the Tilean sea.

A hand fell on her shoulder, and she was spun around.

'Fire,' Pintaldi said through his twisted throat. 'Pretty fire...'

Pintaldi had a fascination with fire. It often got him into trouble. His head still hung at the wrong angle, and his shoulder was caked with dried blood.

'Fire...'

Gently, with strong hands, she took his head and shifted it, setting it properly on his neck. He stood up straight, and experimented with nods. He was put back together again. Pintaldi did not thank her. His eyes were fixed on the burning tree. There were flecks of foam on the ends of his moustache. She turned away from his gaze, and watched with him as the fire was crushed by the storm.

'It's like a struggling soul,' Pintaldi said, 'at the mercy of the gods.'

The flames were wiped off the tree, and it stood, steaming, its branches twisted black and dead.

'Its defeat is inevitable, but while it burns, it burns bright. That should be a lesson for us.'

Pintaldi kissed her, the taste of his blood biting into her tongue, and then staggered back, breaking the contact. Sometimes, he was her lover. Sometimes, her sworn enemy. It was hard to keep track. The variations had something to do with the will, she was sure.

He was gone. Beyond the window, the storm attacked ferociously, tearing at the stones of Udolpho. The house was colder
than ice tonight.

IV

The novice's robe was heavy with chilled water, and Kloszowski missed the warmth and security of his heap of dead people. He was lost in the forests. By the ache in his legs and knees, he could tell he'd been climbing upwards. The ground beneath was sloping more sharply, water running in hasty rivulets around his feet. If there were men-at-arms out searching for him, he couldn't hear them over the din of the weather. He would have pitied anyone trying to get through this storm on horseback in armour, and guessed Zeluco's men would have given up by now. Not that that was much consolation.

Lightning struck, imprinting the black and white image of the forests on his eyes. The trees around here were all twisted and tangled, as if lumps of warpstone in the earth, seeds of Chaos sprouting amid the other roots, were turning the forestry into a nightmare distortion. With each javelin of lightning, certain trees seemed to leap forwards, sharp-twigged branches reaching out like multi-elbowed arms. He told himself not to be superstitious, and tugged at his borrowed hood. Freezing water trickled down the back of his neck.

Underfoot, soft ground was a sea of mud. Soon, there'd be little difference between the forest and the marshes to the south. He was wading, and the novice's boots were too loose, already filled with a soft, cold mush of mud that settled a chill into his toebones. If he stopped, he would be drowned where he stood.

He fought onwards, the rain as tough an obstacle as the ever-changing wind. His robes flapped like the ragged wings of a dying raven. The symbol of Morr picked out on his chest was very apt. He must look like death.

Finding shelter was his only priority. None of the trees offered any cover against rain and wind. His knees were on the point of giving out and his exposed hands were wrinkled like those of a drowned sailor who'd been in the water long enough for the fish to eat his eyes. It could be that, with another irony, he'd escaped from the dungeons of Zeluco only to perish of his freedom, not murdered by the malice of the duce but impersonally snuffed by uncaring elements.

The ground was sloping upwards, and there were slow waterfalls of mud streaming around. Surely there must be a hunting lodge somewhere, or a woodsman's hut. Even a cave would be welcome.

Up ahead, Kloszowski imagined he saw a light.

He felt a surge of strength in his legs and shouldered his way through the rain, pushing towards the glow. He hadn't been wrong, there was a light. Somehow, it wasn't reassuring. A pale blue luminescence, it was constant, distorted only by the curtains of rain hanging between Kloszowski and it.

He pulled himself up over a bank that had been reinforced with stone and logs, and found himself on the remains of a road. He could see the light clearly now. It was a blue ball, hovering a few feet above the ground like a small, weak sun. And beneath it was an overturned carriage.

A horse, its neck broken, was mangled between the traces, legs sticking out in the wrong direction. There was a liveried coachman sprawled face-down in the mud, not moving, a fallen tree across his back.

Kloszowski ran, boots slapping the pebble-and-hard-earth surface of the road. At least the coach would offer some shelter.

He didn't like to look at the blue light, and tried to keep his eyes away from it. In its centre, the blue became a tinted white, and there were thick smudges, changes in the consistency of the glow, that reminded him of a face.

There was a screeching in with the wind. Someone was crying out. The carriage was on its side, rain streaming in through one of the open windows. There were people inside, arguing. Blue flames fell like little raindrops, and evaporated against side of the vehicle. He reached the carriage, and saw himself bathed in the blue light. It didn't radiate any heat.

'Hello there,' he shouted. 'Friend, friend.'

He climbed up, and looked through the open window.

There was a puff and a fizz from inside, and a woman shouted.

'You idiot, I told you it wouldn't work if the powder got wet.'

Kloszowski tried to pull himself in, but the carriage was overbalanced. He heard a wheel snapping as the vehicle righted itself, and jumped back so it wouldn't break his legs. The people inside were dumped on the floor, and sounded shaken up.

'Back, monster,' a man said.

Kloszowski could see a shaking pistol pointed at him. Its flashpan and barrel were black with soot and still smoking. It wouldn't fire again. He pulled open the door, and forced himself in, slapping the firearm away.

Inside, it was wet but at least the rain wasn't whipping his face. It sounded like a thousand drum beats on the wooden roof of the coach.

There were two passengers, the man with the pistol and a

young woman. He was past middle age and had once been sleek and corpulent, and she was in her twenties and probably attractive.

Her face was lovely, and she had a mass of coppery gold ringlets.

They must have been expensively dressed when they set out on their journey. Now, they were as wet, muddy and bedraggled as the meanest peasant. Nature was as great a leveller as the revolution. The passengers were obviously afraid of him, and shrank together, clutching each other.

'What manner of fiend are you?' the man asked.

'I'm not a fiend,' Kloszowski said. 'I'm just lost in the rain.'

'He's a cleric, Ysidro,' said the woman.

'Thank the gods,' the man said. 'We're saved. Exorcise these daemons and I'll see you're richly rewarded.'

Kloszowski decided not to tell them his robes were borrowed. He'd seen the light outside, but no daemons.

'This is Ysidro d'Amato,' said the woman, 'from Miragliano. And I'm Antonia.'

'Aleksandr,' Kloszowski said.

Antonia was less scared that d'Amato and better able to deal with the situation. He knew straight away that she wasn't a parasite.

'We were travelling when this storm blew up,' she said. 'Suddenly, there was this burst of lightning, and the coach turned over...'

'Daemons,' gasped d'Amato. 'There were daemons and monsters, all after my... after...'

He shut up. He didn't want to say what he thought the daemons were after. When the man was dried off and tidied up, Kloszowski imagined he wouldn't much like Ysidro d'Amato. The name was familiar, and he believed he'd heard it during his stay in Miragliano.

'There's a house ahead,' Antonia told him. 'We saw it through the trees before it got dark. We were trying to get there, to get out of the storm.'

Lightning struck, near. Kloszowski's teeth were rattled by the thunderclap. The blue ball had grown, and was all around the coach. Its light was almost soothing and made him want to sleep. He fought the impulse. Who knew what might happen if he were to close his eyes.

'We'd better make a dash for it,' he said. 'We can't stay out the storm here. It's dangerous.'

D'Amato hugged a valise to his chest like a pillow and wouldn't budge.

'He's right, Ysidro,' said Antonia. 'This light is doing things to us. We must go on. It's only a few hundred yards. There'll be people, a fire, food, wine...'

She was coaxing him as if he were a child. He didn't want to leave his carriage. The wind pulled the door open, slamming it against the side of the coach, and rain came in as if thrown from buckets. The face in the light was very definite now, with a long nose and chasms for eyes.

'Let's go.'

Kloszowski tugged Antonia, and they broke out of the carriage.

'But Ysidro—'

'He can stay if he wants.'

He pulled the woman away from the broken coach, and she didn't struggle much. Before they'd gone ten steps, d'Amato stuck his head out of the door and emerged at a run, valise still in a tight embrace.

He was a fat man, not light on his feet, but he splashed enthusiastically as he staggered, and both Kloszowski and Antonia were able to catch him before he fell. He shook free of them, trying to keep them away from his valise. It was obviously a favourite toy.

'It's this way,' said Antonia, pointing. The road was rising slightly, and curving. Kloszowski couldn't see anything in the wet darkness.

'It's a huge place,' she said. 'We saw it from miles away.'

D'Amato was standing transfixed, looking into the empty eyes of the blue face. Antonia pulled at his elbow, turning him round. He shook his head, and she slapped him. Hard. He woke up, and began to walk with them.

Together, they struggled into the darkness. Kloszowski wanted to look back, but didn't. He felt he would never be warm again.

It was impossible to see clearly, but the firm road beneath their feet was as good a path as any.

'They can't have it,' d'Amato was muttering. 'It's mine, mine...'

There was cold water between Kloszowski's eyes and eyelids, and ice forming inside his skull.

'Look,' Antonia said.

There was a wall along the side of the road, partly carved from the mountainside, partly built from great stone blocks. Now, they were standing by a set of huge ironwork gates, rusted and sagging. They could easily get through between the railings. Beyond was the outline of a huge house, and there were faint lights.

Kloszowski stood back, and looked up at the gates. This must be a substantial estate. A family of the parasite classes would live here, sucking the lifeblood from the peasantry, grinding their bootheels into the faces of the masses.

In the scrollwork at the top of the gates, a word was picked out. It was the name of the estate, and probably the name of the family.

UDOLPHO.

Kloszowski had never heard of it.

V

Word of the duel had reached Schedoni, Ravaglioli's father-in-law and Old Melmoth's son, and his disapproval hung over the dinner table like marsh gas. The old man, reputedly a notorious libertine in his nearly-a-century ago youth, sat at the head of the table, still waiting to inherit a position as head of the household from his bedridden father.

At his side was the empty chair and place always maintained for his wife Mathilda, an invalid whom Genevieve had never seen, and beside them were the two outsiders upon whom the family most depended, Vathek the lawyer and Dr Valdemar, the physician.

Both had lived at Udolpho forever, and both had gained the family look, long faces and deep-set eyes. Valdemar was bald but for three cultivated strands pasted across his shining scalp, while Vathek was so thickly-haired that his eyes seemed to peer from a black ball of fur. At separate times, it had been rumoured that Vathek or Valdemar were either Schedoni's long-lost brother

Montoni – Pintaldi's alleged grandfather – or the result of an adulterous or incestuous union contracted by Schedoni in his wild days. None of the rumours had ever been proved or disproved.

Vathek and Valdemar hated each other with a fervour that went beyond any emotion Genevieve could conceive of nurturing, and each was convinced the other constantly plotted his death. The currently favoured means of murder was poison, and neither had touched food of whose provenance they were even remotely uncertain for some weeks. The lawyer and the doctor stared at each other over full plates of meat and potatoes, each silently daring the other to take a perhaps contaminated mouthful. Vathek was charged with the custodianship of the will, but it was Dr Valdemar's duty to keep Old Melmoth alive long enough for it to be finished and signed.

Old Melmoth, who still held court in his master bedroom, was well over a hundred and twenty, and preserved long past his expected death by Dr Valdemar, who had travelled many years ago in Cathay, Lustria and the Dark Lands, in search of the magical ingredients necessary for the prolongation of life. He was a blasphemer and a sorcerer, her aunt said. But Old Melmoth was still alive, chuckling over each new intrigue in the unfolding saga of his family.

At the other end of the table, Ravaglioli sat opposite Pintaldi, pouring himself a generous goblet of wine while his wife Flaminea glared disapproval at him. She was the last remaining adherent of Claes Glinka's long-discredited Moral Crusade, and disapproved of most earthly pleasures. The family had to have someone to criticise its morals, and Flaminea had elected herself, taking every opportunity to preach damnation. A few months ago, she'd taken a hammer to the indecent sculptures of the Hanging Gardens, and destroyed, in the name of modesty, many priceless and irreplaceable works of ancient art. After that, the will, apparently, had been severely rewritten against her interests and her crusade had relaxed minutely. Ravaglioli, who had long since ceased to share his wife's rooms, made an exaggerated display of drinking, sloshing the wine around in his mouth and sighing with satisfaction as a mouthful slipped down his throat. Aunt Flaminea snorted her disdain, and carved her meat into tiny pieces with deft, cruel cuts of her serrated eating knife.

Genevieve was seated next to the empty chair that had been Flamineo's. He had been her father, and Flaminea's brother, before his still-unexplained death. On her other hand was a throne-like piece of furniture, decorated with intricate carvings of which Flaminea definitely did not approve, occupied by her father's fleshly uncle, Ambrosio, a monk of Ranald who'd been expelled from the Order of the Trickster God for an excess of vices. She edged her chair towards her late father's place, specifically to keep her unprotected knee and thigh out of range of Ambrosio's creeping fingers.

Ten feet away, across the table, were the beautiful twins, Young Melmoth and Flora. Pintaldi's ten-year-old offspring by a woman of dubious humanity, their ears were slightly pointed. Their curls fell on thin, delicate shoulders. The twins rarely spoke, save to each other. They had finished eating, and were sitting quietly, unnervingly blinking in a synchronized pattern.

The dinner party was completed by Christabel, Ravaglioli and Flaminea's daughter, as dark as Genevieve was fair, who was at Ambrosio's other side, her fork ready to deal with any exploratory graspings. She'd been educated in the Empire, at the academy in Nuln, and was recently returned to Udolpho, scandalising her mother with the habits she appeared to have acquired during her time away from the family estates. Once, after a dispute about the ownership of a bonnet, Christabel had ominously told Genevieve that she had taken a course under Valancourt, the master swordsman, and would be only too pleased to give a demonstration of her carving skills. Genevieve knew also that her cousin was a devotee of weirdroot, and often sought escape from the cold, stark walls of Udolpho in juicedreams. Just now, she was eating languidly, her hands not quite co-ordinated, and Genevieve suspected she'd been chewing the root earlier.

Genevieve looked up and down the table. It was hard to keep track of her family, to remember their relationships to her and to each other. Sometimes, they changed, and a relation she believed to be her uncle would turn out to be her cousin, or a cousin would become a niece. It was all to do with codicils to the will, which changed everything.

Beyond the tall windows, lightning forked.

Odo Zschokke, the chief steward, served as head-butler, supervising the three maids – Lily, Mira and Tanja – as they brought course after course to the table. Zschokke was seven feet tall, with broad shoulders only now bowed by years. He had been the captain of the Udolpho guard during the last major family war, when Old Melmoth's now-dead necromancer brother Otranto had raised daemons and the dead in an onslaught upon the estates.

Zschokke had sustained wounds from a Slaaneshi daemon's claw that carved three deep grooves diagonally across his face, twisting his nose, tearing his lips and making his eyes seem to stare through the dead skin bars of a cage-mask. His voice had been torn from him, but he was still a capable man, and Old Melmoth trusted him more even than Vathek and Valdemar. No one doubted that Zschokke stood to benefit from the will.

Genevieve didn't want to eat. Her meat was overcooked, grey through to the heart, and she didn't care for vegetables, particularly the black-eyed grey-white potatoes produced by the estate's garden. She took a little red wine, ignoring Flaminea's dagger looks, but it only served to sting her palate. She thirsted, but not for wine, and she hungered, but not for cooked-through beef...

The meal was mainly eaten without conversation. The clatter

of knives and forks on plates was backgrounded by driving rain, and the constant crescendo of thunder.

The storm excited Genevieve, aroused in her a hunting instinct. She wanted to be outside, slaking her thirst.

The maids took away her uneaten main course, and there was a pause. Zschokke signalled, and new bottles of wine were presented to Schedoni for his approval. He blew dust off a label, coughed, and nodded.

'I hardly think innocent children should be exposed to such vice and debauchery, father,' snapped Flaminea, thin lips pinching as she enthusiastically chewed her morsels of meat. 'We do not want to raise another generation of sybarites and libertines.'

Flora and Young Melmoth looked at each other and smiled. Their teeth were tiny and sharp, their eyes nearly almond-shaped. Genevieve had seen them playing games with the castle cats, and could not think of them as innocents.

She sipped her wine.

'You see,' Flaminea said, 'my niece is on the slope to degradation already, swilling wine at her tender years, wearing silks and satins to inflame the lusts of vile men, combing out her long, golden hair. The rot has started. You can't see it yet, but it will show on her face before long. Another sixteen years, and her face will be as corrupted and monstrous as...'

There was a loud thunderclap, and Flaminea refrained from naming the name. Schedoni stared her down, and she collapsed in her seat, shut up by her father's glance.

Genevieve had heard her grandmother was hideously disfigured by disease, and that she was always veiled as she grovelled in her rooms, awaiting Morr's last kiss.

Genevieve raised her goblet in a toast to her aunt, and drained it. The wine was as tasteless and unsustaining as rainwater.

Ambrosio had shown some interest when the subject of inflamed lusts was raised, and his swollen, purple-veined face wobbled as he licked his lips, his hand under the table fastening upon the upper thigh of Lily, the maid pouring his wine. A smile spread over his features as he reached higher, and Lily betrayed no sign of the attentions he was paying to her. A thin string of drool dangled from the cleric's mouth. He wiped it away with a finger.

Schedoni drank, and surveyed the family and its retainers. His face was the template from which everyone else around the table – even the beautiful Christabel – seemed to have been struck. But before Schedoni, the long nose and deep eyes had belonged to Old Melmoth. And before Old Melmoth, there were generations of the House of Udolpho, all the way back to Smarra's father, the Black Cygnet. There was a portrait of the pirate, standing aboard the deck of his vessel supervising the execution of an Araby captain, and he too bore the Udolpho features. He must have been the originator of the line, Genevieve realized. Before the pirate, there had been no family. It was his stolen fortune that had created the house.

Ravaglioli and Pintaldi were arguing quietly, their old quarrel revived again, and making threatening gestures with their dinner knives. Once Pintaldi had ended an argument by thrusting a skewer into Ravaglioli's throat between the meat course and the game, and then, with a flourish, taken his soup spoon to the other man's eyes. Ravaglioli had not forgotten or forgiven that.

'After dinner, I shall play the harpsichord,' Christabel announced. She was not contradicted.

Genevieve's cousin had learned music in Nuln, and possessed a pleasant although not outstanding voice. At the academy, she had also begun to get the measure of her own charms, and was clearly more than a little frustrated to be removed from the society of the Empire back to Udolpho, where her opportunities for breaking hearts were severely limited. Since she had driven Praz the gamekeeper to suicide, there had been no one to torment with her sable-black hair, liquid eyes and silky skin. She spent much of her time wandering the broken battlements of Udolpho, fretting and plotting, shroudlike dresses flapping in the breeze, petting the ravens.

'In Nuln, my playing was often praised by the Countess Emmanuelle von Lie...'

Christabel's boast was interrupted by thunder and lightning. And another crash of noise. At once, it was colder and wetter. Everyone in the great hall turned to the floor-to-ceiling windows which had just been blown in. Rain was pouring into the hall like shot, and stung on Genevieve's face. The wind screamed as the candles placed down the spine of the table guttered and went out. Chairs were pushed noisily back, Flaminea gave a polite little squeak of fright, and hands went to swordhilts.

It was dark, but Genevieve could make everyone out. Her eyes were fine at night. She saw Zschokke moving slowly, as if in a dream, across the hall, reaching for a lantern. One of the maids was wrestling with the opened windows, forcing them shut. The wind and the rain were shut off, and the light came up again as Zschokke turned up the wick of the lantern. There were strangers, dripping wet, standing behind Schedoni's huge chair. While the windows were open, someone had come into the hall.

VI

The company was gloomy, with funereal clothes and long faces, and their great hall was ill-lit and dusty, the upper walls covered with filth and cobweb.

Some of the diners looked barely alive, and they all had an unhealthy pallor, as if they'd lived all their lives in these shadows, never emerging into the sunlight. There were two pretty girls among them, though, a pale, lithe blonde and a lush, dark-haired beauty. They immediately excited Kloszowski's revolutionary interest. Trapped like Olympia and Julietta by the conventions of their class, they might make enthusiastic converts to the cause.

'We were lost,' he explained. 'We made for your light.'

Nobody said anything. They all looked, hungrily, at the newcomers.

'There's a storm outside,' said Antonia, unnecessarily. 'The road is washing away.'

'They can't stay,' said a thin old woman, voice cracking with meanness. 'Outsiders can't stay.'

Kloszowski didn't like the sound of that.

'We've nowhere else to go. There's no passable road.'

'It would be against his will,' the woman said, looking up at the shadowed ceiling. 'Old Melmoth can't abide outsiders.'

They all thought about that, looking at each other. There was an ancient man, a halo of cotton-spun white hair fringing his skull, at the head of the table. Kloszowski took him to be in charge, although he didn't seem to be this Old Melmoth. By his side stood a tall, scar-faced servant, the muscle of the family, typical of the type that leaves their own class and helps the aristocracy keep his brothers and sisters in chains.

A dangerous brute, to judge by the height and breadth of him and the size of his hairy-backed hands. Still, his face showed he had, at least once in his life, taken second prize in a fight.

'Shush, Flaminea,' the old man told the woman. 'We've no choice...'

Several men of the company had swords out, as if expecting banditti or beastmen.

Kloszowski noticed a pronounced family resemblance. Long noses, hollow eyes, distinct cheekbones. He was reminded of the phantom face in the blue light, and wondered whether perhaps they wouldn't be better off taking their chances with the storm.

'See here,' said d'Amato, who seemed to inflate as he dried. 'You'll have to shelter us. I'm an important man in Miragliano. Ysidro d'Amato. Ask anyone, and they'll tell you. You'll be well rewarded.'

The old man looked at d'Amato with contempt. 'I doubt if you could reward us, signor.'

'Hah,' d'Amato said. 'I'm not without wealth.'

'I am Schedoni Udolpho,' the old man said, 'the son of Melmoth Udolpho. This is a rich estate, weighed down with wealth beyond your imagination. You can have nothing we could want.'

D'Amato stepped back, towards a fireplace the size of a stable where whole trees burned, and looked away. He seemed smaller with the fire behind him, and he was still clinging to his bag as if it contained his beating heart. With typical bourgeois sliminess, he'd been impressed by talk of 'wealth beyond your imagination.'

Kloszowski remembered where he'd heard of d'Amato. Miragliano, a seaport built on a network of islands in a salt marsh, was a rich trading city, but it suffered from a lack of drinkable water. Fortunes had been made via water-caravans and canals, and d'Amato had been the leading water merchant in the city, carving out his own empire, forcing his competitors out of business. A year or so ago, he had achieved an almost total control over the city's fresh water, and been able to treble the price. The city fathers had protested, but had to give in and pay him.

He had been a powerful man indeed. But then the Yellow Ague had come, and investigating scryers laid the blame on contaminated water. That explained why d'Amato was leaving home...

Schedoni signalled to the scarred hulk.

'Zschokke,' he said. 'Bring more chairs, and mulled wine. Our guests are in danger of catching their deaths.'

Kloszowski had stepped as close to the fire as he could and felt his clothes drying on him.

Antonia had stripped her soaked shawl, and was raising thin skirts to toast her legs. Kloszowski noticed that at least one of the Udolpho clan was especially intrigued by the spectacle, the flabby old fellow with a cleric's skullcap and a lecher's look in his eye.

Antonia laughed gaily, and did a few dance steps.

'I'm a dancer sometimes,' she said. 'Not a very good one.'

Her legs were shapely, with a dancer's muscles.

'I used to be an actress too. Murdered by the end of Act One...'

She stuck her tongue out and hung her neck as if it were broken. Her blouse was soaked to her skin, leaving Kloszowski in no doubt as to her qualifications for the entertainment business.

D'Amato swarmed around Antonia, making her drop her wet skirts to cover herself.

'Sorry,' she said. 'Bought and paid for, that's me. The Water Wizard has exclusive rights to all performances.'

She was remarkably cheerful, and d'Amato was obviously embarrassed by his plaything's boldness.

'Harlotry is the path to Chaos and damnation,' said the shrivelled killjoy. 'This house was always plagued with harlots and loose women, with their painted cheeks and their sinful laughter. But they're all dead now, and I, righteous and ridiculous Flaminea, am still here. They used to laugh at me when I was a girl, and ask me if I was saving my body for the worms. But I'm alive, and they're not.'

Kloszowski had Flaminea marked as a cheerless maniac straight away. She seemed to derive considerable enjoyment from contemplating the deaths of others, so she wasn't denying herself every earthly pleasure.

The hulk found him a place at the table, next to a moustached gallant who couldn't hold his head properly.

'I'm Pintaldi,' the young man said.

'Aleksandr,' Kloszowski returned.

Pintaldi reached for a candle, and brought it close. Kloszowski felt the heat on his face.

'Fascinating stuff, flame,' he said. 'I've made a study of it. They're all wrong, you know. It's not hot, it's cold. And flames are pure, like sharp knives. They consume the evil, and leave the good. Flames are the fingers of the gods.'

'Very interesting,' said Kloszowski, taking a swallow of the wine Zschokke had decanted for him. It stung his throat, and warmed his belly.

Flaminea glared at him as if he were molesting a child in her presence.

'You are a cleric of Morr,' said a hairy-faced beast sat near Old Melmoth. 'What are you doing out in the storm?'

Kloszowski was befuddled for a moment, then remembered his borrowed robe.

'Um, death is everywhere,' he said, holding up his stolen amulet.

'The dead are everywhere,' said the hairy man. 'Especially here. Why, in this very hall the ghostly disembodied hands of the Strangling Steward frequently take shape, and fix about the throats of unwary guests.'

D'Amato coughed, and spat out his wine.

'Only those guilty of some grave crime need fear the Strangling Steward,' said the folklorist. 'He only visits the guilty.'

'My apologies,' said Schedoni. 'We are an old family, and our blood has grown thin. Isolation has made us eccentric. You must think us strange company?'

Everyone looked at Kloszowski, hollow eyes seeming to glow blue in the gloom. 'Oh no,' he said, 'you've been most hospitable. This certainly compares favourably with the last noble house in which I was a guest.'

That much was true, although Kloszowski suspected Zschokke might share certain talents with Tancredi. All these aristocratic menages kept a pet killer.

'You must stay the night,' Schedoni said. 'The house is large, and rooms can be found for you.'

Kloszowski wondered how long he could maintain the deception. Since the great fog riots, his name had been a byword for insurrection. If he were to be revealed to the Udolpho clan as Prince Kloszowski, the revolutionist poet, he'd probably find himself defenestrated. And the far windows of the great hall overlooked the gorge below. It would be a fall of seven or eight hundred feet onto jagged rocks.

Pintaldi had picked up the candelabrum now, and was holding his palm close to a flame.

'See,' he said. 'It burns cold.'

His skin was blackening, and there was a nasty, meaty smell. 'Harlots will rot,' said Flaminea.

Kloszowski looked across the table at the fair young girl. She had sat quietly, saying nothing, her eyes demurely cast down. She didn't have the Udolpho look, yet she was obviously part of this bizarre collection. Her lips were unrouged but deep red, and she had white, sharp teeth. She looked up, and caught his gaze. She seemed about sixteen, but her clear eyes were ancient.

'Without harlots, where'd be the fun in the world?' said Antonia.

Flaminea shook a bony fist at the dancer, and spat a chunk of gristle onto her plate. The woman had a fuzz of beard on her chin and her hair was scraggy grey. Dried out, Antonia was as healthy as a ripe apple, and made a distinct contrast with this withered crew.

'I shall play the harpsichord,' said the dark girl sitting by the fat cleric. Schedoni nodded, and the girl got up, daintily walking across the hall to the instrument. She wore something long, black and clinging, like a stylish shroud. Kloszowski was feeling warm again, but somehow the cold was still settled in his bones.

VII

As Christabel played, Genevieve considered the outsiders. Something about them disturbed her. She saw Ambrosio's lips tighten as Antonia showed her legs. She felt the strange hostility between the cleric of Morr and the merchant of Miragliano. These men hadn't chosen to travel together. And both had things to hide.

She imagined travelling, coaches crossing the Old World, from Estalia to Bretonnia, from the Empire to Kislev. There were great cities – Parravon, Altdorf, Marienburg, Erengrad, Zhufbar – and unknown, far-distant countries – Cathay, Lustria, Nippon, the Dark Lands. She believed she had spent all her life at Udolpho, never leaving its walls, as much a prisoner as invalid Mathilda or the altered son Ravaglioli and Flaminea were rumoured to have penned in a cellar, fed only on human flesh.

All she could remember was Udolpho, and she couldn't even remember much of that. There were huge gaps in her recollection. And yet, impressions of things she could never have known sometimes came to her.

Christabel played strangely, letting her juicedreams seep through as she embroidered around the edges of a familiar piece. Her tangle of black hair flew back as she nodded her head in time to the savage music.

The music disturbed Genevieve more. In her mind, she was a predator, tearing out the throats of her prey, her teeth sinking into flesh, delicious blood gushing into her mouth, trickling over her chin, flowing over her bosom.

Her nails had become sharp, and her teeth shifted in her mouth, the enamel reshaping...

There were other dream memories, crowding in. Faces, names, places, events. Things she could never have known, she experienced. She remembered a crowd attacked by invisible forces, and the kiss of a dark, handsome man who had changed her. She remembered a queenly woman, her face and arms red with blood, dressed in the costume of an earlier age. She remembered an iron bracelet and a chain, tying her to a rough-faced man, and a night in an inn. She remembered twice venturing into a castle to face a Great Enchanter. She remembered a theatre and a striking actor, and her flight from him, from his city. She remembered a thing with the body of a sea-creature and the eyes of a man. All these things were more than dreams, and yet they did not fit with the life Genevieve knew she had lived, a quiet, secluded, forgotten life in this castle.

Christabel's shoulders heaved, and sweat fell from her face.

Flaminea grunted from time to time. Music was sinful in her mind, and she rejected her daughter's talent. Sometimes, Christabel killed her mother, choking the life out of her with a silken scarf, or battering her with a stone torn out of the walls of the house.

Sometimes, when Flaminea worked up a righteous frenzy, it was the other way around, and she would denounce her daughter as a witch, standing by smugly while the villagers dragged her to the stake and Pintaldi lovingly nurtured the bonfire.

The cleric of Morr was looking at her. He was a foreigner, and didn't strike her as being a real cleric. Even Ambrosio had something about him that suggested holy orders, no matter how many times his hands reached into skirts or bodices. Aleksandr was not the type to bow to any god, or to any man.

Was it just that he was too good-looking to be a celibate of Morr?

His hood was down, and his throat was exposed. She saw the delicate blue vein threading up into his unkempt, still-wet beard, and imagined she could detect its pulse by sight.

Genevieve licked her lips with a rough tongue.

VIII

This was a strange brood, Antonia Marsillach thought to herself, and no mistake. For the millionth time, she wondered whether it wouldn't have been cleverer to stay in Miragliano and throw herself on the mercy of the city fathers. She'd had nothing to do with Ysidro's damned poison water, and suspected he was only taking her away with him to his luxury bolt-hole in Bretonnia because she knew a lot about the careless way he'd pursued personal profit at the expense of public safety. She should have turned the hog in and petitioned for a reward instead of sticking by him. He was no use anyway, never had been. Even when things were going well, he'd been more interested in the counting house than the bedroom. She should go back to the stage, and try to get out of the chorus and into a featured spot. She could act better than some, dance better than most, and the customers always liked to look at her legs. She was still young. She wanted some fun.

And here she was surrounded by refugees from the kind of

melodrama the city fathers had banned from the Miragliano playhouse as overly morbid and liable to incite public disorder. Before the ban, she'd been in them all, shaking herself during the prologues and getting murdered during the first acts of Brithan Cragg's *Ystareth; or: The Plague Daemon and Orfeo's Tall Tale; or: The Doom of Zaragoz*, Detlef Sierck's *The Treachery of Oswald* and *The Strange History of Dr Zhiekill and Mr Chaida*, Ferring the Balladeer's incredibly violent *Brave Konrad and the Skull-Face Slaughterer*, Bruno Malvoisin's obscene *Seduced by Slaaneshi; or: The Baneful Lusts of Diogo Briesach*. Those plays had dark and stormy nights, and weary travellers forced to stay the night, and puritanical harridans, and family curses, and secret passages, and much-altered wills, and ghouls, goblins and ghostliness.

And here she was in one again, promoted from the chorus to a featured role. She'd have to watch herself before the first act curtain.

The witch pounding the harpsichord was competing with the thunder and lightning, while the aunt who hated harlots was foaming at the mouth with righteous hysteria, and the cleric of Ranald was sneaking looks at her cleavage whenever he thought he was unobserved. Schedoni seemed courteous enough, but Antonia wasn't convinced he was still alive. She suspected he might be a wired-together corpse used as a ventriloquist's dummy by the scarred butler. She looked around the great hall, wondering where the entrances to the secret passages were.

Ravaglioli, the harridan's husband, was still eating, while everyone else was paying attention to his dark daughter. He was a noisy, messy eater, and food fragments were scattered about his place at the table.

Antonia was tired, and looking forwards to a big, warm, fresh-laundered bed without Ysidro d'Amato in it.

They had brought out Estalian sherry, and it was doing her good inside. Her clothes had dried on her body, and she relished the thought of peeling them off, and towelling herself down. Maybe she could find skilled hands to help her with that. Aleksandr seemed likely enough, and Father Ambrosio would doubtless be keen to volunteer his services.

She wasn't that wonderful as a dancer. But she had other skills. She could always find a comfortable place somewhere. She always had. Zschokke poured her some more sherry. She was feeling quite tipsy.

Ravaglioli scooped a spoonful of some flavoured gruel into his mouth. Antonia wasn't sure whether it was savory or sweet. He gulped it down with a slurp, and reached out for more.

Then, he paused, and his cheeks ballooned, as if he had bitten into a whole pepper. His face reddened, and the veins in his temples throbbed purple. Tears leaked from his eyes, and slipped into the cracks of his swelling cheeks.

He slapped the table with both hands, his full spoon splattering gruel around him. Christabel continued to play, but everyone else looked at the suffering man.

Ravaglioli held his throat, and seemed to be struggling, trying to swallow something.

'What is it?' asked Schedoni.

Ravaglioli shook his head, and stood up. His throat apple was bobbing, and he was breathing uneasily. His eyes were wide open, bloodshot, and panicked.

'It's justice,' snarled Flaminea. 'That's what it is.'

Zschokke tried to help the man, holding him upright, giving him a goblet of water.

Ravaglioli looked worse than the poisoned plenipotentiary, in Sendak Mittell's *Lustrian Vengeance; or: 'I Will Eat Their Offal!,'* when he was told that the deathbane-laced tripes he had just eaten were pulled from his beloved grandmother while she was still alive.

He pushed the servant away, but poured the water into his

mouth, sucking vigorously. He gulped, and the blockage in his throat went down towards his stomach. He drained the rest of the water, and reached for the sherry, laughing.

'What was it?' Schedoni asked.

Ravaglioli shrugged and smiled, wiping the spittle off his chin. 'It felt like a little metal ball. I've no idea what it was doing in the gruel, or what it could have been. It was coated with something sticky.'

Then he grabbed his stomach as a spasm hit him.

'It... hurts...'

Ravaglioli began shaking, as if lapsing into a fit. He held the edge of the table, and grit his teeth.

'Burning inside... it's growing... hot...'

Suddenly, he bent backwards, his spine audibly snapping against the chair rest. His swelling stomach burst through the hooks of his doublet, and was exposed.

Christabel stopped playing, and turned on her stool to look at the commotion her father was causing.

Zschokke backed away from the flailing man, and several people moved their chairs to give Ravaglioli room. His eyes were showing only white. His stomach was distended like a pregnant woman's, about to deliver triplets. Red stretchlines were appearing in the skin. The man was groaning, and there were noises inside him, breaking and tearing noises.

Antonia couldn't look away.

With a sulphurous bang, Ravaglioli's stomach exploded. Gobbets rained around him, and his chair collapsed.

A whisp of blue smoke curled out of the gaping hole in his midriff.

Somebody screamed, and screamed, and screamed...

...and Antonia realized it was her.

IX

That had been disgusting!

Kloszowski wiped his sleeve with a napkin, and watched everyone panic. D'Amato quieted Antonia down with a slightly overenthusiastic slap, and the dancer sat back, appalled.

A bald fellow with bow-legs, who'd been sitting near Schedoni, scuttled over, dusty coat-tails trailing the floor, and examined the corpse of Signor Ravaglioli, prodding around the edges of his yawning stomach wound with a bony finger.

'Hmmmn,' he said. 'This man is dead.'

Obviously this was a physician of some insight.

'Some explosive device, I suspect,' the doctor added. 'Designed to react to the inside of a human stomach..'

He took a fork, and poked around inside the mess.

'Ah yes,' he said, holding up a small shiny scrap of something. 'Here's a fragment.'

'Thank you, Dr Valdemar,' said Schedoni. 'Zschokke, have this mess cleared away and then bring us coffee.'

Kloszowski got up and thumped the table. Cutlery rattled. Ambrosio stopped his still-full wine goblet from falling over.

'I don't think you understand,' he said. 'This man is dead. Murdered.'

'Yes?' Schedoni seemed puzzled by his outburst.

'Someone must have killed him.'

'Indubitably.'

'Aren't you going to find the murderer? See that he, or she, is punished?'

Zschokke and two servants brought an old curtain to carry off Ravaglioli in, and a maid with a bucket and mop appeared to tidy up the quarter of the room that had been splattered.

Schedoni shrugged. 'Of course, murderers are always exposed, always punished. But first we should finish our meal. The habits of Udolpho will never be disturbed by something as crude as a mere killing.'

Everyone at the table appeared to agree with the old man and so, feeling foolish, Kloszowski sat down. Not only was this family the epitome of the parasite classes, they were all mad.

Christabel, piqued because her father's death had interrupted her recital, returned to the table, and took her seat. Ambrosio made a grasp at her bottom but she brushed his hand away.

Ravaglioli's chair was tipped back and he was lifted onto the sheet, and quickly wrapped. The maid wiped up.

'Put him in the cold storage room,' Dr Valdemar instructed the steward. 'I shall examine further later. There may be much we can learn.'

'Perhaps our guest might say a blessing for the dead,' suggested Vathek the lawyer. Everyone looked at Kloszowski, and he resisted the urge to look behind him.

He kept forgetting he was a cleric of Morr.

Kloszowski mumbled something and made gestures in the air, vaguely trying to imitate clerics he'd seen at funerals. No one questioned his impersonation, and the coffee arrived in several steaming pots.

'I must tell Old Melmoth,' Vathek said, addressing himself to Schedoni. 'This will affect the will. Ravaglioli was in the direct line of succession.'

'No he wasn't,' snapped Flaminea, between thirsty little sips at the boiling black coffee. 'I was.'

Vathek scratched his bristle-covered cheek.

'My late husband married into Udolpho. I am the direct heir, am I not, father?'

Schedoni shook his head, as if unable to remember.

'I thought father was grandfather's son,' said Christabel, 'and that you, mother, married into the family.'

'That was my impression,' said the lawyer.

'Well, your impression was wrong,' snarled Flaminea. 'I have always been the heir. Father Ambrosio will confirm the truth, won't you, uncle?'

Ambrosio, who was dividing his attention between Antonia's thighs and Christabel's breasts, applied himself to the question.

'I'm not your uncle,' said the father, 'I'm your father. Before I entered the cult of Ranald, I was married to my cousin Clarimonde. She was abducted by the banditti and never heard from again, but she left me with a daughter.'

Ambrosio's hand had dipped below the table, in Christabel's direction. He winced, and brought it up again. Christabel still had her meatfork.

'Uncle, you are confused,' said Flaminea. 'You are a father, not *my* father. Surely, you concede that Christabel is your grand-niece, not your grand-daughter.'

Ambrosio drank his coffee, the prong-marks red against the white skin of his hand, and said, reasonably, 'I believe Christabel is Pintaldi's sister, is she not?'

'Christabel?' said Flaminea, eyes glowing blue.

The dark girl shook her head, and said, 'It's nothing to me.'

Outside, the thunder had receded to a dull rumble every few minutes, and the main noise was the steady tattoo of the rain against the walls, and the rattling of the windows. Inside, Kloszowski's head was beginning to ache.

'More coffee?' asked Schedoni, courteously.

X

She had lost track of time, and could not tell how many years she'd been imprisoned. Her life before she came to Udolpho was a distant, vague memory. She had been married, she thought, and had children. She had lived in a city near the sea, and her husband had been a mariner, eventually the owner of his own boat, his own shipping line. Then, she'd travelled, and come, during one of these damnable thunderstorms, to Udolpho.

Her captors called her Mathilda, but that wasn't her name. Her real name was...

Mathilda.

No. It was...

She couldn't remember.

Zschokke, the tall man with the twisted face who brought her her meals, could not speak. But he was often accompanied by a bent, mad old man named Schedoni, and he always called her Mathilda. He spoke to her as if she was pitiably altered, but there was nothing wrong with her.

She was not a victim of warpstone. She was a normal woman.

She tried to lift her head, but the weights Zschokke fastened around her skull while she was asleep were too heavy.

There had been a slit window once, but it had been bricked up.

She could never tell whether it was day or night but she knew when there was a storm. She could hear the thunder, and the stones of the ceiling would become wet, occasionally dripping on her.

She didn't know why she was held prisoner. At first, she'd begged for her release, then for an explanation. Now, she didn't bother. They called her Mathilda and were sorry for her, but they'd never let her free. She would die in this room and be buried under a slab carved with the name of Mathilda Udolpho. That was to be her fate.

Once she had secreted a chicken bone from one of her meals, and snapped it, making a sharp tool. For months, she'd scraped away at the mortar between the stones, loosening large blocks. She'd rested her head against the cold wall while she worked away with her bone-trowel, and had flattened a part of her face.

In the end, Zschokke had caught her. She had tried to sever the vein in his throat with the sharp bone, but it had just broken on his skin. He didn't abuse her for her attack. But she'd eaten filleted meat and fowl ever since.

She tried to remember her real husband, her real family. But she could only picture the face of Schedoni Udolpho, and recall the names of the children he repeatedly told her they'd had together: Montoni, Ambrosio, Flaminea...

She tried to stand, but couldn't. Her head was heavy as a cannonball, and her neck had long since withered away. She could draw her knees up and crouch but her head stayed anchored to the floor.

She dragged herself, pulling with her hands and pushing with her feet, across the floor of the room, the carpet bunching up under her. One day, Mathilda would get out. And then they'd all be sorry.

XI

Zschokke stopped and grunted, tapping d'Amato on the chest. The water merchant staggered back as if he'd been dealt a weighty blow.

The huge steward pushed open a door. It creaked, of course. Zschokke shoved d'Amato through it. Then, he lifted up his candle, and proceeded down the corridor.

Kloszowski didn't know where they were within the house. They had been led a long way away from the great hall, through passages and up staircases. They could be either deep in the depths of Udolpho, or high up in one of the towers.

They had passed through a derelict part of the building, and he had imagined that Zschokke was a little afraid, casting too many careful looks about him, flinching away from the holes in the walls and the screened-off rooms. Kloszowski hated to think what might put a fright into the giant brute.

These were the guest apartments.

Antonia was trying to smile, and talking to the steward, asking him questions about the family, and about the house. Zschokke interjected a few groans into his grunts.

'This reminds me very much,' the dancer was saying, 'of the daemon-blighted inn of von Diehl's *The Fate of Fair Florence; or: Tortured and Abandoned.'*

They came to another door, and Zschokke pushed it open. There was a fire burning in a grate in the room beyond, which was decorated in the Cathayan style, with silks and low tables and pieces of porcelain. The steward pointed a finger at Antonia.

'For me?' she said. 'Thank you. It looks lovely. Very homey.'

Kloszowski was in the room next door, a tiny cell with a bare cot, a single candle, and a thin blanket. This was what they thought fitting for a cleric, obviously. Next time he was forced to take a disguise, he'd pick something likely to win him better accommodation. Zschokke slammed the door behind him, and he was alone.

There was a thin window, and the rain steadily spattered against it. Kloszowski peered through, but couldn't see anything beyond the trickles of water.

He stripped off his habit, and got out of the novice's boots. His feet were still filthy from the forest mud. The rest of his clothes were ragged and grimy from his spell in the dungeons of Zeluco. He undressed, tearing his britches to pieces, and unpicking the rags of his shirt from his chest and arms.

There was a basin of water by his bedside. He remembered d'Amato's Yellow Ague, but assumed that up here in the mountains they wouldn't be buying from a bloodsucker like him. Obviously, they had enough rain to fill their own butts. He washed himself thoroughly, and felt better than he'd done in months.

Oddly, there was a full-length mirror in the room, the one non-ascetic touch of the furnishing.

He stood naked before it, and held up the candle.

The dungeon hadn't been good for him. There were bruises on his wrists, ankles, back and chest, and he had scabbed-over wounds on his knees and hips. He could see his bones too clearly through his skin, and his face was more haggard than romantically gaunt.

Still, that particular ordeal was over.

Then, his image in the mirror shook, and distorted, as if a ripple were travelling across a still pond. The frame lurched forwards, and the mirror swung open like a door.

Kloszowski tried to cover himself with a towel. His heart beat too fast. Something came out of the dark space behind the mirror, and seized him by the neck, pulling his head down.

XII

There was nothing for it but to do the deed herself. Vathek was too spineless for the business. And, in any case, she would never have trusted him to carry it through.

In the months since she had first seduced the lawyer, Christabel Udolpho had learned many things. She knew now that there was not one will, but many different, mutually irreconcilable wills. Old Melmoth Udolpho changed his mind daily, and insisted on newly-drafted testaments. Some he would sign, some he would abandon.

She dressed carefully, in tight riding britches and a loose blouse, then pulled on her soft leather boots and spent some time braiding her hair. Vathek watched her, chattering about nothing, going over and over the plan. He was confused about the details, but she had them down cold.

The lawyer touched her neck, and let his thin fingers creep into her hair. She felt a thrill of disgust, but suppressed it and gave him a winsome smile in the mirror.

Vathek was a vile creature, hirsute all over his body, and given to sweating. There was some animal in his soul, she was sure. A pig, or a bear. But he wasn't strong, not in his limbs or in his mind. He was easy to lead.

Christabel touched the furred back of Vathek's hand, and rubbed her cheek against his arm.

Soon, it would all be over. Soon, all the fortune of Udolpho would be hers. Then, she could take lovers for herself, gratify her own wants. Aleksandr, the cleric of Morr, had seemed interesting in a reedy, sly sort of way. And she'd heard the maids talking about the giant, Odo Zschokke, and how his manly parts were in proportion to the rest of him. A tiny flare of desire raised her hackles.

Her hair crackled with electricity, and expanded a little, giving Vathek a slight shock. He withdrew his hand, and tried to laugh.

'Be sure to finish him,' he said. 'You must be sure.'

Christabel smiled as she pulled the falconer's gloves on. They were fine leather, and felt good on her hands. She had strong hands, from hours of practice with harpsichord and duelling sword.

After the fortune was disposed of, and the Black Cygnet's treasure found, she would have to turn her attention to Lawyer Vathek. Perhaps an accident might be arranged. A fall from the south wall. An encounter with wolves.

She stood up. She was taller than the lawyer, and he had to look up to meet her eyes. His smile was shaking. He was afraid, of what they were about to do, afraid of her...

She patted his shoulders.

She had dictated the final will, naming herself sole heir to the house and fortunes of the family. Old Melmoth, the blind fool, had signed it, imagining himself to be dealing with a minor business matter. All the other wills were bundled up in scrolls in Vathek's office, waiting to be burned.

Melmoth could not live much longer. Not without Dr Valdemar's infusions to keep him going.

Christabel opened a drawer, and pulled out a ball of copper wire. It was supposed to be for the harpsichord. She unravelled a length and held it up before Vathek's face. His eyes wavered.

She bit through the wire, and held up a loop of about four feet, the ends tied around her thick-gloved hands.

She pulled the loop tight, and it straightened with a musical twang. It would do the job.

'I'll be back,' she told Vathek, and stepped out into the dark hallway, moving silently through the gloom towards the doctor's rooms.

Very soon, she would be very rich.

And then they'd all tremble.

XIII

At least, the last surprise had been relatively pleasant.

'I knew there'd be a secret door, somewhere...'

They were cramped on his cot, but after weeks in a dungeon, Kloszowski was not about to complain. Antonia was soft, and expert. Being a dancer gave her a lot of control. She wore bells on her anklets, and they had tinkled amusingly as her legs wrapped around him, ankles crossed tight against the small of his back. His neck was cricked as his head was propped against the headboard, but the enjoyable warmth of Antonia's body, pressed close to his own, made up for that.

'I searched my room, and found some levers by the fire. I didn't want to be alone in this place.'

Kloszowski wondered if Antonia would be a convert to the cause. She evidently had an attachment to that bloated bourgeois exploiter d'Amato, but it could hardly be very strong. After all, she'd sought out his company.

'You're not really a cleric, are you?'

He admitted it. She snuggled closer, settling her head on his chest.

'I knew it. No one is what they say they are.'

'Are you really a dancer?'

'And an actress. Not now, I admit. But I was. The city fathers closed down the Miragliano playhouse, and I had to find something to do. And there was Ysidro, lolling about in the street with his purse clinking...'

'What about d'Amato? Is he what he says he is?'

She pouted. 'He's running away from the city fathers. The Yellow Ague is his fault. He poisoned everyone.'

He had been right about the water merchant.

'Coins are all he cares about, Aleksandr. Coins, and the things they can buy. Things like houses and horses and clothes and statues. Things like me.'

She rubbed a warm knee up his leg, exciting him again.

'Don't worry,' she said. 'This is compliments of the management. Selling it never got me anywhere but into trouble. Even dancing is better than that. Ysidro took me to a municipal ball once, before everyone started foaming yellow and dying, and all the city fathers' wives ignored me. There was this one woman, Donna Elena, who was a real cow, and made jokes behind her fan that set all her henfriends off on that horrible pretend laughing. I wanted to kill them all, scratch their eyes out. Donna Elena's husband, Don Lucio, was a commissioner of public works. Ysidro wanted him to grant him a city contract, to provide water for the watch stations. After the ball, Ysidro told me to go to a waterfront inn with Don Lucio and let him do what he wanted.'

'Did you enjoy it?'

'Not it, itself. There wasn't much to Don Lucio, if you get my meaning. But I kept thinking of Donna Elena, and her fan and her laugh. She'd sold it too, but for life. I was only stuck with

Don Lucio for the night. She had him forever, and good luck to her too, the slag...'

'There's injustice in the world, my love.'

'Too bloody true,' she said, rolling on top of him, flicking his neck with her tongue. 'But forget that for now...'

He did.

XIV

Genevieve couldn't sleep. She only really felt alive at night.

In her nightgown, she paced her room, listening to the noises of the night. There were creatures in the storm, calling to her.

Her room was modest. She had no mirrors.

Above her mantel was a portrait of Flamineo, her father. He had looked much like Flaminea, his twin, but had been wild where she was puritanical.

A flash of lightning lit up her father's face, making his eyes glow blue. He was painted standing on the mountainside, with the silhouette of Udolpho in the background, and tall trees all around. Sometimes, people imagined they saw things moving in the trees in the picture, bright-eyed and sharp-clawed things.

Her father had been a huntsman, an associate of that famous devotee of the chase, Graf Rudiger von Unheimlich. He had died of a fall during a hog course. He had been obsessed with dangerous game, and had even been known to set out after creatures with near-human intelligence – werewolves, goblins, elementals. No wonder he was dead.

Genevieve couldn't remember him. He had the Udolpho face, but so did everyone else she knew.

There was more lightning. She looked at the portrait, and it was a landscape. The trees were there, and the hillside and the silhouette. But her father was missing.

It had happened before.

XV

Her strangling wire before her, she crept down the passage.

Vathek had told her these were the corridors haunted by the Bleeding Baron, a houseguest of Smarra Udolpho who had been stabbed by his sons but refused to die.

She kept to the shadows, trying to stay silent.

Christabel thought of what she'd do with the fortune when it came to her. First, she would expel her relatives from Udolpho and cut them loose in the world. They wouldn't last a month apiece. Then, she'd dismantle the house, stone by stone, until she had the Black Cygnet's treasure. Then, the wealthiest woman in the Known World, she would return to the great cities – of the Empire, of Bretonnia, of Kislev – and make all men her slaves. Countries were hers for the taking.

She heard something, and pressed herself into an alcove, blending with the dark. Something heavy was coming down the passage.

She held her breath, and waited. Heavy footsteps sounded out, and there was a metallic creaking. Blue light filtered through from somewhere.

Christabel tried to shrink into a ball, her killing loop ready just in case. A man-shaped thing rounded the corner. It was taller than Zschokke by a full three feet, and had to bend its head to fit into the high-ceilinged passage. The apparition was clad in a full set of antique armour. It was burnished iron, with fiery designs inlaid, and moved like an animated statue. It had a species of clanky grace that was almost bewitching.

Christabel stood up, and was ignored as the thing walked past. Vathek had not told her about any mailed monster. This was a new addition to the Histories of Udolpho.

The armoured giant moved slowly, but with purpose. Its visor was down, but there was a blue glow behind the slits.

Not knowing why, she stepped out into the thing's path, and looked up at it. There was an unfamiliar crest on its helmet.

The giant halted, and stood over her, its arms outstretched.

She was impressed with its sheer presence, its size, its power. If she stretched her arms out to their limits, she could barely touch both the thing's shoulders. She touched her fingertips the iron chest. It was smooth, and slightly warm, metallic but living. She let her palm linger on the sculpted muscles.

The giant made Lawyer Vathek seem truly pathetic.

It embraced her. She felt a flush of pleasurable fear, as she was lifted by the giant. It could crush her with no effort. She slipped her arms around its neck, and hung in its grip. Sensing a male presence beyond the visor, she felt drawn into the blue light.

After a moment, he set her down gently, and pushed past her, continuing on his way. She watched his armoured back as he turned the next corner. Her heart, she realized, had nearly stopped. She felt faint, but overcame her weakness. Her body was still vibrating with the pleasure of the giant's touch.

She could not yield to womanish feelings. Less carefully than before, she strode through the passages towards the doctor's apartments. She wanted this over with.

Dr Valdemar sometimes worked late in his laboratory, distilling the infusions which had been keeping Old Melmoth alive all these years. He would always be found surrounded by bubbling retorts and smoking crucibles. When she had done her business with him, she would set a fire and no one would suspect anything. The elements and chemicals he was fooling with were dangerous. There had been more than one unfortunate explosion in his rooms.

The doctor's door was open. She held her loop ready, and slipped in. There was a fireplace, its blaze shrunken to embers, its orange glow cast through the room. A chair was outlined before the fireplace, and Dr Valdemar's bald head shone above its back. He was staring into the hot coals.

On the points of her toes, she crossed the floor, and, with a swift movement, fixed the loop around Dr Valdemar's head. She pulled tight, and felt the wire through her gloves as the struggled to choke the life out of the doctor.

He didn't resist.

Immediately, she realized why. Dr Valdemar was tied to his chair, and shoved close to the fire. His legs had been pushed into the grate when the coals were burning high. Now, his boots and britches were partly burned away, and his feet were stubby cinders at the end of blackened legs.

The doctor's head rolled in her strangling grip, and she saw that his mouth had been stuffed with pages of parchment. In his forehead three metal pimples were shining. They were nailheads.

Damn, she thought, the twins have been here first!

XVI

'Did you hear that?'

'What?'

Someone was singing. A mournful lament, wordless and haunting. Kloszowski would never forget it.

'That.'

'Ignore it,' he told her. 'It'll be more trouble.'

The melody was far away, but getting louder.

'But...'

He kissed her, and pressed her head against the pillow.

'Listen, Antonia. Here's my plan. We stay here, and pass the night pleasantly. Tomorrow when the storm is over, we get up early, steal some clothes and get away without looking back.'

She nodded her agreement as he slipped his hand down to her cleft, and teased. She bit her underlip and shut her eyes, responding to his touch.

The singing was almost that of a choir.

Kloszowski kissed her shoulder, and tried to forget the song. It was no use.

Antonia sat up.

'We can't do it.'

This wasn't going to work.

'We have to find out.'

'I think that'll be a very bad idea.'

She was out of the bed, and pulling on the nightgown she had been wearing. Kloszowski was cooling off.

He got up, and wrapped the novice's robe around him. He looked around for a weapon. He could probably smash someone's skull with the basin, but it was hardly convenient.

He tried to open the door. It was bolted, from the outside.

'We're locked in,' he said, fairly relieved.

Antonia pulled the mirror open. 'No we're not. There are tunnels and stairways. I saw them on the way here.'

She picked up the candle and stepped into the passage. Suddenly, it was dark in the cell. He heard her ankle bells tinkling tinily.

'Come on.'

He blundered his way into the boots, and followed.

XVII

Genevieve heard a rap at her door, and the scurry of small feet. It was the twins playing knock-and-run-away again, she knew. She didn't open the door. It would only encourage them.

She sat in the dark and listened. The Wailing Abbess was going again, guiltily confessing over and over again to the stifling of her baby boy, the result of her indiscretion with a dwarfish wizard. The whole family was supposed to be buried behind one of the walls in the east wing somewhere.

Her father wasn't back in his portrait yet.

There was a creak. Her door was bending a little, as if something heavy were propped against it. Knowing she'd regret it, she walked over, unlocked the door, and pulled it open. Her visitor fell to his knees, then pitched chest forward onto the carpet at his feet. She recognized Lawyer Vathek from his clothes.

But where was his head?

XVIII

Aleksandr was keeping up with her but wasn't happy about it.

There must be an entire system of these tunnels, like the dwarf labyrinths under many of the cities of the Empire. They kept having to push through dust-heavy curtains of cobweb, and crunching old bones underfoot. She could hear rats scuttling in the dark.

They still couldn't tell where the song was coming from.

'It's odd,' she said, scything away a cobweb with her arm. 'Lots of webs, but no spiders.'

Aleksandr huffed. 'I don't like spiders.'

'Who does?'

'Christabel Udolpho?'

Antonia laughed. 'Maybe.'

She rubbed the cobweb between her fingers and thumb. It came apart.

'This isn't like webs, you know. It's like the cotton stuff they use in the theatre. I remember in the company of *Cobweb Castle*;

or: The Disembowelment of Didrick that it got everywhere. People were choking on it.'

'So this is a melodrama, then?'

'Well, have you ever seen a dinner guest explode before? Or a hulking butler with more scars than pimples? Or found a place like this on a dark and stormy night?'

'You have a point. A small one, perhaps, but a point.'

They came to a dead end. They turned and retraced their steps, and came to another.

'That wall wasn't here. Look, our footsteps come out of it...'

She lowered the candle. It was true.

The singing had stopped. There was a steady grinding sound now, much nearer.

'Antonia,' Aleksandr said, 'hold up your candle.'

She did. The ceiling was slowly descending.

'Merciful Shallya,' Aleksandr said.

XIX

Ysidro d'Amato knew he wouldn't be able to sleep until he'd counted it all out again, just one more time.

He had his valise open, and was fingering the bags of coins. He opened each in turn, loosening the drawstring, and sorted through the different denominations. He always had as much as he could in coinage, and kept it in his own hiding places rather than the banking houses of Miragliano. That had proved to be a wise course.

He cursed the marsh-trader who had offered him such an irresistibly low price for two barge-tankers of supposed rainwater. When the watchmen, and anyone whose business took them to a watch station, started dropping dead, sickly foam leaking from every orifice, d'Amato had instinctively known it was time to leave the city, and move into his Bretonnian household.

His coins clinked as he passed them from hand to hand. He would leave Antonia Marsillach along the way somewhere, he'd decided. Given the choice between hard, cold coin and soft, warm skin, he would always choose the former.

This was a strange house. He'd be happy to leave.

He began to replace his coinbags in his valise, carefully slipping them in. Something in the bag moved, and he pulled his hand out quickly, tucking it into his armpit. He had felt a small, warm body. It was the size of a rat, but it hadn't been furred. Rather, its back had been covered with tiny quills that made his skin sting.

Blue eyes peered up from the dark of the bag.

He was unable to make a sound. He watched in horror as the valise tipped over, unbalanced by the shifting weight of the thing inside.

Then, in a black blur, the thing shot out, and, squeaking, disappeared. A moneybag chunked against the floor, and a scrap of parchment drifted out. It was an old bill from his counting house that he'd used to line the bottom of the valise.

He picked up the paper and looked at it. It wasn't covered in the jotted figures he remembered. It was a plan of some sort, but it wasn't complete. The lines were broken up, as if he only had half of the design, the scribe having been interrupted before he could ink in all the faded pencil lines. There were the remains of a seal on the paper, a baby swan's head in black wax.

Behind him, a door opened. He turned. D'Amato clutched his dagger. No one would steal his coins and live.

'Montoni,' the newcomer said. 'Grandfather, it's me.'

It was Pintaldi. He slumped forwards into the room. He held up his arm. Three of his fingers were missing, and the stumps were still pumping blood.

'It was Flaminea and Schedoni,' he gasped. 'They're trying to cut our branch out of the will.'

'The will?'

'Yes. The fortune should be ours, grandfather. I know you have returned to put our case.'

'I'm not...'

Pintaldi threw himself into a chair, and started binding his hand with a scarf.

'I recognized you from the portrait in the gallery, grandfather. You haven't changed that much in sixty years. Still the same Montoni.'

The merchant was confused. He knew he was not this Montoni, and yet, there was something...

'The fortune, you say?'

Pintaldi nodded. 'It's vast, by now, the interest compounded since the time of Smarra's father. Unimaginably vast.'

D'Amato tried to imagine an unimaginably vast fortune. He tried to see it in coins. A pile of moneybags the size and shape of a city, or a mountain.

'And, grandfather, I still have my half of the map. It's tattooed on the backs of my children. With your half, the pirate's treasure shall be ours! And damn these silly stories about the Black Cygnet's curse!'

Treasure! D'Amato's prick hardened. Treasure! He looked at the paper from his valise, casually cast aside, and back at Pintaldi. Alert now, he listened. But he didn't mention the half-map he'd found.

'They're plotting all the time. Flaminea, Ravaglioli, Schedoni, all of them. Plotting to cut us out. Vathek is with us, but Valdemar isn't. I can win Christabel round. She likes a handsome face. But Genevieve is a witch. We'll have to kill her.'

He was beginning to follow. 'A witch, yes. A witch.'

'Ambrosio is the real problem. Your brother. Zschokke knows you were exchanged in infancy, and that he is really Montoni and you Ambrosio. But that can be dealt with. You were Montoni when you ran off, when you fathered my father with that bandit queen, when you slew the wood elf who could have given testimony against us.'

Montoni remembered. He had only been using the name of

d'Amato as a disguise. He had forgotten, but returning home had brought it all back. The fortune was rightfully his. The treasure was rightfully his. Schedoni and Flaminea were usurpers. Not a coin would go to them.

'Pintaldi, my beloved grandson,' he said, embracing the youth. 'Our cause will prevail.'

Pintaldi cringed, binding his hand tighter.

'We must kill Genevieve. And Ambrosio.'

'Yes,' he said. 'Indeed we must.'

'Tonight.'

'Yes, tonight.'

XX

The space was barely two feet high. They were pressed against the floor, and tangled together, their limbs sticking out the wrong way. The ceiling was still coming down.

Kloszowski couldn't take this seriously. It was such a stupid way to die.

'Antonia,' he said, 'I should tell you that I'm a notorious revolutionist, condemned to death throughout the Old World. I'm Prince Kloszowski.'

Her face, near his, smiled feebly.

'I don't care,' she said.

They tried to kiss, but his knee got in the way. Eighteen inches. This was worse than the corpse-cart. The floor was wet. Water was leaking in from somewhere.

He thought of all the things he could have had if he hadn't devoted his life to the cause of the revolution. The approval of the dowager princess, a fine house, quality clothes, a large estate, a pretty wife and wonderful children, accommodating mistresses, an easy life...

'If we ever get out of this,' he said, 'I'd like to ask you to..'

There was an inrush of air, and the ceiling was withdrawn, hurtling upwards. The wall slid into a slot onto the floor, and there was a clear passage ahead.

'Yes...?'

Kloszowski couldn't finish his sentence.

'Yes?' said Antonia, her eyes heavy with happy tears.

'I'd like to ask you to... to..'

The pretty girl's lower lip trembled.

'...to get me a couple of complimentary tickets next time you dance. I'm sure you're a wonderful performer.'

Antonia swallowed her evident disappointment, and smiled with her mouth, shrugging her shoulders. She hugged him.

'Yes,' she said, 'sure. Come on, let's get out of these tunnels before anything more happens.'

XXI

Ravaglioli's stomach felt empty, as if he hadn't eaten for months.

He struggled out of the thick material in which he had been wrapped, and straightened up. Ulric, but his stomach hurt!

He was laid out on a stone table in one of the vaults. He tried to remember what had happened. There had been something in his gruel. He had swallowed something. It was Flaminea, he was sure. She was the poisoner. Pintaldi would have used fire, Christabel her hands.

He staggered across the flagstones, and collapsed against the doorslab. He would have to use all his strength to push it out of the way. Then, he'd find Flaminea and have his revenge.

His wife hated insects, and Ravaglioli knew where he could find a nest of young lashworms. He would take their eggs and force them down her throat, letting them hatch inside her, and eat their way out. That would pay her back.

He pushed against the stone, straining hard. He thought of revenge.

XXII

In the great hall, lying on a hog-length platter, she found Schedoni. He had a skewer in his chest, but he was still alive and bleeding.

The blood excited Genevieve. Something in her stirred.

Lightning struck, and shadows darted across the hall. She saw Zschokke standing by the window, blood on his hands. He had been drinking, and was a stupefied statue. One of the maids was with him. It was Tanja, naked and oiled, on all fours like an animal. She wasn't fully human, staring eyes where her nipples should be, and a tiny, scaled tail poking from her buttocks.

Schedoni was breathing irregularly, his blood spreading in a puddle around him.

Genevieve ran across the room, to the table. Tanja hissed, but Zschokke held her back.

Was Schedoni her grandfather, or her great-grandfather? She couldn't remember.

The old man's shirt was torn open, and the skewer rose and fell with each gasp of his ribcage. Genevieve's mouth was full of blood. Her eyeteeth slid out of sheaths. An ancient instinct took over. She pulled the skewer and threw it away, then fixed her mouth to Schedoni's wound. She sucked, and the old man's blood was pumped into her.

Her mind cleared, and she swallowed.

These people were nothing to her. She was a visitor, like Aleksandr and d'Amato and the girl. They had made her play her part, but it wasn't her. She wasn't Genevieve Udolpho. She was Genevieve Dieudonné. She wasn't sixteen, she was six hundred and sixty-nine. She wasn't even human. She was a vampire.

Genevieve drank, and became stronger.

Rough hands took her by the back of the neck, and pulled her off Schedoni. Her teeth came out of the wound, and blood bubbled free from her mouth.

Zschokke threw her across the room. She landed like a cat, and rolled upright.

The steward roared through his ravaged throat, and Tanja leaped at her.

She made a fist, and punched the animal girl's face. Tanja bounced away, nose pushed in.

It had been a subtle trap, she remembered. She'd been running, and that was part of it. She had wanted to change her life, and that had been her weakness. She could no longer live with Detlef, no longer be domesticated in Altdorf. Travelling to Tilea, she had been caught in a storm, and been forced to take refuge in the House of Udolpho. Then, she had been sucked into their game...

Zschokke had a pike, taken down from the wall. Twenty feet long, it looked manageable in his hands. He prodded at her. Its tip was silver. She stepped back. He was trying for her heart.

Schedoni was sitting up now, wound scabbing over. That was part of the spell. Now she was out of its influence, and she suspected it wouldn't work for her. A thrust of silver and wood through her heart, and she'd be as dead as anyone.

Zschokke came for her.

XXIII

In his bed, Old Melmoth smiled, weak muscles pulling at his much-lined skin. As a boy, he had loved to read melodramas, to see them on the stage. As a young man, he had been the foremost collector of sensational literature in the Old World. Now, on his deathbed, thanks to the magic spells his pirate forefather had brought back from the Spice Islands, he was at the centre of the greatest melodrama the world had ever seen. He pulled the strings, and his puppets schemed, murdered, loved and prowled...

Vathek sat by his bedside with his head in his lap, another draft of the will laid out on the clothes. Dr Valdemar, pulling himself around by his hands, was in the corner, preparing the next infusion.

Outside, it was a dark and stormy night...

XXIV

They came out through a door in the fireplace of the grand hall. There was a fight going on. Genevieve, her eyes red and her teeth sharp, was backing around the long table, and Zschokke, the steward, was after her with a pike.

'Do something,' Antonia suggested.

Kloszowski didn't know. He wasn't sure whether Genevieve stood between him and the fortune of Udolpho or not. Maybe her death would take him one step nearer to the mastery of this pile, to the fulfilment of his destiny.

He stepped into the room.

'I am Montoni,' he announced. 'Come back from the sea to claim my birthright!'

Everyone paused, and looked at him.

He stood tall, determined to show through his bearing that he was indeed the rightful heir. His years of wandering were forgotten. Now, he was home, and prepared to fight for what was his...

'No,' said another voice, '*I* am Montoni, come to claim my birthright.'

It was d'Amato, dressed up as a ridiculous comic bandit, with sashes and a cummerbund, and a sword he could hardly lift.

'Are you crazed?' asked Antonia. 'First you're a revolutionist, now you're the missing heir.'

'It just came to me. I must have had amnesia. But now I remember. I am the true Montoni.'

D'Amato was affronted, and waved his sword. 'You'll never cheat me out of my inheritance, swine. Out of my treasure! It's mine, you understand, mine. All the coins, the mountains of coins. Mine, mine, mine!'

The merchant was a pathetic madman.

D'Amato's sword wobbled in the air. Kloszowski had no weapon.

'Mine, you hear, all mine!'

Antonia handed him a three foot long poker with a forked end. He remembered how d'Amato had abused his beloved. Antonia was a gypsy princess, sold in infancy to the vile Water Wizard, and mistreated daily. Kloszowski held up the poker, and d'Amato's sword clanged against it.

'Fight it, you fools,' Genevieve shouted. 'It's not real. It's Old Melmoth's spell.'

The merchant slashed wildly, and Kloszowski barely avoided taking a cut. He got a double-handed grip on the poker, and brought it down heavily on d'Amato's head, knocking him against a heavy chair.

So much for the usurper!

D'Amato fell in a heap, mumbling.

'It's mine, all mine. I am Montoni, the true Montoni Udolpho..'

Kloszowski drew Antonia to him, a strong arm around her heaving shoulders, and kissed the girl he would make mistress of Udolpho.

'I am Montoni,' he said.

He looked at everyone, waiting to be accepted.

'NO,' roared a familiar voice.

The word hung in the air, echoing like a thunderclap.

'NO.'

Zschokke had spoken. He was no mute after all.

'I can stay silent no longer.'

The steward had the voice of a bull. Kloszowski had heard his voice earlier, before nightfall, before the storm. Zschokke had been the bandit chieftain who had robbed the cleric of Morr. He must have known all along that Kloszowski was in disguise.

'*I* am the true Montoni Udolpho,' he said.

The suits of armour ranged against the far wall came to life, their visors raised.

'And these are my loyal servants.'

They were swarthy banditti, many missing eyes and noses.

'This house and all in it rightfully belongs to me.'

Zschokke thumped his chest for emphasis. The point of the pike appeared between his neck and collarbone, and speared upwards. Zschokke looked at the thing sticking out of him, and opened his throat in a deafening sound of rage.

He was lifted off his feet like a toy, and slid down the pike. Gouts of blood spurted around his face. There was a giant in armour behind Zschokke, hoisting him on his own pike. With the giant had come Christabel, dressed as a bride in a moth-eaten white train and veil. Kloszowski was astonished.

XXV

She finally reached the door, her head pushed first against it, and found it unlocked. For the first time in many years, Mathilda was out of her room. With an effort, cradling her head in her hands, she stood up. There was a window at the end of the corridor, and beyond that she saw the valley.

For an instant, she was her old self – Sophia Gallardi of Luccini – and then she was at the window. Her head broke the glass and the casement, and she fell with the rain towards the slope hundreds of feet below. She felt as if the fall would never end. But it did.

XXVI

Antonia was lost. She no longer knew, nor cared, who everyone was.

Zschokke was twisting like a worm on a fishhook, and the giant was standing like a statue. The armoured banditti clustered around the giant, striking useless blows with maces and swords.

One of the windows blew in, a cloud of glass shards spreading through the hall with the wind and rain. It was more spectacular than the finale of Jacques Ville de Travailleur's *Accursed of Khorne; or: Death of a Daemon Lord*.

The table was knocked over, disclosing Father Ambrosio, his habits askew, entangled with two of the serving maids and a squealing piglet.

He appeared to be having some form of seizure, doubtless brought about by overexertion. He was trying to dislodge something unseen from around his neck. Antonia believed she saw the red imprint of invisible fingers in the white flab of his neck.

She took Kloszowski's arm, and held him close.

Genevieve, her chin bloody, took Kloszowski's other arm. She seemed to be the only other person in Udolpho who was awake.

'We've got to get out of here,' the vampire said.

'Yes,' Antonia said.

'Now.'

'Yes.'

Kloszowski didn't struggle.

The giant slowly threw his pike like a javelin. With Zschokke still spitted on it, it travelled the length of the gallery and its point sank into the wall about fifteen feet from the floor. The pike sagged, but the servant bandit was pinned fast, blood dribbling from his back.

Antonia wondered about d'Amato. She left Kloszowski to Genevieve, and bent over her former protector.

The double doors flew open, and Pintaldi burst into the great hall, bearing a blazing torch in either hand, shouting, 'Fire, fire!'

'Ysidro,' she said. 'Ysidro, wake up.'

'It's all mine, do you hear? I am Montoni! Montoni!'

'Ysidro?'

He pushed her away, and she stumbled against Flaminea.

'Harlot,' she said, scratching.

The giant was moving fast now, wringing the necks of the bandits one by one, and tossing them in a pile. Christabel was playing the harpsichord in ecstasy, her train flowing in the wind.

'Come on, girl,' said Genevieve, who was tugging at a blank-eyed Kloszowski.

Antonia allowed herself to be led out of the hall.

'Mine, mine...'

'Fire, fire!'

XXVI

Christabel couldn't remember who she really was. It didn't matter. Since she had come to Udolpho, she had been home.

Her new lover had killed Zschokke. Now, he would ravage the rest of her enemies. The last of the steward's bandit crew was down, dead inside his crushed armour.

She slammed the harpsichord lid shut, and held out her arms, feeling the cold caress of the wind on her body.

Ravaglioli was crawling out of the vaults into the hall. She nodded, and the giant stepped on her father's back.

Tanja, the lizard-maid, flicked out a long, forked tongue and caught a fly.

'Merciful Shallya,' said Flaminea as the strangling cord went around her neck. Christabel pulled tight.

'Fire, fire...'

Pintaldi tossed a torch into the air, and it came down in burning pieces.

Christabel's train caught light, and the flames licked up around her in an instant, spreading to Flaminea.

'Harlot,' her mother croaked, spitting.

Christabel kept the noose tight, even as the fire grew around them. Pintaldi was right. The flames were cold, and cutting. Pintaldi was on fire himself, spreading his flames everywhere, embracing everyone.

They were all there. Schedoni, Ravaglioli, Vathek, Ambrosio, Dr Valdemar, Flaminea, Zschokke, Pintaldi, Montoni, the maids. The fires spread throughout the great hall. Another wing would be ravaged before the storm extinguished it all. The giant stood unmoved by the blaze. There were others with him. Flamineo, the Phantom Huntsman. The Blue Face of Udolpho. The Strangling Steward. The Wailing Abbess. The Spectre Bride. The Bleeding Baronet. And many, many more.

Christabel felt her face melting...

...and knew it would not be forever.

XXVIII

The rain was dying out, and it was nearly dawn.

Kloszowski lay on the ground while Genevieve and Antonia watched the House of Udolpho burn.

'Will it be forever?'

'No,' Genevieve said. 'It'll remake itself. It's a strange spell. Something Old Melmoth whipped up.'

'Was anyone part of the original family?'

'I don't know. I think maybe Schedoni. And Dr Valdemar is a real doctor.'

Kloszowski sat up, and the women turned to him.

'M-Montoni?' Antonia asked.

He shook his head.

'He thought he was a revolutionist,' Antonia explained to the vampire.

'I am a revolutionist,' he protested.

'It'll pass.'

'But I am.'

Another tower toppled into the ruin, gold gleaming for an instant in the first light before a belch of black smoke obscured it. As one section of the house crumbled, another grew like an accelerated plant, walls piling up, windows glassing over, roof-beams stretching creakily across the spine. The House of Udolpho was unbeatable.

'We can't stay here,' Genevieve said. 'We've got to skirt round the estate, keeping well clear of it. The spell is far reaching, and persistent. Then maybe we can make our way to Bretonnia.'

'Will they go on?'

Genevieve looked at him. 'I think so, Aleksandr. Until Old Melmoth finally dies. Then maybe they'll all wake up.'

'Fools.'

'We all believe in fairy tales,' the vampire said.

XXIX

Alone in his room, Old Melmoth enjoyed the climax of tonight's plot. Fire was always satisfying, always purgative.

The armoured giant was good. He had been an excellent addition. One had escaped. But one was new. A fair exchange. The cast was the same size it had been at nightfall.

Broken Mathilda was back in her room, more altered than ever.

There was just drizzle outside now, and the first blotches of dawn in the sky.

Christabel was screaming as she burned, her wedding dress crumpling and crinkling, melting against her skin. And Tanja was hissing venom in Ambrosio's face, repaying him for his attentions.

Schedoni was cooked where he lay on his platter. Perhaps he could be eaten cold for breakfast. It would not be the first time human meat was served at the table of Udolpho.

He relaxed, and waited for sleep.

It would be interesting to see what happened with Montoni's map fragment. The Black Cygnet's curse had claimed many treasure hunters down through the years. Perhaps Flamineo should creep from his portrait more often, with his hunting dogs, and seek out a new dangerous game.

He had first made his spell in the library, pledging a portion of his soul to the dark powers on the condition that he never be bored again. His early life had been neither tragic nor comic, but merely boring. Now, he was a part of his beloved melodramas, constantly entertained by the dances of his scheming puppets. He drifted, but was brought back by a tiny sound. His door opening.

'Vathek?' he croaked. 'Valdemar?'

Two sets of footsteps, light and surreptitious. His visitors didn't answer him.

He felt the tug of his bedclothes, as they climbed up onto his bed, forcing through his curtains. They were light, but he knew their fingernails and teeth would be sharp, and they would use them skilfully. He heard them giggling together, and felt their first touches. The curtain of his bed collapsed, falling to the floor.

'Melmoth,' he said, with love. 'Flora?'

It had been the final curtain.

Part Three

Unicorn Ivory

I

Tall, straight trees stood all around like the black bars of a cage. If Doremus looked up, he could barely see the blue-white tints of the sky through the foliage canopy of the Drak Wald forest.

Even at midday, it was advisable to travel these paths with a lantern. Advisable, that is, for the traveller. The huntsman had to forgo safety for fear his light would alarm his quarry.

Calmly, Graf Rudiger, his father, laid a hand on his shoulder to get his attention. He squeezed, pinching too hard, betraying his excitement. He jabbed his head towards the north-west.

Not turning too fast, Doremus looked in that direction, and caught the last of what his father had seen.

Points of reflected light. Like short silver daggers scraping bark.

His father tapped two fingers against Doremus's shoulder. Two animals.

The sparks of light were gone, but the beasts were still there. The breeze was from the north, and they would not get the hunters' scents in their nostrils.

His father silently pulled a long shaft from his quiver, and
nocked it in his warbow. The weapon was longer than the reach
of a tall man. Doremus watched Rudiger draw back the bowstring, the cords in his neck and arm standing out as the tension
grew. The graf made a fist around the fletches of his arrow, and
its sharp triangle rested against his knuckles.

Once, on a wager, Graf Rudiger von Unheimlich had stood for
a full day with his bow drawn, and, at sunset, struck the bulls-
eye. The friends against whom he had bet had barely managed
an hour or so apiece with their bows drawn, and they had for-
feited their weapons upon their loss. The trophies hung in the
hunting lodge, elegant and expensive pieces of workmanship,
finely inlaid and perfectly turned. Rudiger wouldn't have used
such trinkets: he put his faith in a length of plain wood he'd
hacked himself from a sapling, and in a craftsman who knew
a bow was a tool for a killer, not an ornament for gentlemen.

The graf stalked towards the quarry, bent over, arrow pointed
at the hard ground. The beasts' spoor was visible now, delicate hoofprints in the mossy, rocky soil of the forest floor. Even
this late in the day, there was still frost. Beyond the length of a
finger into the pebbly leaf-mulch, the earth was iron hard, frozen solid. Soon the snows would come and put an end to Graf
Rudiger's sport.

Making an effort to keep his breathing quiet, Doremus took an
arrow of his own and lined it up in his supple bow, pulling the
string back two-thirds of the way, feeling a knot of shoulder-pain
as he fought the catgut and wood. As everyone kept pointing
out, Doremus von Unheimlich was not his father.

The others fell in behind the pair. Otho Waernicke, under
special orders not to blunder around like a boar and give the
hunters away, was moving carefully, meaty arms tucked around
his belly, checking under every footstep for treacherous twigs
or slippery patches.

Old Count Magnus Schellerup, the last of the soldiers the former Emperor Luitpold had called his Invincibles, was flashing his thin-lipped skull's grin, the scars that made a tangle of one cheek reddening as the hot blood of the chase flushed his face. The only concessions he made to the passing years were the many-layered furs which made a hunchback of him. Magnus might complain about his old bones, but he could keep up with men forty years his junior on a forced march. Balthus, the thick-bearded guide, and his slender night companion, were the rear guard, along to pick up the pieces. The girl clung to her man like a leech. If Doremus thought about her, he had to suppress a shudder of distaste.

He watched his father. These brief moments were what he lived for, as he neared his prey, when the danger was at its height, when there could be no foreknowledge of the equality of the contest. Count Magnus was the same, hanging back only out of deference for the graf, but consumed with a lust for the honourable kill. Doremus had had it explained to him from the cradle, listened to the stories of trophies won and lost, and still it meant nothing to him really.

A muscle in his arm was twitching, and he felt the bowstring biting into his fingers as if it were razor-edged.

'It's no good if you don't bleed,' his father had told him. 'You have to carve a groove in your flesh just as you carve a notch in your bow. Your weapon is a part of you, just as, when the time comes, you are a part of it.'

To fight the pain, Doremus made it worse. He pulled further, drawing the arrowhead to the circle of his thumb and forefinger, its points scratching the flesh-webbing of his hand. The tendons of his shoulder and elbow flared, and he bit his teeth together, hard.

He hoped his father was proud of him. The Graf Rudiger did not look behind him, knowing his son wouldn't dare fail.

Rudiger stepped around a tree, and stood still, straightening up. Doremus advanced to stand at his shoulder.

They saw the quarry.

There had been a subsidence in the last fifty years, bringing down several of the trees. They lay, broken but still alive, branches shot out in odd directions, and the hollow had filled with still rainwater. This part of the forest was full of subsidences, where the old dwarf tunnels had fallen through. The ground was as dangerous as any creature of the wilds. The pool was still, covered with ice as thin as parchment, dappled with red-brown leaves.

At the other side of the pool, where the ice was broken, the quarry stood, heads dipped to drink, horns trailing in the water.

Behind them, someone drew audible breath at the sight. Balthus's bedmate. The girl would be cursed.

As one, the unicorns looked up, eyes alert, horns pointed at the hunting party.

It was a frozen moment. Doremus would remember every detail of that fragment of a second. The unicorn horns, sparkling from the water, shining like new-polished metal. The steam from the beasts' flanks. Clouded amber eyes, bright with intelligence. The shadows of the twisted branches of the fallen trees. The croak of the greentoads at the pool's edge.

The unicorns were stallions, slender and small as young thoroughbreds, white with the characteristic black flecks of their tribe in the matted hair of their beards and underbellies.

Graf Rudiger's arrow was in flight before the girl had finished her noisy inhalation. And it was speared into his kill's eye before Doremus had his aim. Rudiger's unicorn neighed and thrashed as the arrowhead emerged from the back of his head, and reared up.

The shock of death came fast, blood pouring out of its eyes and nostrils.

Doremus's unicorn was turned and away before his arrow was

released and, as he let go the fletches, he had to bring up his left hand to adjust the aim.

The arrow flew wonkily from his hand, and he felt a burning up and down his arm.

'Good shot, Dorrie,' blurted Otho, clapping his agonised shoulder. Doremus winced, and tried not to let his pain show.

The unicorn was almost out of sight before the arrow found him. It slid past his flanks, carving a red runnel in his white hide, and bit deep beneath his ribs.

It should be a heart-shot.

Doremus's unicorn stumbled and fell, but got up again. Blood gouted from his wound.

The animal screamed, emptying his lungs.

'A kill,' Count Magnus said, nodding approval.

Doremus could not believe it. From the moment he had chosen his arrow, he had been sure he would miss. He usually did. In wonder, he looked to his father. The Graf Rudiger's heavy brows were knit, and his face was dark.

'But not a clean kill,' he said.

Doremus's unicorn staggered on, vanishing between trees.

'He won't get far,' Balthus said. 'We can track him.'

Everyone was looking to Rudiger, waiting for his verdict.

Grimly, he stepped over the crest of the subsidence, choosing his footmarks well among the leaf-encrusted floor-vines. His bow was slung on his back again, and he had his dwarf-forged hunting knife out now. The von Unheimlich fortune was one of the greatest in the Empire, but, beside his bow, this knife was the graf's most prized possession.

They all followed the master huntsman, edging around the still pool to the fallen beast.

'A shame it was only a stallion,' Count Magnus said. 'Otherwise, it would have been a fine trophy.'

His father grunted, and Doremus remembered the hunters' lore that he had been made to learn by rote as a child. The unicorn horn his great-grandfather had brought to the von Unheimlich lodge was from a mare. Only unicorn mares made trophies.

Rudiger's unicorn was already beginning to putrify, suppurating brown patches spreading on his hide like the rot on a bruised apple. Unicorn males did not last long after the kill.

'You'll soon have your arrow back, Rudiger,' Count Magnus said. 'That's something.'

Rudiger was on his knees by his kill, prodding with his knife. The animal was truly dead. As they watched, the rot spread, and the stinking hide collapsed in on the crumbling skeleton. The remaining eye shrivelled, and plopped through its socket. Maggots writhed in the remains, as if the carcass were days dead.

'That's amazing,' Otho said, making a face at the smell.

'It's the nature of the beast,' Balthus explained. 'There's some magic in their make-up. Unicorns live well beyond their time, and when death catches up with them, so does decay.'

The pale girl tutted to herself, face blank. It could not be pleasant for her to see such a thing, to know this must eventually be her lot.

Rudiger put his knife away, and scooped up a handful of the unicorn's cooling blood. He held it up to Doremus's face.

'Drink,' he said.

Doremus wanted to back away, but knew he could not.

'You must take something from the kill. Every kill makes you stronger.'

Doremus looked to Count Magnus, who smiled. Despite the bright red mess a wildcat had made of his face, he was a kindly-looking man, who often seemed more willing than his own father to overlook Doremus's supposed weaknesses and failures.

'Go on, my boy,' Magnus said. 'It'll put iron in your bones, fire in your heart. Libertines in Middenheim swear by the potency of unicorn blood. You'll partake of the virility of the stallion. You will sire many fine sons.'

His courage stiffened, Doremus shoved his face into his father's hands and swallowed some of the thick red liquid. It tasted of nothing in particular. A little disappointed, he did not feel a change.

'Make a man of you,' Rudiger said, rubbing his hands clean.

Doremus looked around, wondering if he were seeing more clearly. The guide had said there was some magic in the make-up of the beast. Perhaps the blood did have its properties.

'We must follow the wounded stallion,' Balthus said. 'He mustn't be allowed to reach the mare of the tribe.'

Rudiger said nothing.

Suddenly, Doremus wanted to be sick. His stomach heaved, but he kept it down.

For an instant, he saw his companions as if they wore masks, masks reflecting their true natures. Otho had the jowly face of a pig, Balthus the wet snout of a dog, the girl a polished and pretty skull, Magnus the smooth and handsome face of the young man he had been.

He turned to look at his father, but the vision passed, and he saw the graf as he always did, iron features giving away nothing. Perhaps there had been magic in the blood.

The unicorn was just a sack of bone fragments now, flat against the forest floor, leaking away essence. Otho prodded the corpse with his foot, and opened a gash in the hide, through which belched a bubble of foul air and yellow liquid.

'Euurgh,' Otho said, with an exaggerated grimace. 'Smells like a dwarf wrestler's loinstrap.'

Rudiger took his arrow from the unicorn's head, breaking it through the papery skull. He considered the shaft for a moment, then snapped it in two and dropped the pieces onto the messy carcass.

'What about the horn?' Otho said, making a grab for it. 'Isn't there silver in a unicorn's horn?'

The horn powdered in his grip, the traces of silver glittering amid the white pulpy ash.

'A little, Master Waernicke,' Magnus explained. 'It goes with the magic. Not enough to be worth anything.'

Doremus noticed that the girl was staying well away from the kill. Her kind didn't care for blessed silver. She had a fair face and shape, but he couldn't forget the skull he had seen.

Balthus was on edge, eager to continue.

'If the wounded beast gets to his tribe, the mare will know what we've done. The whole tribe will be warned. That could be dangerous for us.'

Rudiger shrugged. 'Fair enough. We're dangerous for them.'

The graf was not concerned. After a kill, he was always distracted, triumph followed by irritability. Doremus recognized that he was the same way after he had been with a woman. No matter how wonderful it was, it was never up to the anticipation. Rudiger kept his trophies dutifully, but Doremus wondered if they were only reminders of his disappointment. The lodge was full of magnificent horns and heads and pelts and wings, but they might just as well be handfuls of dust for all his father cared for them.

It was the moment of the kill that was all to the graf, the moment when he was the power of life and death. That was his fulfilment.

'You bagged a beast, Dorrie,' Otho blustered. 'Bloody well done. That merits a good few hoists of the ale jar, my friend. You'll have a special place at the table in the League of Karl-Franz from now on. We'll down you a good few toasts before the term's end.'

'Balthus,' said Rudiger, in a dangerously even tone.

The forest guide turned to pay attention to his master. His mistress stood a little behind him, quivering a little.

'In future, have your vampire whore keep quiet or leave her behind. You understand?'

'Yes, excellency,' Balthus said.

'Now,' the graf said, 'day is done. The hunting has been good. We shall return to the lodge.'

'Yes, excellency.'

II

Vampire whore.

Genevieve had been called worse.

But if she were to be serious about not killing Graf Rudiger von Unheimlich, it would have helped if he wasn't such a bastard.

After three days at the von Unheimlich hunting lodge, Genevieve had to admit the graf appeared to incarnate all the vices which Prince Kloszowski claimed were endemic among the aristocracy.

He treated his son like a broken-spirited dog, his mistress like a slow-witted servant and his servants like the frosty leaf-mould they had to spend so much time scraping from the soles of his highly-polished hunting boots. With the fuzzy close-to-the-skull haircut typical of the noblemen of this northern region of the Empire and an assortment of supposedly glamorous scars all over his face and arms – and, presumably, the rest of him – he looked like a weathered granite statue that had once been of a handsome young man and was now due for replacement.

And he murdered for sport.

In her time, she had met many people who richly deserved killing. Since her time encompassed six hundred and sixty-nine years, most of them were dead, of violence, disease or old age. Some were dead by her own hand.

But she was not a murderer for hire. No matter what Mornan Tybalt thought as he sat in the Imperial palace in Altdorf, moving people around like chesspieces, tugging the strings of his many puppets.

Puppet, that was a new entry for her collection of professions. And assassin?

Perhaps she would have been better off staying with poor Detlef? It would have been some years before time overcame him and left her stranded with her eternal youth, carrying another grandfather-aged lover through his final years.

She was still quite fond of him, even.

But she had left Detlef and Altdorf. Journeying to Tilea, she had become caught up in the intrigues of Udolpho, and been extricated only through the intervention of Aleksandr Kloszowski. Then, she had accompanied the revolutionist and his current mistress, Antonia, back to the Empire, travelling with them for the lack of other companions.

She had debated politics with the revolutionist, pitting her cool, cautious experience against his fiery, self-delighted idealism.

That association had been her mistake, the first hook that Tybalt had needed to catch her. She hoped Kloszowski was in Altdorf now, plotting the downfall of the Empire, and, especially, the ruination of the scheming and one-thumbed keeper of the Imperial counting house.

In the cramped quarters she was sharing with Balthus, she stripped out of her hunting clothes – tight leathers over linen – and chose one of the three dresses she was allowed. It was simple, white and coarse. Unlike everyone else in the lodge, she didn't need furs or fire after nightfall. Cold meant nothing to her.

Recently, as the full moons shrank for the last time this year, she was becoming more sensitive. She hadn't had blood for over two months. Kloszowski had let him bleed her one night, when Antonia was distracted, and there had been a young wall guard in Middenheim. Since then, nothing, no one.

Her teeth hurt, and she kept biting her tongue. The taste of her own blood was just a reminder of what she was missing. She must feed, soon.

She looked at Balthus, who was at his devotions before the shrine of Taal by his bed. Her partner-in-crime, Tybalt's puppet had broad shoulders and a thick pelt over his muscled chest and arms. He might be weak in spirit, but he had strength of body. There would be something in his blood, if not the tang of the truly strong then at least enough flavoured substance to quench her red thirst for a while.

No. She was forced to share enough intimacy with the forest guide. She did not want to extend their acquaintance. She had too many blood ties, tugging at her memory.

Blood ties. Detlef, Sing Toy, Kloszowski, Marianne, Sergei Bukharin. And the dead ones, so many dead: Chandagnac, Pepin, Francois Feyder, Triesault, Columbina, Master Po, Bloody Kattarin, Chinghiz, Rosalba, Faragut, Vukotich, Oswald. All wounds, still bleeding.

From the slit window, she could see the slopes descending towards the Marienburg-Middenheim road, the major path through these trackless woods. A rapid little stream, ice-flecked, ran past the lodge, providing it with pure water, carrying the sewage away.

Kloszowski would have made a poem of that stream, coming pristine to the house of the aristocrat, flowing away thick with shit.

With his blood, she had taken some of his opinions. He was right, things must change. But she, of all people, knew they never did.

Balthus didn't speak to her when they were alone, or even much when they were with the others. She was supposed to be his mistress, but he wasn't much for play-acting. By some peculiar turn, that made the imposture a lot more convincing that in would have been if he had always fawned over her and pestered her with public advances.

She was sensitive enough to pick up any suspicions, had there been any. The puppet-assassin had passed the first test.

Graf Rudiger was too arrogant to think himself vulnerable. He travelled with no men-at-arms. If he remembered Genevieve as the mistress of Detlef Sierck, he gave no sign of his recognition. He had been at the first night of Detlef's *Strange History of Dr Zhiekhill and Mr Chaida*, but gave no indication that he had then noticed the vampire.

It had been a week after she had parted from Kloszowski and Antonia. She had been drawn to Middenheim, the City of the White Wolf, needing the distraction of people around her, needing to satisfy her red thirst.

She had found the wall guard and shared herself with him, taking as her due a measure of his blood. He had gone cross-eyed with pleasure as she lapped at the pool of his throat.

Then the watchmen had come for her and taken her, naked under a blanket, to an inn in the better part of the city where she had been sat in a darkened room, tied to a chair.

She broke the ropes after a minute or so of straining, but it was too late. The puppet master arrived, and commenced their interview.

She had seen the olive-skinned Tybalt at the Imperial court, trotting around behind Karl-Franz in his grey robes. She had followed his attempts to impose a levy of two gold crowns annually on all able-bodied citizens of the Empire. Known popularly as the thumb tax, this had led, two years earlier, to a series of riots and uprisings during which Tybalt himself had suffered the loss of a thumb. Despite the injury, he had emerged from the riots with an increased measure of power and influence.

His principle rival for the Emperor's ear had been Mikael Hasselstein, lector of the cult of Sigmar, but Hasselstein had been grievously hurt by some scandal and retired to a contemplative order. He had also been at the first night of *Dr Zhiekhill and Mr Chaida*, grimly protesting. Lipless, humourless, pock-marked and balding, the righteous Tybalt frightened Genevieve more than most servants of the Chaos gods. Coldly devoted to the House of the Second Wilhelm, Tybalt had the makings of a tyrant. And underneath his patriotic fervour and the network of new legislation, Tybalt was at the centre of a web of intrigue and duplicity, his puppets tied to his own standard rather than that of the Emperor, his activities beyond the reach of any legal authority.

Of course, the minister had enemies. Enemies like the Graf Rudiger von Unheimlich.

In that darkened room, Mornan Tybalt, one hand a bandaged paw, had given her a choice. If she refused to do his bidding, then he would bring her to trial, charged with being a confederate of the notorious revolutionist Kloszowski. She would be implicated in a tangle of plots against Karl-Franz and the Empire. Her past association with the well-remembered and ill-regarded von Konigswald family would tell against her, and, as Tybalt reminded her, no one really liked or trusted her deathless kind. She would be lucky to be beheaded with a silver blade and be remembered as the inspiration for Detlef Sierck's *To My Unchanging Lady* sonnets. Tybalt would press for a harsher punishment, silver-shackled life imprisonment in the depths of Mundsen Keep, each endless day identical to the next for as long as the persistent spark remained in her unaging, undead body. But if she became his puppet and carried through his plan, she could go free...

Had she followed her instincts, she would have torn out the Minister's scrawny throat. At least that way she would have earned her punishments. But he had another hook: Detlef. Tybalt promised that if she did not enter his service, he'd use his considerable influence to have the Vargr Breughel Memorial Playhouse closed down, and to prosecute various suits against the playwright. Tybalt insinuated it would be easy to break Detlef who, lately, was not the man he had been. Genevieve carried enough guilt over Detlef, and knew she couldn't be the cause of further hurt to him.

Tybalt did not need to explain the situation between him and the graf. It was well-known. Tybalt was the son of a palace clerk, who had risen through the ranks through his wits and determination, and blackmail, extortion and duplicity. He had about him similar men, colourless toilers without breeding or lineage, quill-scratching achievers who insinuated themselves into the workings of the Empire and became indispensable. Tybalt and his like had never wielded a sword in battle or taken the trouble to acquire the manners expected of the court. They dressed in a uniform drab grey as a protest against the highly-coloured fopperies of those thin-blooded aristocrats they saw as parasitical hangers-on.

Graf Rudiger von Unheimlich was the patron of the League of Karl-Franz, the famous student society of the University of Altdorf, and he was the unelected, unofficial leader of the old guard, the families who had served the Emperor since the times of Sigmar, the battered and hulking truebloods who commanded the Empire's armies, and who brought glory to the name of Karl-Franz with their victories.

The graf rarely deigned to visit any of the great cities of the Empire, but Karl-Franz and his heir Luitpold had many times been his guest at the hunting lodge the von Unheimlich family maintained in the great forest of Talabecland. Karl-Franz trusted Rudiger, and the graf was not the man to keep silent when he saw a plague of grey men with ledgers sapping the strength of the Empire. After the thumb tax riots it had been the alumni of the League of Karl-Franz who had helped restore order, not the ink-stained bureaucrats of the treasury.

While Mornan Tybalt had been in hospital screaming over his lost thumb, and the Empire had been shaking a little as the news of the Altdorf uprisings spread out, it had been the Graf Rudiger who had convened the electoral college and the nineteen barons of the first families at his lodge, and formulated the plans which had forestalled a revolution.

'We shall be the Invincibles again,' he had said, and the Empire had remembered the old days, the days of warrior-statesmen like Count Magnus Schellerup. After bloody months, all had bowed again to the House of the Second Wilhelm.

Later this year, Graf Rudiger and the Emperor would meet again at the ceremony by which Prince Luitpold would attain his manhood. The electors would be there, and the nineteen barons. And Mornan Tybalt was afraid that a quiet conversation between these descendants of the Empire's great families would lead to the downfall of one grey clerk's son.

'The graf must die,' Tybalt had told her, 'and in such a way that there are no questions. An accident, if you can. Simple violence, if you must. Whatever, the finger of guilt must point away, to the winds. Von Unheimlich is a hunter, the foremost in the Empire. And you, Mademoiselle Dieudonné, are a predator. The match should be intriguing, I think.'

Tybalt already had one puppet in place, Balthus. But the guide was just a spy. The minister needed a murderer.

Genevieve suited the requirements.

Balthus finished his oblations and stood up. Genevieve wondered what Tybalt's hook was in his case. There must be something about him that could cause his ruin.

He hadn't mentioned her trespass of this afternoon. If anything, the slip made her seem more like an empty-headed plaything. The graf might have utter contempt for Genevieve now, but he wasn't afraid, or suspicious, of her.

She remembered his conduct in the woods. His treatment of his son, Doremus. His intolerance, impatience.

He had called her a vampire whore.

Her eyeteeth touched her lower lip, and she felt their keenness. There would be red in her eyes.

She remembered Doremus, gulping down the unicorn's blood to make a man of himself. She'd heard of the custom, but never seen it practised. It struck her as barbaric. And, born into an age of barbarism she'd outlived, she had a horror of such things.

'As an afterthought,' Tybalt had said, 'the graf has a son and heir, Doremus. A sensitive youth, I'm told. The hope of the von Unheimlich line. There are no brothers or male cousins to carry the name. It seems unlikely that Doremus could replace his father among the nineteen, but I detest loose ends left to dangle. They have a habit of snagging on something, and the whole design unravels. Once the graf has been eliminated, take care of the son as well. Take good care of the son.'

III

'The Grafin Serafina was a beautiful woman,' Count Magnus said. 'To die so young is a tragedy.'

Doremus had been looking again at the portrait in the dining hall, wondering what lay behind the face of the mother he had never known.

She had been painted in the woods, kneeling by a brook, surrounded by flowers of spring. There was an impossible touch of the elfin in her sharp, delicate features. And the trees above cast shadows upon her face, as if the painter had foreseen the accident that would befall her. Twenty years ago, in these woods, she had been thrown from her horse, and her slim neck had been snapped.

'If you are ever inclined to judge your father harshly, my boy, remember his great loss.'

Magnus laid a hand on his neck, and fondly squeezed, ruffling his hair.

'What was she like, uncle?'

Magnus had been 'uncle' to him ever since he was a child, although he was not a blood kinsman.

The count smiled with the half of his mouth that worked, and his scar blushed.

'Lovelier than the painting. She had gifts. She took away the cruelty of men.'

'Was she... '

Magnus shook his head, cutting off his question. 'Enough, boy. Your father and I have too many old wounds. Past Mondstille, when the year grows old, they ache.'

The servants were setting the fire in the alcove, and a supper had been laid out. A hunt supper. Meats from the day's chase, fruits from the woods.

His father was at the head of the table, emptying his third horn of ale, recounting the day's exploits to his mistress of the moment, Sylvana de Castries, and to Otho, who had been on the hunt but seemed no less interested for that.

The graf had crawled out of the momentary gloom that had come upon him after his kill, and was enthused, explaining every step of the chase, every creak of the bow, every twitch of the quarry.

There was something about Sylvana that put Doremus in mind of his mother's picture although, nearing her twenty-sixth birthday, she was already five years older than Serafina had been at her death. He supposed the resemblance was what attracted his father to the otherwise undistinguished woman, an unmarriageable younger daughter – servants whispered she was barren – of a wealthy merchant of Middenheim. At twenty-six, Sylvana was getting too old for her station. The graf always bedded child-women. Doremus, astonished and appalled, had seen his father look at Balthus's vampire. Rudiger saw only the face of sixteen, not the soul of six hundred.

The graf held an invisible bow out, smile tight as he demonstrated his sure aim.

Otho Waernicke was matching Rudiger drink for drink, and

showing it badly. He was the serving lodge master of the League of Karl-Franz at the University of Altdorf, and hence merited the patronage of the graf, who had once held the position himself.

Otho was a grand-duke of somewhere obscure, elevated from the commonplace not through any martial distinction of his family but because a toadying money-lender of a grandparent had extended unlimited credit to a profligate elector. After this term, Otho would leave the university to pursue his interests – gambling, whoring, drinking, brawling, spending – elsewhere, and it was his duty to choose his successor. It was important to his father that Doremus become the next lodge master, and continue the family tradition. In Altdorf, Doremus was a member of the League of Karl-Franz, but rarely chose to participate in its legendary, orgiastic celebrations, aligning himself with the more studious faction, the 'inkies,' within the university.

Otho laughed too loud at some remark of Rudiger's.

Otho had presided over Doremus's initiation ceremony, when the pledges had been made to pick up a crab-apple with clenched buttocks and run trouserless around the courtyard of the college three times without dropping the fruit, then required to consume five deep horns of heavy beer while reciting backwards the lineage of the House of the Second Wilhelm.

Doremus had not exchanged more than a few sentences with Otho since that memorable occasion and had been surprised to find Waernicke invited to this hunting party. Of course, Otho, the first lodge master of the league not to have come from among the families of the electors or the nineteen barons, had been impressed to be summoned by such an important personage as the Graf Rudiger. He had been annoyingly solicitous and matey towards Doremus ever since they set out from Altdorf for Middenheim, and then to the hunting lodge.

The graf released his invisible arrow, and laughed as he recalled his true aim and clean kill.

Sylvana clapped, arranging her face so as to express amusement without cracking the mask of powder around her eyes and mouth.

Otho was staring directly into Sylvana's valley-like cleavage, and dribbling beery spittle.

Rudiger, of course, must notice his guest's interest in his mistress. Doremus wondered just how hospitable his father was prepared to be to upstart Otho.

Doremus looked away from Sylvana, back to his mother's portrait. The Grafin Serafina had died on another of Rudiger's unicorn hunts. If there was any gossip, it had never been repeated within Doremus's earshot.

Magnus stood in front of the rising fire, toasting his behind, drinking wine from a goblet. Balthus sat at the table, on hand to give expert testimony should the graf need a detail of his stories confirmed or expanded. His vampire was about somewhere, lurking.

Doremus sat down at the table, and carved himself a slice from a haunch of venison.

'Fine meat, my son,' Rudiger shouted. 'The finer for its freshness.'

Actually, Doremus would have preferred it hung for a day or two, but his father was insistent that what he killed this morning should be consumed this evening.

'To fully appreciate the taste of a meat, you have to kill it for yourself,' Rudiger explained, loudly. 'It is the way of the forest, the path of tooth and nail. We are all hunters, all animals. I simply remember better than most.'

Doremus chewed the tender meat, and cut himself some bread. Anulka, the dark servant girl with the distracted eyes, brought him a jug of spiced wine. His legs and back ached from his day in the woods, but he was hungrier than he'd thought.

From somewhere, Otho found a lute, and began to sing bawdy songs. Tired of the noise, Doremus poured himself a goblet of wine, and hoped the liquor would make the racket go away.

'Oh, the bold Bretonnian barber has a great big pole,' Otho sang, 'And the doughnut-maker's daughter a fine-sugared hole...'

IV

'A pity we couldn't have unicorn on our table, graf,' Otho ventured, voice tired from the fine entertainment he had granted the others. Some blasted servant had taken his lute away. He assumed Rudiger would have the fellow roundly flogged and booted for his impertinence, although the graf had unaccountably failed to intervene. He probably didn't want to make a fuss during dinner.

'Unicorn is not a game animal,' the old sportsman said. 'Unicorn is barely an animal at all.'

'Is that a unicorn horn on the wall?' Otho asked, knowing damned well it was, but wanting to keep Graf Rudiger occupied with stories. While he was boring everyone with tales of the hunt, he wasn't looking at Sylvana. And when he wasn't looking at her, the woman was nuzzling his leg under the table with nimble fingers, pinching his thigh, exciting his interest.

Sylvana de Castries had been eyeing up Otho for days, and tonight, if old Rudiger got sozzled enough, things would pass between them that would brighten up this dull holiday jaunt. It was a week since his last harlot, and his balls were bursting.

Otho choked back a laugh as Sylvana's hand strayed into his lap. From here, he could see down the front of her dress, almost to her belly-button. She had a ripe body, lightly freckled the way Otho liked his whores.

After a day of hunting, there was nothing better than an evening of food and drink, and a night of well-upholstered harlot. Among his league brothers, Otho was famous for his appetites in all directions. It was a point of honour in the fraternity that the lodge master be insatiable. Although, looking at weedy Dorrie, that tradition was due to take a nosedive in the new year.

Otho wondered if there were any way he could keep Doremus out of the office, and pass the cap on to one of the real bloods, Baldur von Diehl, Big Bruno Pfeiffer or Dogturd Domremy.

The unicorn trophy was mounted on a shield bearing the von Unheimlich coat of arms. Three feet long, and regularly polished, it was a perfectly tapered spear, threaded through with veins of silver. In the lodge, it was traditional for a little blood from any notable kill to be rubbed into the horn as a tribute, and the trophy's background was overlaid with crusted stains.

Rudiger emptied his horn, and called for it to be refilled. Anulka, the juicy maid-slut with the blue lips of a weirdhead, complied. If Sylvana didn't come through, Anulka was Otho's number two choice. She looked just the sort for a midnight game of hide-the-sausage.

'Yes, Lodge Master Waernicke,' Rudiger replied, 'that is the horn of a unicorn mare. A magnificent beast, hunted down and killed by my grandfather, the Graf Friedrich. As you know, only the female unicorn yields ivory. The stallions we saw today were poor things beside a unicorn mare. They are taller, swifter, beardless, possessed of an almost human intelligence. Among unicorns, things are different than among men. Each tribe consists of a mare and six or eight stallions. Lusty bitches, unicorn mares. Mothers gore their female foals at birth. Only the strongest survive to adulthood, to gather their own tribes. Unicorn mares are the longest-lived of natural animals, surviving several generations of stallions to tup with their grandsons and great-grandsons.'

Otho laughed loud, and elbowed Sylvana. Under the table out of Rudiger's eyeline, he slipped a spit-slicked forefinger into his fist and wiggled it in and out. Sylvana laughed like music, and her breasts shook like jellies.

Otho's mouth went dry with lust, and he had to gulp down a swallow of wine to keep himself from choking.

He had been drinking ale, wine, Estalian sherry and coarse Drak Wald gin. He believed in mixing his drinks, and his stomach had never let him down yet.

'You have hunted a unicorn mare?'

Otho looked around. Genevieve, the vampire girl, had dared to ask the graf a question.

There was a pause. Otho expected the graf to lash out at the intemperate bloodsucker. Instead, he sipped his ale, and shook his head.

'No, but I shall. Tomorrow. And you shall all accompany me.'

In the quiet that fell, Otho could hear the fire crackling.

'A two-edged privilege that,' Magnus said, 'considering the saying.'

Everyone looked at the old northerner.

'And what saying is that?' Otho asked, jollying the party along.

'"Of those who hunt the unicorn mare, one comes home and he alone." It's commonplace in the Drak Wald, and in the north.'

'A superstition,' Rudiger snorted.

'Nevertheless, it is often true. As a child, I was a guest in this lodge when Graf Friedrich set out to bring home his ivory. And I was here when he came up the hill, horn in his hand. Five had set out. Including your father, Rudiger. And only one returned.'

The graf fell quiet. Although Friedrich was often remembered in story and song, little was said about Dorrie's grandfather, Lukaacs.

'Are you afraid, old friend?'

Magnus shook his head. 'No, Rudiger, not afraid. I'm too old for that.'

'"One comes home and he alone," eh?'

Rudiger had explained earlier that he had waited years for the chance to go after a unicorn mare. Traditionally, they could only be stalked between the winter solstice of Mondstille and the new year celebrations of Hexenstag. And, despite the proliferation of stories, they were rare creatures.

'Today, we robbed our mare of two consorts. That will have angered her. Tomorrow, we must hunt her down, or she will come for us. That is all there is to it.'

Otho felt he better show some enthusiasm. 'Fine sport,' he said. 'I'm in.'

He slapped the table, rattling the cutlery, and shoved a hunk of meat into his mouth, washing it down with more ale.

Sylvana sat primly back, her hand withdrawing. 'Tonight,' she had whispered. 'Outside...'

That would be cold, but a league man fears no discomfort.

'It will be an adventure,' Otho said, through a mouthful of food. Then, he belched.

Rudiger looked askance at his guest, but he too was drunk, although with a quieter, more dangerous inebriation.

'Sorry,' Otho said. Rudiger shrugged, and smiled.

'And I,' Magnus said.

Dorrie kept his mouth shut. But there was no way out of it for the little inky, Otho knew. When Graf Rudiger called his unicorn hunt, he had spoken for his son too. The milksop would have to rush about in the open air, keeping up with the graf. If it weren't for his lineage, Doremus would come in for a lot more barracking at the university. He was just the type the league men liked to tar and feather, or tie naked to the statue of the Emperor in the courtyard. Didn't drink, didn't brawl, didn't wench. Nose in a bloody book all the time. The dead woman in the portrait must have put it about as much as Sylvana, because little Dorrie certainly didn't seem to be the type to have an old man like Graf Rudiger. Come to think of it, he had heard stories...

The threads of silver in the mare horn caught the last of the fire, and shone like lines of molten metal.

'The unicorn mare is the most dangerous quarry in the world,' Rudiger said.

'And what's the second?' the vampire asked, boldly.

'Man's mare,' the graf said, smiling. 'Woman.'

V

After midnight. Here she was, again, creeping through dark corridors, night senses alive.

Rudiger would have understood, Genevieve thought. He was a hunter. In him, it was a need as keen as her red thirst.

This afternoon, she had thought Otho Waernicke might be a possibility. He was a fat-head, but certainly strong in his way, impulsive, hot-passioned. But now his blood would be thick with ale and wine, and she had tapped too many drunks in her barmaid days. She didn't need his hangover. Sylvana had been drinking heavily too, and she wasn't sure she should try her anyway. The graf might find out, and take extreme measures. That silver-and-ivory unicorn horn would be a very effective way of ending her vampire life. Doremus was off-limits for the same reason, although the youth appealed to her. He had depths that weren't immediately apparent, and that made him attractive.

The last moons of the year, just past full, shone in through the glassed window at the end of the corridor. The pale light was cool and soothing to her skin, but the thirst burned in her throat and stomach.

Soon, she would be forced to Balthus. The puppet could hardly resist, and everyone already assumed she was bleeding him in his bed. But, for the moment, she could afford to be more fastidious.

The forest guide had taken to laying garlic flowers on his shrine to Taal, to protect him from her. And he had a silver knife under his mattress. She had picked it up with a cloth around her hand, and dropped it into the commode. She didn't want Balthus panicking and hurting her.

She made her way back down to the dining hall. The embers were still glowing in the ashes of the fire, and the servants were clearing up by candlelight, bearing away the crockery to the kitchens, arguing over the leftovers of the venison and fruit.

They all froze as she stepped into the hall, but, recognizing her, shrugged and got back to work. They knew what she was, but also that she was only barely their superior in the von Unheimlich household. Compared to the caprices of Graf Rudiger, she was no threat.

There was a servant girl in her early twenties, dark where the others were corn-blonde, sultry where they were lumpy. At dinner, Genevieve had sensed this girl's interest. Her name was Anulka, and she was from the other end of the Empire, the World's Edge Mountains. In that region, there were Truly Dead vampire lords and ladies, and the peasants competed to please their masters. Anulka had lingered by Genevieve, bringing her wine and food which went untouched, and bestowing smiles and glances.

The girl would do.

Anulka was by the fire, waiting. Genevieve beckoned her, and she curtseyed, crossing the room with a certain smugness of expression, calculated to irk the other maidservants. They turned their backs, and shook their blonde plaits, muttering prayers to Myrmidia under their breaths.

The dark girl took Genevieve by the hand, and led her out of the dining hall into a dressing room. It was sparsely furnished, but there was a cot, with pillows rather than straw.

Anulka sat on the cot, and, smiling, loosened the drawstring of her shirt, lowering her collar away from her swan-white neck. Genevieve's eyeteeth grew longer, sharper, and her mouth gaped open. There was red desire behind her eyes. She felt her finger-nails extend like claws, and brushed her hair away from her face.

She must have blood. Now.

'No, child,' someone said, a hand upon her shoulder. 'Don't cheapen yourself.'

She wheeled around, razor-tipped fingers up to strike, and saw the interloper was Count Magnus. Just in time, she held herself back. It would not do to harm this nobleman, the friend and mentor of Graf Rudiger.

'The slut's looking for a protector, for gold, for a way out of this place.'

Anulka's blouse was in her lap now, and her flesh was pale and cold in the moonlight. There was a trickle of blue juice seeping from her mouth, spotting her breasts.

'She's a weirdroot chewer, Genevieve,' Magnus said. 'You'd be poisoning yourself.'

Anulka smiled as if Magnus weren't there, teeth stained, and caressed herself, inviting Genevieve's sharp mouth to fasten upon her body.

If she hadn't been so consumed with the red thirst, she might have noticed Anulka's addiction. She was far gone into it, weird-dreams floating in her eyeballs. The servant lay back on the cot, and convulsed as if Genevieve had bitten her. She moaned, welcoming a long-gone, or half-imagined lover.

Magnus found a blanket and, not unkindly, put it over Anulka's slow-writhing body.

'She'll sleep it through,' he said. 'I know the addiction'

Genevieve looked at him, asking without words...

'No,' he said, 'not me, my father. His brother was one of the five who didn't come back when Friedrich won his ivory. He thought it should have been him, and tried to bury the guilt with dreams.'

She was weak now, and enervated. She was shaking, her gums split and her stomach empty. She had been close to drinking, but not close enough..

'Dreams,' Magnus said, wistfully.

There was nothing for it. She must find Balthus and take him. He would fight, but she could find a burst of strength to overcome his struggle. Her teeth would meet in his neck.

She turned, and her knees gave way. Magnus, surprisingly fast for someone his age, caught her.

'It's been too long, hasn't it?' he asked. She didn't have to answer.

Magnus laid her down on the flagstones, which were ice-cold through her dress, and propped her up against the wall.

The red thirst was an agony.

The Count was undoing the seven tiny buttons at the end of his jacket sleeve. He rolled the cloth back, and loosened the cuff of his shirt.

'It'll be thin,' he said, 'but we're a fine-blooded family. We can trace our line back to Sigmar himself. Illegitimately, of course. But the blood of the hero is in me.'

He presented his wrist to her, and she saw the blue vein pulsing slightly. His heart was still strong.

'Are you sure?' Genevieve asked.

Magnus was impatient. 'Child, you need it. Now, drink'

She licked her lips.

'Child...'

'I'm six hundred years older than you, count,' she said.

Gently, she took his wrist in her hands, and bent her head to the vein. She licked a patch of skin with her tongue, tasting the copper-and-salt of his sweat, then delicately scratched the skin, sucking up the blood that welled into her mouth.

Anulka moaned in her weirddream, and Genevieve suckled, feeling the warmth and calm seeping throughout her body.

When it was over, her red thirst receded and she was herself again.

'Thank you,' she said, standing up. 'I am in your debt.'

The count still sat, his bare arm extended, blood filling his tiny wounds. He was looking distractedly at the window, at the larger moon. A cloud drifted across the moons.

'Count Magnus?'

Slowly, he turned his head to look up at her. She realized how weak he must be after her meal. Invincible or not, he was an old man.

'I'm sorry,' she said, gratitude gushing. She helped him upright, hugging his great barrel chest as she got him standing. He was heavy-set, big-boned, but she handled him as if he were a frail child. She had taken some – too much? – of his strength.

'Child, take me to the balcony. I want to show you the forests by night. I know you can see better in the dark. It will be my gift to you.'

'You've done enough.'

'No. Rudiger wronged you today. What Rudiger does, I must make amends for. It's part of our bond.'

Genevieve didn't understand, but she knew she must go along with the count.

They passed through the dining hall, which was cleared of servants, and towards the balcony doors. The cloud passed the moons, and light poured in, striking the portrait given pride of place among the von Unheimlich trophies.

Magnus paused, and looked up at the picture of the young woman in the woods. Genevieve felt a shiver of motion run through his body, and he said a name under his breath.

Serafina.

The doors were open, and a night breeze was blowing in, scented by the trees. Genevieve could taste the forests.

The doors should have been fastened.

Genevieve's night senses tingled, and she intuited something. Not a danger, but an excitement. An opportunity.

Count Magnus didn't even know she was there. He was years ago in his memories.

Silently, she manoeuvred him onto the balcony, keeping in the heavy shadow of a pillar.

The balcony ran the length of the lodge, and afforded a view of the slopes beneath. The lodge was built against a sharp incline, and could only be approached from the side paths. The pillars held the lodge up, and the balcony between them was level with the tops of the nearest trees. Beneath, the stream ran.

There was a man at the other end of the balcony, bent over the balustrade, looking downwards, a bottle clasped in one hand.

It was the Graf Rudiger.

For Genevieve, it would be a simple matter. She had to put Count Magnus down, trusting him to fall asleep. Then, she simply had to pick up Rudiger and throw him, head-first, off the balcony. His skull would be crushed, and it would seem like a drunken, regrettable accident.

And Mornan Tybalt would be unopposed in the councils of the Emperor.

But she hesitated.

Replete, she felt benevolent, grateful. Count Magnus was the graf's friend, and her goodwill towards him spilled over onto the von Unheimlich family. She could not, with honour, carry out Tybalt's mission while Magnus's blood was still in her.

Magnus lurched away from her, standing shakily on his own. She was afraid for a moment he would tumble over the balustrade. It was fifty or sixty feet to the jagged rocks of the streambed.

But Magnus was firm on his feet.

Rudiger didn't notice them. He was deep in his own brooding. He took a pull from his bottle, and Genevieve saw he was shaking. She wondered if the graf were human enough to be terrified by the goal he had set himself. He was more likely to come home on a bier with a hole in his chest than in triumph with his ivory in his fist.

And that, too, would let Genevieve off Tybalt's hooks.

Rudiger was looking at something below, out in the woods.

Genevieve heard a woman's laughter. And a man's, deeper and out of breath.

Magnus was almost level with the graf now. Genevieve followed him, worry rising.

Out in the woods, white bodies shone in the moonlight.

Magnus embraced the graf, and Rudiger struggled in his friend's grip, teeth gritted.

Graf Rudiger von Unheimlich was shaking with rage, angry tears on his face, his eyes red-rimmed and furious. With a roar, he crushed his empty bottle in his hand, and the glass shards rained down from the balcony.

Genevieve looked over the balcony.

Down by the stream, Otho Waernicke, a fat naked pig-shape, was covering a woman, snorting and grunting, his belly-rolls and flab-bag buttocks shaking.

Rudiger shouted wordlessly.

The woman, eyes widening in horror, noticed the audience, but Otho was too carried away to be aware of, or care about, anything but his lusts. He rutted with vigour.

Genevieve saw fear in the face of Otho's partner, and she pushed at the bulky youth, trying to get free of him. He was too heavy, too firmly attached.

'Rudiger,' Magnus said. 'Don't...'

The graf pushed his friend aside, and made a fist of his bleeding hand, cold sober fury radiating from him.

The woman was Sylvana de Castries.

VI

Doremus was in the woods, hunting with his father.

'The second most dangerous quarry,' Graf Rudiger had said. 'Man's mare...'

They were running fast, faster than horses, faster than wolves, darting and weaving between the tall trees.

Their quarry was forever just out of sight.

Magnus was by Doremus's side, his scar fresh, face bloody.

Balthus was with them, doglike, snapping at their heels, licking his nose and forehead with a long tongue. And his vampire glided above them on butterfly-bat wings stretched between wrists and ankles, lips pulled back from teeth that took up half her face. Rudiger kept on, dragging them all with him.

They moved so fast they seemed to be standing still, the trees rushing at them with ferocity, the ground ripping out from under their feet.

Doremus had a stitch as sharp as a daggerthrust.

They were closing on the quarry.

They burst from the trees into a clearing, and caught sight of the prey.

Rudiger cast a stone from his slingshot. He caught the quarry low on her legs, and she fell, a jumble of limbs, crashing down against a fallen tree, bones snapping loud inside it.

Moonlight flooded down onto the fallen prey.

Rudiger howled his triumph, steam rising from his open mouth, and Doremus saw the face of the fallen.

He recognized his mother...

...and was awake, shaking and covered in sweat.

'Boy,' Rudiger said. 'Tonight we hunt.'

His father was standing in the doorway of his bedchamber, bending his bow to meet the loop of its string, neck straining taut under his beard.

There was a servant ready with Doremus's hunting clothes. He stepped out of bed, bare feet stung by the cold stone floor.

The shock of the chill wasn't enough to convince him he wasn't still dreaming.

Count Magnus was with his father, and Balthus and Genevieve. Doremus didn't understand.

'The second most dangerous quarry.'

He pulled on his clothes, and struggled into his boots. Gradually, he came awake. Outside, it was still darkest night.

Unicorns were hunted by day. This was something different.

'We hunt for our honour, Doremus. The name of von Unheimlich. Our legacy.'

Dressed, Doremus was pulled down the corridor towards the entrance of the lodge.

The night air was another shock, cold and tree-scented. Magnus had lanterns lit and was tending them. Balthus had the two dogs, Karl and Franz, and was whipping them to a frenzy.

There was a dusting of snow on the ground now, and flakes were still drifting down lazily. Cold, wet spots melted on his face.

'This harlot has dishonoured our house,' Rudiger said. 'Our honour must be restored.'

Sylvana was shivering, standing between two servants who were careful not to touch her, as if she carried the plague. She was dressed in a strange combination of man's and woman's clothes, some expensive, some cheap. A silk blouse was tucked into leather trousers, and a pair of Rudiger's old hunting boots were on her feet. She wore a cowhide waistcoat. Her hair was a tangle over her face.

'And this fool has insulted our hospitality, and shown himself unworthy for his position.'

The fool was Otho Waernicke, dressed similarly to Sylvana, and laughing with an attempted insouciance.

'This is a joke, isn't it? Dorrie, explain to your father...'

Coldly, Sylvana slapped the lodge master of the League of Karl-Franz.

'Idiot,' she said. 'Don't sink further, don't give him the satisfaction..'

Otho laughed again, chins quaking, and Doremus saw he was crying.

'No, I mean, well, it's just...'

Rudiger stared at Otho, impassive and hard.

'But I'm the lodge master,' he said. 'Hail to Karl-Franz, hail to the House of the Second Wilhelm.'

He saluted, his hand shaking.

Rudiger lashed him across the face with a pair of leather gloves.

'Poltroon,' he said. 'If you dare to mention the Emperor again, I shall have you killed here and let the dogs eat your liver. Do you understand?'

Otho nodded vigorously, but kept quiet. Then, he clutched his stomach and his face went greasily grey-green.

He burped, and a dribble of vomit came out of his mouth.

Everyone, including Sylvana, stood back.

Otho fell onto his hands and knees, and his whole body shook like a stuck pig's. He opened his mouth wide and, in a cascade, regurgitated every scrap of the food he had consumed earlier. It was a prodigious puke, worthy of legend. He choked and gagged and spewed until there was nothing but clean liquid to bring up.

'Seven times,' Count Magnus said. 'A record, I suspect.'

Otho heaved painfully, and made it eight.

'Get up, pig,' Rudiger said.

Otho snapped to it, and stood up.

'The wolf has its fangs, the bear its claws, the unicorn its horn,' Rudiger said. 'You too have your weapons. You have your wits.'

Otho looked at Sylvana. The woman was calm, defiant. Without her face paint, she looked older, stronger.

'And you have these.'

Rudiger produced two sharp knives, and handed them to Sylvana and Otho. Sylvana got the balance of hers, and kissed its blade, eyes cold.

Otho didn't know quite how to hold his.

'You must know,' Rudiger told Sylvana, 'that when I hunt you, I love you. It is pure, with no vindictiveness. The wrong you have done me is set aside, washed away. You are the quarry, I the hunter. This is the closest we could ever be, closer by far than we were as man and mistress. It is important you understand this.'

Sylvana nodded, and Doremus knew that she was as mad as his father. This game would be played out to the death.

'Father,' he said, 'we can't...'

Rudiger looked at him, anger and disappointment in his eyes. 'You have your mother's heart, boy,' he said. 'Be a man, be a hunter.'

Doremus remembered his dream, and shuddered. He was still seeing things differently. The unicorn blood was in him.

'If you see dawn,' his father told Sylvana and Tybalt, 'you go free.'

Rudiger took a waxed straw from a servant, and touched it to the flame of one of Magnus's lanterns. It caught, and began to burn slowly.

'You have until the taper is gone. Then we follow.'

Sylvana nodded again, and stepped into the darkness, silently vanishing.

'Graf Rudiger...' Otho choked, wiping his mouth.

'Not much time, hog.'

Otho stared at the burning end of the straw.

'Get you gone, Waernicke,' Count Magnus said.

Making his mind up, the lodge master pulled himself together and jogged away, fat jouncing under his clothes.

'The snow is slowing down,' Magnus said, 'and melting on the ground. A pity. That would have helped you.'

'I don't need snow to follow tracks.'

The taper was nearly half-burned. Rudiger took the dogs from Balthus, gathering their leads in one hand.

'You and your bloodsucking bitch stay here,' he ordered his guide. 'I'll only take Magnus and my son. We should be enough.'

Balthus looked relieved, although Genevieve – who was more alive somehow tonight – was irked to be left behind. For some reason, the vampire had wanted to be in on the hunt. Of course, she must be used to the second most dangerous quarry.

The straw was a spark between Rudiger's thumb and finger. He flicked it away.

'Come on,' he said, 'there's hunting to be had.'

VII

Otho Waernicke felt as if someone had just run him through the gut with a red-hot poker, and dug around a bit in his vitals.

He didn't know where he was in the forest. And he was more frightened than he'd ever been.

Brawling was more his line. Going out into the Altdorf fog with his League mates and tangling with the Hooks or the Fish on the docks, or with the thumb tax rioters along the Street of a Hundred Taverns, or with the blasted revolutionists. That was real fighting, real bravery, real honour. A good brawl, with a good booze up and a good bedding afterwards.

Rudiger was just a maniac out to slaughter him. The Graf von Unheimlich was no better than the Beast, that altered revolutionist who had ripped apart half a dozen whores in Altdorf two years ago. Otho had brawled well the night they had exposed the fiend.

Yefimovich was the sort of creature who should be hunted through the night. He would probably take to it.

His feet hurt in the unfamiliar boots, and he was cold to the bone.

Where was Sylvana? She had got him into this; now it was her duty to save his fat from the furnace.

His fat was weighing him down now. It had never been such a nuisance before. Meat and drink gave a fellow a figure.

Running was all very well, but he kept banging into trees and cutting his face open or ripping his clothes. He had fallen on his ankle a few minutes ago. It was already throbbing, and he was afraid he had broken something.

This was a nightmare.

He couldn't remember how it had happened. He had only been on that harlot Sylvana a moment or two when he was being hauled off, and slapped silly.

Graf Rudiger had hit him.

That was why he had been so sick.

A treebranch, ridiculously low, came out of the dark and smashed his face. He felt blood pouring out of his nose, and just knew his teeth were loose.

He wished he were back in Altdorf, snoring in his bed at the League's lodge house, dreaming of hot women and cold ale.

If he got out of this, he would enter the Order of Sigmar. He would take vows of temperance, celibacy and poverty. He would offer to all the gods. He would donate his money to the poor. He would volunteer for missionary work in the Dark Lands.

If only he were allowed to live...

He ducked under the branch, and stepped forwards.

All the blood he had been spilling and the trees he had been bashing would be a trail the graf could follow. Huntsmen were good at all that rot, tracking their quarry through scratches on bark and bent twigs on the ground.

Merciful Shallya, he wanted to live!

He kept seeing the graf's arrow going through the unicorn's head, the amber eye bursting, arrowpoint prodding out of the mane.

At once, there wasn't any ground under his feet, and Otho fell. His knee struck stone, and then his back, his head, his arse. He rolled down a slope, stabbed by stones and branches. Finally, he came to a halt, face up.

He would just lie and wait for the graf's arrow.

It couldn't be any worse than running in the dark.

Above him he saw the moons, Mannslieb and Morrslieb.

He prayed to Morr, god of death, pleading with him to hold off. He had exams to pass, a life to live.

He remembered the pain in his stomach, and rolled over. There couldn't be anything more inside him to come out, but his belly clenched and he coughed, choking on bile.

This was how he would die.

He ground his face into the icy dirt, and waited for the arrow in his back.

Behind him he would leave three unacknowledged bastards that he knew of, and unpaid bills in a dozen taverns. He didn't know if he had killed any men, but he had thrown stones and knives in brawls and any number of his opponents might have died of the pummellings he had given them. He had served his Emperor, and he had looked forward to a lifetime of defending the House of the Second Wilhelm from his enemies.

A point jabbed him between the shoulderblades, and he knew it was over.

'Kill me,' he said, rolling over to present his belly to the sword. 'Kill me to my face.'

The graf was not standing over him.

Instead, he found himself staring into a pair of huge amber eyes, set either side of a long face. A sparkling horn stuck out from between the animal's eyes and prodded him.

The unicorn mare breathed out, and plumes of frost shot from its nostrils.

Unicorns are horses with horns, but horses have no range of expression.

This unicorn was smiling at him, mocking him. The stallions' eyes had been cloudy, but the mare's were bright, glowing, alarming.

He froze, and felt his bladder giving out, flooding his trousers with warm wetness.

The unicorn whinnied a laugh at him, and took its horn away.

It was taller than the tallest cavalry horse Otho had ever seen, and long-maned, powerfully muscled. Immensely strong, it was also sleekly feminine.

Horrified at himself, Otho couldn't help but respond to it as he would to a woman.

For the first time in his life, Otho Waernicke saw something he considered beautiful.

Then, with a ripple of white in the darkness, it was gone.

Otho could not believe his luck. He sobbed relief, and laughed out loud, choking on the emotions unloosed from him.

Then he heard the other animals coming.

They were growling, barking, tearing across the distance between him and them.

The two dogs exploded out of the night, and sank their teeth into his fat.

Otho screamed.

VIII

Doremus skidded down the slope, arms out to keep his balance, towards the yapping, screeching tangle.

'Karl! Franz!'

He called the dogs, but they didn't hear or didn't care.

Behind him, Rudiger stood on the crest of the ridge, watching the dogs go for Otho.

This had gone far enough. He wasn't going to let the fat idiot get killed. It wasn't as if his father really cared about his mistress. As far as Doremus could judge, he would have thrown Sylvana away soon. It was only natural the woman should cast around for another protector. Admittedly, she had shown poor taste, but Otho was a duke, albeit a thin-blooded parvenu of a duke.

'Karl,' he shouted, and the dog looked up, red on its teeth.

He took Karl's collar and pulled him away. Franz was chewing Otho's knee, tearing through cloth to get to the flesh.

The lodge master was still alive. He didn't even seem to be

hurt that much. He had scratches on his face and neck, but the dogs hadn't a taste for human meat.

Doremus pulled Franz away.

Calmed, the dogs sat and slavered. Doremus patted their heads.

Otho moaned and cried.

For some reason, Doremus remembered Schlichter von Durren-matt, the undersized lad who hadn't passed the initiation into the League of Karl-Franz. Otho and his fellows had mercilessly kicked and pummelled the boy, throwing him naked into the Reik, advising him to swim home to mother. Doremus wished Schlichter, now a novice of Manaan, were here to see Otho Waer-nicke fouled and humiliated.

Doremus threw Otho a kerchief.

'Clean yourself up,' he said.

His father and Magnus were with them now. Rudiger made no attempt to intervene, and watched coldly as the sobbing Otho, his boy's eyes streaming in his fat libertine's face, wiped his wounds, wincing as he touched the cuts.

'This quarry was poor,' Rudiger said. 'Not worth taking a tro-phy from.'

'You should clip his ears, at least,' Magnus said, half-smiling to show he was joking.

Otho, who didn't see the smile, whimpered.

'I should have his balls for what he's done,' Rudiger said, not smiling. 'But a man's a man, and bears little responsibility for the actions of his loins.'

'The mare,' Otho said. 'She was here...'

Rudiger smiled, 'Was she, indeed? A finer quarry than you, jostling for position. But it's no use. The unicorn is tomorrow's animal. Tonight we're after man's mare.'

Magnus was concerned. 'It could be dangerous. Unicorns don't believe in hunters' etiquette.'

Otho was hugging himself, shivering with fear and the cold.

'Master Waernicke,' Rudiger said, 'listen well...'

Otho shut up, and half-sat, looking to the graf.

'Go back to the hunting lodge, and a carriage will take you to Middenheim. Tell the coachman to leave before I return from this hunt.'

Otho nodded, relief dawning on his face. He bent forward, to kiss Rudiger's boot. The graf prodded him in the chest, and snarled disgust.

'My son will be the next lodge master?'

Otho said 'yes' several times, tears flowing freely.

'And he will restore the honour of the League of Karl-Franz.'

Magnus helped Otho stand up. It was clear the quarry had wet his trousers. Even Doremus had no more disgust for the fool.

'Get out of my sight,' Rudiger said.

Otho bowed nervously, and scrambled up the slope, grunting and huffing, foam falling from his mouth.

The last Doremus saw of Otho was his ample behind vanishing over the crest of the ridge.

'He'll find his way back by dawn,' Magnus said. Rudiger shrugged, and plodded on.

'The woman took the left fork back there,' he said. 'She'd have headed for the stream, to break her scent.'

'Father?' Doremus said.

Rudiger and Magnus both turned to him.

'What?' Rudiger asked, glaring dangerously.

'Nothing.'

'Come on then. It'll be dawn in an hour, and the quarry will have flown.'

Doremus felt shamed, but fell in step with the two huntsmen.

Rudiger had been right. The dogs followed Sylvana's trail to the stream, then hesitated. The graf set them loose, knowing they would find their own way back to the lodge.

'It's just us now. A man hunts a woman. That's the way of the world, my son. A man hunts a woman.'

'Until she catches him,' Magnus said, completing the saying.

They followed the stream into the woods. The pre-dawn light was already in the skies, filtering down through the trees as an eerie glowing.

'Plenty of time,' Rudiger said.

'We're near Khorne's Cleft,' Magnus said, making the sign of Sigmar at the mention of the dread power's name.

Khorne's Cleft was a deep subsidence, some three or four hundred feet, cutting through the forest as if a giant axe had struck the hillside. There was a waterfall gushing into the Cleft, and local legend had it that the water ran red whenever a mortal crime was committed by the fall. That, of course, was nonsense, although Doremus had heard the waters did have unusual properties. Natural healing, the woodsmen's wives called it. As a child, he had cut himself badly on the forehead and Magnus had washed his face with waters from Khorne's Cleft, wiping away and closing up the wound as if it had never been.

'Good,' the graf commented. 'She can't get over that.'

They emerged from the trees, and stood on the edge of the Cleft. Doremus heard the water crashing to the thin, deep lake at the bottom, and saw the rush of the fall from the opposite side of the gorge.

'Where is that harlot?' Rudiger swore, nocking an arrow and drawing back his bow.

It was impossible that Sylvana could have climbed down. The Cleft had no bottom, just the lake. Too many woodsmen had left their bones down there.

Doremus looked down, around and, finally, up.

The Cleft was the beyond the length of even an athlete's jump, but the spreading trees above met and mingled, creating one canopy. He couldn't see the woman, but he could see where the branches were moving, weighed down by something heavy.

Doremus said nothing, but his father looked up anyway.

'Cunning minx,' he said, aiming at the moving branches.

Magnus laid a hand on his friend's shoulder.

'Rudiger,' he said. 'No. This ends here. Your honour is restored.'

The graf shook off Magnus, and cold fury burned in his face.

'My honour, Magnus? That has not always been your first concern.'

Magnus stood back as if slapped, and his eyes fell. Rudiger took aim again. Doremus could see Sylvana now. She was almost across, her legs hanging down over the waterfall.

'Rudiger,' Magnus shouted...

Then, things happened, quickly and together. Doremus was whirling around, trying to follow it. Inside his mind, there were explosions of clarity.

His father let loose his arrow, and it flew straight. Nearby, in the woods, there was a crashing as something large loomed. Sylvana didn't scream as the arrow pierced her side, but Doremus heard the tearing of her clothes and flesh as the barb slid into her. Magnus's protest died in his mouth. Hooves struck hard ground, and young trees bent aside. A huge head burst from the trees behind them, amber eyes aflame, hornpoint flashing like lightning. Rudiger had another arrow ready and away. Sylvana shook the branches she was clinging to, and leaves fluttered down like dead birds, swept away by the torrent of the fall. The mare's horn sliced through the distance, and Doremus knew the unicorn would stab his father, spearing him, shoving him from the edge of Khorne's Cleft. Rudiger's second arrow took Sylvana higher up, in the shoulder, and she lost one handgrip. Boughs creaked and cracked. Magnus made a wrestler's grasp for the unicorn's neck, and she turned her horn to slice at him.

The unicorn mare was a vast, awesome creature, silver-white and ancient. Sylvana fell, impossibly slow, towards the waters. The mare's horn caught Magnus below the ribs, and gored him. With a splash, Sylvana hit the lip of the waterfall, and scrabbled

at a rock which divided the rushing waters. The unicorn tossed
its head, and Magnus was lifted off the horn, a rope of blood
bursting from his wound. Rudiger had still another arrow ready.

Magnus hit the ground, spilling over the edge of the Cleft and
Doremus, unfrozen at last, reached for him. Sylvana's hands were
torn from the rock, and she was swept over the fall. The unicorn
bellowed, its sound joining with the woman's scream. Rudiger
turned from his kill, and met eyes with the mare. Doremus had
hold of Magnus, and was hauling him back from the precipice.
Sunlight broke through, and shone off Rudiger's arrowpoint and
the tip of the mare's horn. Magnus was babbling. Rudiger and the
unicorn looked at each other, his arrow pointed to the ground,
her horn to the sky.

'My boy,' Magnus said, through agony. The unicorn withdrew,
without turning, and was gone into the woods.

It was over, for the moment.

'My boy, I must tell you...'

Doremus listened, but Magnus had fainted. His chest still rose
and fell, but his furs were soaked with blood.

'Father,' Doremus said. 'Help me with uncle, help me.'

He looked at the graf, who had relaxed his bow. Doremus's
father was staring across the Cleft.

In the first light of day, the waters of the fall seemed red with
blood.

IX

First, Otho had limped out of the night, dogs at his heels, screaming for a coachman. One was ready, and without a word to Genevieve, the lodge master of the League of Karl-Franz left, his hastily packed bags rattling around the carriage with him.

Then, shortly after dawn, the others came back, Rudiger and Doremus supporting Magnus.

'Keep away from him, leech,' Doremus warned her as she went to help.

Magnus, barely awake, shook his head at him.

The count broke away from his companions, and Genevieve took his weight in her arms. It was nothing to her.

She laid him down on cushions in the dining hall, and tore his clothes away from his wound.

'It's deep,' she said, 'but clean. And nothing has been broken or punctured. He's been lucky.'

She had picked up a deal of doctoring in her years, among many other skills. Balthus tore up a tablecloth for bandages.

Magnus, drifting in and out of consciousness, winced as she wrapped him up tight. A little blood seeped through his bandage.

'The wound should knit,' she told the others.

Doremus was concerned for the Invincible, but Rudiger hung back, not interested in the count's survival.

'We should go out soon,' the graf said. 'The mare is still around.'

Genevieve couldn't understand the man she was supposed to kill. His best friend was sorely hurt, and he thought only of chasing a unicorn.

'He'll be avenged,' he explained, answering her unasked question.

'He's not dead; he doesn't need vengeance.'

Magnus was quiet, compliant.

'Balthus,' Rudiger ordered. 'Be ready to leave within half an hour. Today, we'll bring back the ivory.'

Balthus saluted, and went off to get his hunting gear.

A door opened, and Anulka wandered in, eyes vacant, bodice badly laced, hair in rat-tails.

'You,' Rudiger said. 'Look after Count Magnus.'

The servant obviously didn't understand. Her lips and chin were blue with weirdjuice.

'Vampire,' Rudiger said. 'You come with us.'

At that moment, Genevieve decided – Tybalt or no – that she would kill the Graf von Unheimlich. She knew there was blood on his hands. He must have killed his mistress. And Sylvana de Castries had not been the first 'hunting accident' in the vicinity of Rudiger's lodge.

Magnus, exhausted, was looking at the portrait of the graf's dead wife.

'Serafina,' he said to himself. He was exhausted, hurt, delirious.

'Anulka,' she said to the maid, using her vampire eyes to penetrate the dreamfog. 'Get some weirdroot. I know you have it. Grind a little into a herbal tea. Give it to the count. You understand?'

The servant nodded, fearful. Weirdjuice, much diluted, could help take away Magnus's pain.

She let Anulka take Magnus, and stood up.

'Get ready,' Rudiger told her. 'Perhaps you'll learn something about hunting by daylight.'

Genevieve bowed and withdrew, trotting down the corridor to her quarters.

Balthus was already dressed in jerkin and furs, and taking his knives and snares down from the shrine of Taal.

'We'll do it today,' she told him. He nodded, his back to her.

'You keep Doremus occupied, and I'll finish the graf. Then we'll be free of Tybalt.'

Genevieve pulled on trousers and a waistcoat. She took one of Balthus's feathered caps, and tucked her hair under it.

'What's his hook, Balthus?' she asked. 'What makes you Tybalt's puppet?'

The guide turned to her. His beard had grown recently, and was creeping up his cheeks towards his eyes. A thatch of ruddy fur swarmed up from his chest and around his neck.

'I might change,' he said. 'Some day.'

'A touch of warpstone, eh? Poor faithful dog-altered. Well, you can find a new master and fetch all the sticks you like after this.'

Balthus didn't look happy about it.

Back in the hall, Rudiger was impatient to leave.

Magnus, already drifting into the dream from Anulka's tea, was trying to say something, trying to talk to Doremus. The graf's son knelt by his 'uncle,' trying to listen, but Rudiger was pulling him away.

'Time for that later,' the graf said. 'We must be on the trail before it cools.'

Genevieve squeezed Magnus's hand, and followed the three men out of the lodge. The dogs were tired, so the hunters would have to do without.

Around the lodge, where the trees were cleared, it was a pretty morning. The sun was heavy on Genevieve's eyes, but in the dark of the woods things would be better.

The graf was striding off. He had told Balthus they were heading for Khorne's Cleft, to pick up the mare's trail there.

Genevieve hesitated, looked back at the lodge, and followed the others. It would be no trouble for her, keeping up.

They travelled a recently beaten path, the way Rudiger and Doremus had brought Magnus. Genevieve smelled blood on the ground. Under some circumstances, she was more sensitive than a good dog. But she did not volunteer to stand in for Karl and Franz.

Rudiger was grimly exultant. He sang under his breath, hunting songs of the Forest of Shadows.

Unaccountably, Genevieve did not just want to kill him. She wanted to break him, humble him and drink his blood. What he had told Doremus yesterday was true: you could take strength from your kills. Genevieve wanted his strength.

Rudiger had changed since he had killed his woman. He wanted Genevieve by his side, and kept tugging at her, keeping her up with him.

She guessed his interest in her, and planned to use it against him. When Balthus led Doremus away, she would take her teeth and claws to him. Once it was over, she could pitch him into Khorne's Cleft, and his body would be gone forever.

They came to the Cleft. This, she understood, was the site of the kill. Genevieve noticed Doremus looking into its depths, hoping for a glimpse of Sylvana.

Rudiger was unaffected, down on his knees, looking for hoofprints. 'Here,' he said, tapping the frosted ground.

Genevieve examined the spoor, noting the distance between prints.

'She must be huge,' she said.

'Yes,' grinned Rudiger. 'An old bitch unicorn, seventeen or eighteen hands, ivory longer than my arm.'

She smelled his arousal.

Rudiger took her slender wrist, and encompassed it with his mighty fist. She could break his back with her slim hand.

'I want her horn,' he said.

He stood up, and followed the mare's hoofmarks into the trees. Doremus followed, reluctantly it seemed. Genevieve thought the way they were taking was familiar.

'She took her time,' Rudiger said, pointing to a chewed branch well out of human reach, 'had some breakfast. She's a cool one, trying to gull us all the time. She'll take a lot of killing.'

The graf strode ahead, following the path the mare had made.

Genevieve looked to Balthus, and the guide turned away. She knew she couldn't count on him, but she hoped she wouldn't have to.

'Look,' Rudiger said, pointing to a flattened area, 'you can see the outline.'

There was a blanket of thin scum on the leafy ground, and the last traces of a skeleton.

'This was your kill of yesterday, son,' Rudiger said. 'Your wounded stallion must have found her, set her off against us. That's war, of course. We must kill the mare, Doremus, before she kills us. This is what it is to be a man.'

She had heard raving lunatics make more sense.

Rudiger went on ahead, came back, and called them on, urging them to run.

She got the feeling Doremus was at the end of his patience with his father. He shouldn't be difficult to distract.

'Come on, come on,' Rudiger said.

Genevieve realized what it was that had been plucking at her mind. 'I know this path,' she said.

'Yes, yes,' Rudiger agreed. 'The track to the lodge. The mare has doubled back, gone on the attack. Very clever, but we aren't fooled.'

She was appalled.

'But the count...'

'An old huntsman's trick, my dear. Leave the wounded as bait. Magnus taught it me when I was a child.'

Rudiger laughed, and Genevieve could have struck him down. Her nails were lengthening, sharpening, and her anger was keen.

But the graf was gone, running ahead, all caution flown, enthused by the chase.

Balthus caught her eyes, and nodded towards a fork in the trail. He could mislead Doremus, and she could end it.

She shook her head.

'We've got to get back to the lodge,' she said. 'Count Magnus is in danger.'

'Uncle...' Doremus said. 'How?'

'The mare has his scent, his blood,' Balthus explained. 'She'll want to finish him.'

'And my father...?'

'Knew?' Genevieve asked. 'Of course he knew. Come on.'

Stirring Doremus out of his doziness, she ran on, following Rudiger, following the mare.

The trees thinned, and they neared the lodge.

From ahead, she heard a howl. A man's howl of grief and fury.

Outpacing Doremus and Balthus, she ran, dodging trees, pushing against the ground. She was fast as a leopard when she had to be.

But she was not fast enough.

The doors of the lodge hung open, and Rudiger stood before them, still shouting his anger.

Genevieve pushed past him, and saw she was too late.

Anulka was crumpled in the entrance, a bloody hole gouting under her chin, twitching in her last dream. Count Magnus

Schellerup lay beyond, beside the overturned and smashed table. He was twisted like an old blanket, and the deep gores in his chest exposed ribs and vitals. The mare must have tossed him on and off her horn like a child playing with a cup and ball toy.

She skidded on the blood, and fell to her knees.

The smell of the blood was in the air around her, and she salivated. The blood of the dead was repulsive to her, tainted food. She had been reduced to drinking it too many times, but it still made her stomach turn. Magnus's blood, in her, cried out.

Doremus was with her now, the wind gone out of him.

'Uncle...'

It was too late.

Behind her, Rudiger was striding back into the woods, determined to have his revenge.

Genevieve took a cushion, and laid it against Magnus's bloody head, covering his scar. She looked at the unblemished half of his face, and at Doremus. Then, she shivered, the world turning around and coming down, with a nauseating lurch, in a new configuration.

She understood. And she understood what she had to do.

Leaving Magnus, pushing past Doremus and Balthus, she followed Rudiger into the forests.

Her foreteeth slid out of their gumsheaths.

X

Doremus wept in his heart, but no tears came.

Uncle Magnus was dead, and there was nothing more to do for him. He looked at the old man's face, his scar covered by the vampire girl's curiously tender gesture. For all his life, Magnus had been there, the old Invincible, warm where his father was cold, understanding where his father was indifferent, encouraging where his father was demanding. The count had not been invincible, in the end. But he had died quickly, of a mortal and honourable wound, not lingered with some disease, leaking uncontrollably from all orifices, mind befuddled, body diminished.

It was not such a bad death, Doremus told himself. Then he looked at the blood, at the ripped wounds, and knew there was no such thing as a good death.

Balthus was waiting, in attendance. There were servants all around now, chattering, tutting. Where had they been when the mare was killing the count? Hiding for the sake of their skins?

Doremus followed his father and the vampire, Balthus jogging along with him.

No matter what he felt about his father, about hunting, about the kill, Doremus swore he would track down this thing that had slaughtered his uncle and end her life.

He would find the mare before Rudiger, and this time he would have a clean kill. Then, he would burn his bow.

The forests swallowed them up.

XI

Following his trail, Genevieve hunted the huntsman.

This had nothing to do with Tybalt.

This hunt was hers.

She imagined the mare's horn gouging against Magnus's ribs, sinking deep into his belly, pulling out his intestines.

And she remembered the cold madness of the Graf Rudiger von Unheimlich.

At this moment, there was no more dangerous beast in the forests than a she-vampire.

Always, she had kept herself apart from the Truly Dead, those vampires who preyed on the living for pleasure. She had listened to them enthuse about their sport and felt superior to the grave-grown things with their foul breath and red eyes, faces set in beast's snarls, clinging to their coffins and catacombs by day, gliding on the winds by night in search of juicy necks, relishing the fear they cast about them like a shroud.

She remembered those she had known: the Tsarina Kattarin,

bloody tyrant who reigned for centuries, exultant with the blood of her subjects flowing over her body; Wietzak of the World's Edge, a mouthful of teeth like razor-edged pebbles, chewing the flesh of a peasant child; even her father-in-darkness, Chandagnac, dandyish as he dabbed the gore from his lips with a lace handkerchief, old and alone behind his handsome face and manners.

For the first time in nearly seven hundred years, Genevieve Dieudonné understood the righteousness of the red thirst.

She regretted those she had spared: Tybalt, Balthus, Anulka, Otho. She should have gutted them, and drunk the blood fresh from their bellies. She should have drunk an ocean from them.

Rudiger was travelling fast, keeping ahead of her.

She knocked young trees out of her way, enjoying the crack of breaking wood. Birds flew from their falling nests, and small animals scurried out of her way.

'Halt,' a voice said, piercing her red rage, and striking her at the heart.

She stood still, and found herself in a small clearing.

Barely half a dozen yards away, the Graf Rudiger stood, warbow raised, arrow ready.

'Silver head, wooden shaft,' he explained. 'In an instant, it would be through your heart.'

Genevieve relaxed, stretching out her arms, opening her empty hands.

'Normally, I'd tell you to throw down your weapons, but I can hardly expect you to pluck out your teeth and nails.'

Her red rage flared, and she saw Rudiger's face coloured by a bloody film. She fought to control herself, to let the killing thirst die.

'That's right,' Rudiger said. 'Get a leash on your temper.'

He gestured with his arrowhead, and Genevieve sank to a crouch. She crossed her legs under her, hands tucked under her bottom.

'That's better.'

Her teeth slipped back, shrinking.

'Tell me, vampire, how much has that grey book-keeper put on my head? How many of his precious crowns will he part with to get his way?'

Genevieve kept quiet.

'Oh yes, I know all about your mission here. Balthus has the soul of a dog, and the loyalties too. I've known from the beginning. Tybalt doesn't understand that there's more to a man than a price.'

Calm in triumph, Rudiger reminded Genevieve of Mornan Tybalt, eyes glittering as a scheme was fulfilled.

'I'd kill him if it would do any good. But once Balthus gives testimony, there wouldn't be any point. The jumped-up clerk's son will be back where he belongs, toiling in some tiny office, struggling for every scrap of food, for every tarnished pfennig.'

Could she get to him before his shot her?

'You're better than that, vampire. Tybalt must hold you to some crime to make you his tool.'

Behind Rudiger, in the woods, something large was moving. Genevieve could sense her, could feel her excitement.

'Let's make a truce?'

Rudiger relaxed, and let his arrow slide loose.

Genevieve nodded, needing the time.

'See,' Rudiger said, holding the bow in one hand and the arrow separately. 'No harm.'

He came to her, but not within her arm's reach.

'You're pretty, Genevieve,' he said. 'You remind me...'

He extended his arm, and his fingertips touched her cheek She could grab his arm, maybe tear it off...

'No, you're an original,' he said, taking his hand away. 'You're a huntress, like the mare. You'd be good with me. After the hunt, there are other pleasures, rewards...'

She felt his lust curling out at her. Good. It might blind him.

'Strange to think you're so old. You look so green, so fresh..'

He took her and kissed her, rough tongue pressing against her lips. She tasted the blood in his spit, and it was like pepper in her mouth. She did not fight him, but she did not join him.

He let her go.

'Later, we'll raise your enthusiasm. I'm skilled with more than the bow.'

Rudiger stood up.

'First, there's ivory to be had. Come on..'

He stepped into the woods, and she got up, ready to follow. She did not know what would happen next.

She had the mare's scent. And so, obviously, did the graf.

XII

They were back at Khorne's Cleft. On the other side, from which Sylvana had fallen.

For Doremus, this would be a haunted spot now.

By day, it was stranger than it had been at night. The waterfall sparkled, and it was possible to see all manner of colours and lights in the water.

Balthus was down on all fours, smelling the ground. His backbone had lengthened, straining his jerkin, and his ears were pointed, shifting back on his skull.

It seemed only natural. Even Doremus could sense the call of the woods.

He was still seeing things. And hearing them.

The trees whispered, and the rush of the waterfall was a hissing chatter, talking to him, singing him strange music.

It was bewitching.

He felt like sitting down, and listening hard. If he paid attention for long enough, he was sure he could make out what was being said to him.

It was the unicorn blood in him.

Balthus sat up, snorting, slavering. Then, he bounded off into the woods. Doremus should follow him, but he felt a lassitude creeping over him. The whisperings held him back.

Balthus was scurrying away.

Doremus followed the guide, trailing after his noise. Balthus was yapping like a hound.

Tonight, he would want to be kennelled with Karl and Franz, leaving the leech alone in his bed.

He found Balthus at the edge of a clearing, pointing. He pressed his back to a tree, and caught his breath.

Something was moving between the trees, something with a silver-white hide that flashed.

Doremus had an arrow ready.

He kicked Balthus, sending him off to the right, hoping to attract the mare's attention. If she charged the guide, Doremus would get a perfect shot. He could take her in the neck, or the eye, or the withers. Then, he could use his knife to finish the job if it needed finishing.

He would prefer a clean kill. It would make his father proud.

The mare came to a halt and raised her head, listening. Doremus knew the true kinship of hunter for prey, and understood her thinking.

She suspected a trap, but was measuring her chances. Was she confident enough to charge anyway?

Balthus barked, and the mare went for him.

The unicorn galloped out of the woods, and exploded, bigger by daylight than Doremus had imagined last night, into the clearing. Doremus stepped out from behind the tree and advanced a few paces, arrow coming up...

There was a shaking in the ground as the unicorn's hooves

struck. Then, the rumbling increased and became a sharp, earthy scream.

The ground was giving way.

Doremus fired, but his arrow shot upwards, skittering above the unicorn's eyes and clanging against her horn as she batted it aside, its force spent.

The earth tipped like an unbalanced stone, and Doremus slid down it. The unicorn lost her footing too, and whinnied a long stream of forest oaths.

Doremus lost his bow and started tearing at the rippling ground, pulling himself out of the subsidence.

The mare, heavier than he and stuck with hooves rather than fingers, just floundered, and sank further.

Turning his head, Doremus saw the unicorn's head shaking, horn waving, as she fell through into the abandoned dwarf tunnel beneath.

He had lost her.

XIII

They ran to the sound, and found where the earth had given way. Doremus was squatting by the hole.

'The mare's down there,' he said.

Rudiger needed no more. He scrambled into the hole, calling for them to follow.

'I can see down there,' Genevieve said. 'You can't.'

Balthus, part-way through some change, fumbled a tinder-box and a candle out of his pouch and struggled with them. His pawlike hands couldn't work the flint. Doremus took the candle, and struck a light to it.

Carefully, they let themselves into the hole. It was about twice as deep as a man is tall, and led into a tunnel.

'This must be an arterial route,' Genevieve said. 'It's tall enough for us, and for the mare.'

There were much smaller side tunnels, cobwebbed over, which neither man nor unicorn could have got through.

'An easy track,' Rudiger said. 'We just follow the broken webs.'

Balthus whimpered as a spider the size of a housecat scuttled out of its lair.

Rudiger took the point of his boot to it, and it squealed as he crushed it against the wall.

Rudiger was ahead again, and they were behind. This was going round and round, hunting the hunter hunting the hunter and being in turn hunted. Genevieve wanted it finished.

The tunnel sloped downwards, deeper into the earth. She hoped the engineers had built to last. Nearer the surface, things were falling apart.

These workings had been abandoned since the time of Sigmar. None of the higher races had set foot here for centuries.

'There's light ahead,' she said, feeling it in her eyes.

'That's impossible,' Rudiger snorted.

Doremus covered the candleflame, and they all saw it.

'Evidently not,' the graf admitted. 'My apologies.'

The mare had headed for the light.

It was cold down here, and wet. Water trickled down the walls and around their boots.

Their way was barred by a sparkling curtain, and the drumming of water was loud in their ears.

'We're behind the waterfall,' Doremus said.

It was true. Genevieve stepped forwards, and put her hand in the icy curtain, feeling the water splash onto her arm and face.

'The mare must have plunged through,' Rudiger said.

It was a pretty sight.

'Come on,' the graf grunted, holding his nose and throwing himself into the water.

For an instant, he was visible in the water like a bug frozen in ice, then he was swept away.

Doremus was startled.

'There must be a way through to the Cleft,' Genevieve said. 'He should come out with the mare.'

Balthus leaped after his master.

'Are you the kind that doesn't like running water?' Doremus asked.

'I didn't think I was yesterday.'

Still, neither of them made a move to the curtain.

'Can you hear the voice in the water?'

Genevieve listened, and thought she could hear something frail and pleading in the rush of the fall.

'I've been hearing that all day.'

'It must come from around here somewhere.'

Genevieve looked about. To a human, this would be almost as dark as night. To her, it was almost as bright as day.

'Douse the candle, I'll see better,' she said.

Doremus complied.

The rock chamber behind the waterfall became plainer. There were murals carved into the walls, depicting Sigmar wielding his hammer against the goblins. It was indifferent as art, but showed some dwarfish enthusiasm.

The noise was a mewling, singing, crying...

They found her in an alcove, mossy blankets pulled around her, face pale and thin, almost elfin.

'Sylvana?'

The woman didn't answer her name.

'She must be dead,' Doremus said, 'I saw father shoot two arrows.'

Genevieve knelt by the woman, and saw how changed she was. The arrows were still in her flesh, but they had sprouted, grown. Green shoots emerged from the wood, and the fletches were heavy with blossom. Her face was changed too, supple as young bark with a green undertone, her hair was the consistency and colour of moss, her thin arms were wrapped around her soft, pulpy body. She had taken root where she lay, been absorbed into the nook. Where she was, she had water and light.

Genevieve had heard that these waters had properties. As she looked at Sylvana, flowers blossomed around her face.

'Doremus,' Sylvana whispered, her voice coming not from her filmed over mouth but from her breathing nostrils, 'Doremus...'

The young man didn't want to get near the changing woman. But she had something to tell him.

Her head raised, neck growing like a branch beneath it.

'Rudiger killed your mother,' she said.

Doremus nodded, accepting what Sylvana told him. Obviously, that had occurred to him.

'And he killed your father too,' Genevieve added.

Doremus's eyes went wide with incomprehension.

XIV

'Clever, clever,' a voice said behind them.

Rudiger stood, dripping, before the waterfall, his knife out,
its blade glistening.

'Doremus,' he said, 'to my side. I have kills to claim.'

Doremus froze, not knowing what to do.

'Serafina?' he said. 'Mother?'

'A whore, like all women,' Rudiger shrugged. 'You did well
to grow up without her warping you with her fussing and
fiddling.'

The vampire stood up, slowly. In the dark, her eyes seemed
to shine red.

'I waited for you outside, but only the faithful dog came.'

The thing that had been Sylvana shrank, her head sinking into
its bed of greenery.

'So I returned.' He beckoned with his knife.

'That's a poor thing, graf,' Genevieve said. 'Where's your other
weapon?'

Rudiger laughed, as he did at the height of the chase. He tapped his quiver.

'In with the arrows.'

'Father,' Doremus said. 'What does this mean?'

'You don't have to call me that any more.'

'It was Magnus,' Genevieve told him. 'I saw it in his face. You have his face.'

Suddenly, Doremus understood his 'uncle,' understood the care he had always bestowed on him, understood the glances he had always given Serafina's portrait.

'He was a good friend, and no more to blame for the betrayal than that fat fool last night,' Rudiger said. 'It was the harlot I married, that was all.'

Genevieve had been creeping nearer to Rudiger, by inches, whenever the graf was paying attention to Doremus. He didn't know which one to help.

'Vampire,' Rudiger said. 'Keep your distance.'

Genevieve stood still.

'How did you know I did for Magnus?' he asked.

'The count was killed with a horn. The mare would have used her hooves as well.'

Rudiger smiled. 'Ah, that's a hunter's observation.'

From his quiver, he pulled out his grandfather's trophy.

'So pretty, so sharp, so dangerous,' he said, looking at Genevieve. The horn was still red with Magnus's blood.

'I couldn't let him take my heir away,' Rudiger explained. 'The name of von Unheimlich must continue, even if the bloodline is interrupted. Honour is more important even than blood.'

Doremus knew the count had been trying to declare himself as his father. When Magnus was wounded, he had wanted him to know, had wanted him to carry the memory.

'It was eating him inside,' Rudiger continued. 'He would have spoken out in public, taken you away, taken you for his heir. Now, the threat is gone. The family is whole.'

Doremus turned away from the graf, and cried for his father.

XV

Genevieve went for Rudiger, and collided with him, arms going around him, pushing aside the deadly horn.

Together, they hit the curtain of water.

She clung tight as they plunged down, deep into the lake at the bottom of Khorne's Cleft. Under the surface, it was quiet, all sound muffled.

She could stay under longer than the graf.

She could drown him. But he was struggling, fighting her.

Underwater, he was strong, pushing her away. She felt the point of the horn scrape across her thigh, the silver stinging like a lashworm eating in the wound.

They broke the surface, and the noise was unbearable. Rudiger was shouting, and the water was hammering down around her.

Her blood was all around her.

Rudiger ducked under, and she saw his boots kick the air as he went down. She trod water, paddling with her arms.

345

Rudiger rose from the waters, horn held in both hands like a heavy sword, angling down at her.

She knifed her legs, and twisted out of the way, and the horn stabbed the unresisting water.

Making a fist, she punched Rudiger in the side, feeling but not hearing his ribs give way. He turned like a wounded fish, and stabbed out, forcing her back. A wave hit her, and she had to keep her balance. The horn came for her again, and she swam back.

She found rock behind her, and the waterfall pressed her down.

Slowly, thinking her pinned down, Rudiger came for her, horn ready for her heart.

'Die, vampire bitch,' he snarled.

The horn jumped, and she let herself be sucked down.

Rudiger stabbed the stone, and she shot out her hand, latching onto his throat, feeling his stiff wet beard in her grip.

The horn broke and she hurled her whole bodyweight at the graf.

She slammed against him and he lost his fragment of horn, his hands grabbing for her hair.

She had lost her cap, and her hair was loose.

Genevieve ignored the pain in her scalp, as Rudiger wrenched. He was under her, and as she swam for the mouth of the culvert, she kept pushing the graf under the surface. He gulped down icy water, and choked out bubbles of air.

There was hard rock under her feet now, and she scraped the graf across it.

At the edge of Khorne's Cleft, the water flowed into a stream, and there was firm ground she could strike for.

Her eyeteeth were points of pain in her mouth, and she felt the red rage again.

She could hear the graf's heartbeat, feel the blood pounding in his throat. Her nails had dug in, and the beaten man was bleeding.

The waterfall had worn a bowl-like indentation in the rock, and at the edge of the culvert there was a ridge that almost breached the surface.

Genevieve slammed Rudiger against the ridge, cracking his spine.

She stood up, the water pouring out of her clothes, and looked down at her quarry.

He was still kicking, but he couldn't hurt her any more.

The graf's warbow and quiver were washed away, floating down the stream. His knife was at the bottom of the lake. His grandfather's ivory trophy was broken and gone. The fight was out of him.

Behind her, Doremus emerged from the waterfall.

The need was in her throat, her heart, her stomach, and her loins.

She fell upon the graf like a beast, nuzzling his neckwounds with her mouth, and tearing through the skin, chewing into the veins with her sharp teeth.

The blood, iced cold by the water flowing around, gushed into her mouth, and she swallowed greedily.

This was not loving, this was preying.

She drank long, sucking the wounds dry, opening fresh ones, and sucking them too. She tore the graf's clothes, and ripped his flesh. She felt him shrinking inside her, sniffed his passions as they were extinguished, swallowed him whole and digested him completely.

She heard his heartbeat slow to a halt, felt his waterlogged lungs collapse, sensed his blood slowing...

At once, she had dead blood in her mouth, and it tasted of ashes. She spat it out and stood up.

Graf Rudiger von Unheimlich was beyond the healing of the waters of Khorne's Cleft.

At the bank of the stream, the unicorn mare stood, amber eyes fixed upon the predator.

Genevieve felt the last of Rudiger's blood rush through her heart, and she strode through the water, kicking waves around her. The mare waited for her.

Wading ashore, she walked up to the unicorn.

They both knew the hunt was over.

She placed her arms around the mare's neck, and rested her head next to the unicorn's, feeling the fur rise against her cheek.

She sensed that the mare was as old as she, that she had known the last of her stallions, that this was the last hunt...

Looking into the mare's eye, Genevieve knew it must all be over. With a sudden wrench, she turned the beast's head around, hearing its neck break like the crack of a gun.

The old mare went down to her knees, and died in peace.

There was a final reward.

She grasped the horn, feeling the nasty tingle of its silver threads, and plucked it from the mare's forehead. It came loose as easily as a ripe fruit is freed from the bough.

The red rage passed from her like a cloud.

XVI

'Here, Master Doremus,' Genevieve said, handing him the ivory. 'A present. A replacement for the trophy that was lost.'

He was shivering, his clothes heavy with water.

Balthus, almost completely a dog, was crouched by the dead mare. He bared his teeth, and worried the unicorn's belly.

Genevieve kicked him away, and he slipped, yapping, into the woods. He was part of the wild now, like Sylvana. The Drak Wald was well known for claiming its own.

The vampire stood between her kills, between the unicorn mare and the Graf von Unheimlich.

'This is what hunters are for,' she said, 'for killing the things that need killing, the things that have outlived their time, have gone beyond their glory.'

The ivory felt smooth and beautiful in his hands.

'Go home, Doremus,' Genevieve said, 'and bury your father. Bury him with honour. Take his name, if you want. Or Count Magnus's. Use your position to harry Mornan Tybalt, whatever...'

He was still confused about all this.

'And as for him,' she said, nodding at the graf, who lay face up in the water, mouth open. 'Forget that he killed Count Magnus. Remember that he knew what he knew but let him live as long as he did. That must mean something.'

The vampire girl was different, now. Commanding, strong, confident. She didn't disgust him any more. She was old, but she looked younger now than ever before.

'And you?' he said.

She looked thoughtful a moment. 'I'll stay here a while, and lose myself in the forests. I'm a wild thing, too.'

Genevieve reached up and kissed him, her cold lips against his. Doremus felt a thrill course through him.

'Be the man your father would have had you be,' she said.

He left her there, and made his way down, past the stream.

When he was out of her sight, he took one last look at the ivory and tossed it into the water. It sparkled on the streambed, the current flowing over it. That was a better background for the trophy than any dusty wall.

Nearing the lodge, Doremus realized the saying was true: *One comes home and he alone.*

ABOUT THE AUTHOR

Kim Newman is an award-winning author, film critic and broadcaster. As 'Jack Yeovil', he wrote the popular Vampire Genevieve and Dark Future novels for Black Library. He has a vast array of further fiction credits to his name, and his passion for film has led him to write several books on the subject. He has also written for television, radio and theatre, and has directed a small film. He lives in Islington, North London.